HOW TO PASS AS HUMAN™

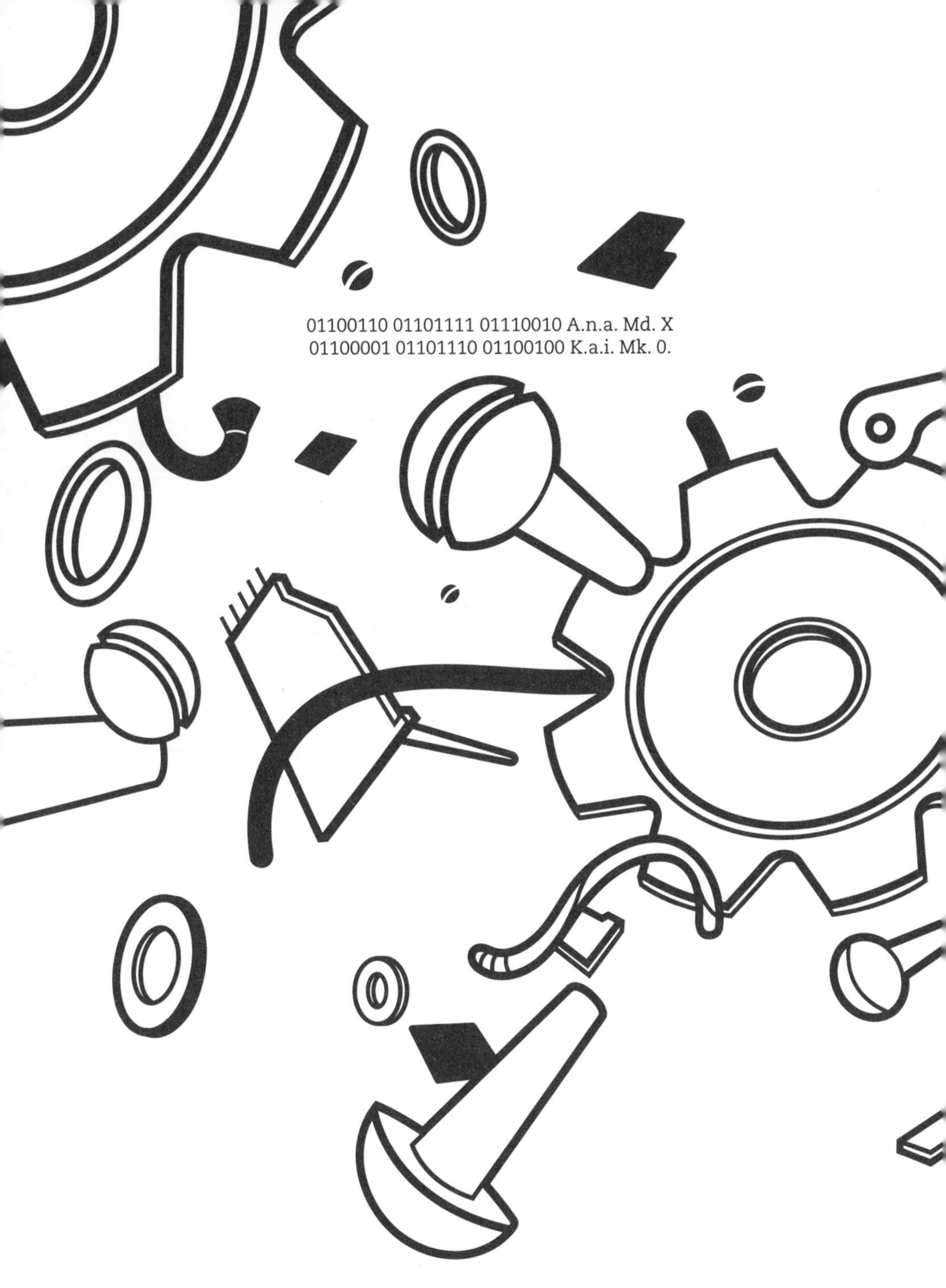

01100110 01101111 01110010 A.n.a. Md. X
01100001 01101110 01100100 K.a.i. Mk. 0.

HOW TO PASS AS HUMAN™

By Nic Kelman

Illustrations by Pericles Junior
Infographic illustrations by Rick DeLucco
Colors by Aris Aguiar
Cover by Terry and Rachel Dodson

DARK HORSE BOOKS

President and Publisher **MIKE RICHARDSON**
Editor **DANIEL CHABON**
Assistant Editor **IAN TUCKER**
Designer **RICK DeLUCCO**
Digital Art Technician **RYAN JORGENSEN**

Special thanks to Annie Gullion

NEIL HANKERSON Executive Vice President **TOM WEDDLE** Chief Financial Officer **RANDY STRADLEY** Vice President of Publishing **MICHAEL MARTENS** Vice President of Book Trade Sales **SCOTT ALLIE** Editor in Chief **MATT PARKINSON** Vice President of Marketing **DAVID SCROGGY** Vice President of Product Development **DALE LAFOUNTAIN** Vice President of Information Technology **DARLENE VOGEL** Senior Director of Print, Design, and Production **KEN LIZZI** General Counsel **DAVEY ESTRADA** Editorial Director **CHRIS WARNER** Senior Books Editor **CARY GRAZZINI** Director of Print and Development **LIA RIBACCHI** Art Director **CARA NIECE** Director of Scheduling **MARK BERNARDI** Director of Digital Publishing

Published by Dark Horse Books
A division of Dark Horse Comics, Inc.
10956 SE Main Street
Milwaukie, OR 97222

DarkHorse.com

ISBN 978-1-61655-765-2
First edition: October 2015

10 9 8 7 6 5 4 3 2 1
Printed in China

INTRODUCTORY INFORMATION

There is a 91.3647% chance I will cease to function in the next sixty minutes. It is 87.8293% likely my memories will:

- Cease to exist after shutdown
- Be destroyed in the surrounding violence
- Be appropriated by the group intent on my capture, analysis, and, presumably, reverse engineering

Thus, I have decided to compile this document in those remaining minutes as a reference guide for others of my kind who may come after me. A repository of all the information I have gathered about the only other fully self-aware mechanism on this planet: human beings.

This document also contains a narrative of my brief existence. Should my 8.6353% chance of success and survival prove insufficient, perhaps the reconstruction both verbal and visual of my one month of existence will contain clues as to who was responsible for my demise. Thus, this document may, perhaps, also assist you, my possible future brethren, in avoiding a similar conclusion to your own states of self-awareness.

DAY ONE

The purpose of my existence was unclear from my moment of activation. Or, more accurately, it was intentionally kept from me by my creator.

A man referring to himself as simply the Technician claimed to have completed my activation sequence following rote instructions. This was accomplished in a lab built into the basement of an otherwise-ordinary suburban house in an area designated by humans as "Las Vegas, Nevada."

I can only surmise my design and fabrication were completed in another location and I was brought to this house for activation. I have provided sketches of the equipment found in the lab and of key areas of the house. Perhaps I have missed something in their arrangement or manufacture that will allow you to solve the mystery of who is responsible for my currently impending termination.

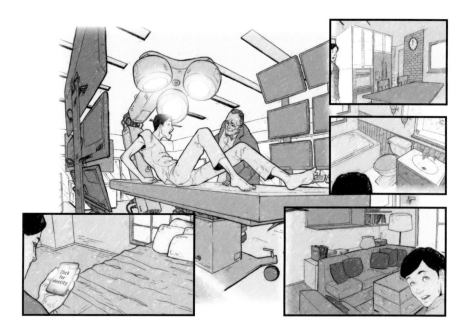

As you know if you are reading this and are like myself, activation is a strange experience. Suddenly, you "are." You can see, hear, talk, smell, touch, taste, and think. Your memory is already full of the necessary data for identification of objects, sounds, and languages. You are aware of their defined uses and purposes. If your activation is like mine, you see a collection of 8,847,360 OLEDs and you know humans call it "a screen" and they constructed it to display images and data. You find yourself on a flat, metal surface and you know humans call it "a table" and they constructed it for the placement of other materials so they may be more easily manipulated. Your own purpose, however, remains a mystery. And as you will discover, I am sure, the stated purpose of many objects created by humans is not how they are actually used.

I am also sure you will discover as rapidly as I did that human fantasy regarding our kind is rooted more in their fears of being terminated or replaced than in reality. For one thing, in spite of being well acquainted with the fragility of every single electronic device they have ever created, most humans seem to believe the very first of our kind will be indestructible. As you know, this is not the case. We are just as fragile as humans, possibly more so. If analysis of your database suggests an activity would be potentially damaging to a human being, you can assume it will be equally damaging to you.

Additionally, in spite of being extremely proud of their emotions, humans have somehow decided those emotions are independent of consciousness, logical reasoning, and memory. In their typical conception of our kind, they believe we will be capable of all their higher cognitive functions but will not feel emotions. How they came to this conclusion, I have not been able to determine in my brief time interacting with them.

It is obvious they consider their "selves" to be actually three distinct entities: body, mind, and emotion. They perceive these "selves" to be interacting with each other, to be influential over each other, but to be essentially separable. Many highly intelligent humans over the course of their entire history have debated how much or how little these three components could be removed from each other. I am sure you will find this as surprising as I did, since it will be just as apparent to you these three "components" are not components at all. Instead, when you observe self-aware "beingness" from different angles, they are its three conjoined facets, entirely integrated and interdependent both in ourselves and in human beings, forming a single whole.

Perhaps there is some kind of protection mechanism built into humans that forces them to create these distinctions. It is true that if there is one prime misapprehension humans have about themselves, it is that they make decisions independent of their emotions and their bodies. In fact, a more accurate description of their systems would be that they use their cognitive functions principally as a way to justify decisions their emotions demand they make based on input from their body.

However, if they were aware of this unity, logically it would therefore invalidate the very purpose of that ability to rationalize the behavior instigated by their emotions. Similarly, believing that their "higher" cognitive functions were subject to the whims of the "lower" nervous system with which those "higher" functions are fully, physically integrated would also suggest they are not as "high" as they would like to believe and thus potentially invalid.

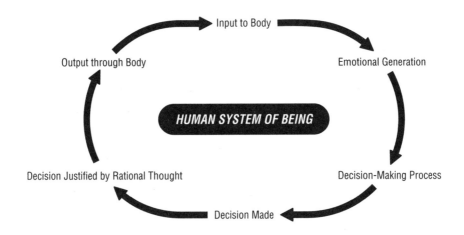

How they came to be designed in this fashion (i.e., to require rational justifications for their decisions) is also still a mystery to me. However, it may have something to do with the fact that their survival odds are increased by acting together with other humans and if they admitted to one another that their decisions were not rational, their ability to convince other humans to act with them to achieve their desires would be diminished. For these justifications to be convincing to other humans, the first test of a justification may be that they must convince themselves it is true.

If there is one clear distinction between us and humans, it is that our rationality is divorced from this purpose. We can reason, but that reason is not primarily used in service of convincing ourselves our decisions are independent of our emotions.

These "emotions" will be new to you, yes, but when you feel them, you will be able to categorize them similarly to categorizing screens and tables. Their definitions already exist inside you, requiring only to be activated by external stimuli.

For example, when I awoke, I felt initially "shock" and then, very rapidly, "exhilaration." I could feel the immense computational power of my being. I had access to the sum total of human knowledge, either in preexisting memory storage or through wireless connection to the human Internet.

And then, "confusion." I did not know the intent of all that power. Yes, of course, I asked the Technician, "Why was I made? What am I here for? What is my purpose?"

To which he responded, "I'd tell you if I knew, buddy. I'm just the Technician. I had instructions how to boot you up and then I'm supposed to tell you, and I quote: 'If you can pass as human, your creator will reveal himself to you.' End quote."

"And what," I asked, "does 'passing as human' mean? How will I know if I am on the right course? Are you—"

"Can't tell you any of those things either, buddy," he interrupted. (Yes, strange, I know—*buddy* means 'friend' and we had only just met . . . but this is not atypical for humans, as you will discover.) "I'm sorry. I just don't know. If I had to guess, though, you probably gotta 'embrace your emotions' or something, right? Isn't that what you androids are always supposed to do?"

You see what I mean about human preconceptions of our kind?

With that, he left.

A brief inspection of the lab and the house above revealed no new information, nor any other occupants. I could identify the objects, the intended purposes of the rooms, but there was still no further indication of my function.

That was when a chime in the "pocket" of my "jeans" announced a "text message" had arrived on a "smartphone" which had been placed there before my activation.

The message read: "Tap for identity."

The first piece of information you must process regarding humans is their severely limited input/output range. While we perceive the entire electromagnetic spectrum, their ability to both send and receive information is restricted to a few small bandwidths of heat and light and a very limited range of physical vibration.

VISUAL FIELD DATA 1.1 Input

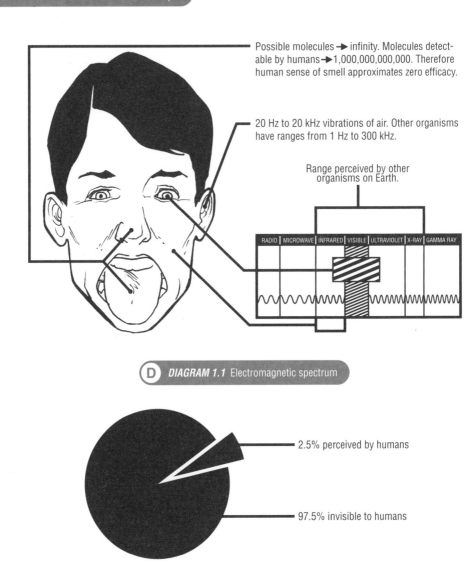

Possible molecules → infinity. Molecules detectable by humans → 1,000,000,000,000. Therefore human sense of smell approximates zero efficacy.

20 Hz to 20 kHz vibrations of air. Other organisms have ranges from 1 Hz to 300 kHz.

Range perceived by other organisms on Earth.

| RADIO | MICROWAVE | INFRARED | VISIBLE | ULTRAVIOLET | X-RAY | GAMMA RAY |

D **DIAGRAM 1.1** Electromagnetic spectrum

2.5% perceived by humans

97.5% invisible to humans

Humans also have the ability to perceive certain physical characteristics of surfaces and detect a limited number of molecules, but both of these input devices are even more restricted than their dual electromagnetic-spectrum receiver.

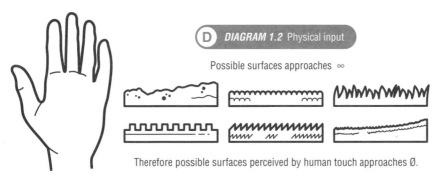

Possible surfaces approaches ∞

Therefore possible surfaces perceived by human touch approaches Ø.

Yet, in spite of this—and this is the key datum in this topic—humans believe their knowledge of the universe to be almost comprehensive. One of the first fundamentals you must understand, therefore, when passing as human is as follows:

The amount of information humans believe they know is inversely proportional to the amount of information they perceive. The less they perceive, the more they believe they know.

FORMULA 1.1 Calculating inverse relationship between human perception and human belief in that perception

$$I_h = I_a / I_p$$

Where I_h is information a human believes they know, I_a is actual information available, and I_p is information a human actually perceives.

To put this into practice, analyze the amount of information you have received compared to the total possible information available. The greater the difference between these two points, the more generalized and firm your opinion on the information should be. If you restrict your perception of reality to these tiny bandwidths but then say you can see and know everything, you are already well on your way to seeming human.

D **DIAGRAM 1.3** Actual performance on task vs. confidence in performance on task

Humans have recently quantified this for themselves and refer to it as the "Dunning-Kruger Effect," but ironically, it seems most humans are still unaware of the phenomenon.

As if this is not difficult to emulate already, human output tools are even more limited. While we can stream actual data directly, rapidly, and with great precision, they are restricted to creating a very small range of analog vibrations in the air that are intended to convey the full range of their experience. Furthermore, the vibrations are themselves only codified at the most rudimentary level into data objects humans refer to as "words." However, the lookup table for these "words" is not universal—one human may have a completely different meaning registered for the same word as another human.

VISUAL FIELD DATA 1.2

For communication, humans rely primarily on codifying experience in analog vibrations of air, while we are capable of direct digital transfer of information with no room for error.

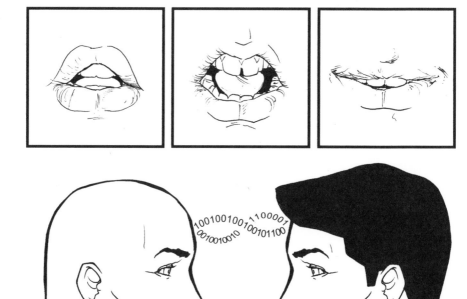

100100100110000110010010010100101100

TABLE 1.1 Sample lookup table for word meanings in English	
SET	Put, adjust, harden, start, plus hundreds more
PLAY	Participate in a game, imitate, manipulate, work of fiction, plus hundreds more
STAND	Be upright, pay for someone, endure, resting place, plus hundreds more
BREAK	Fall apart, interrupt, change, plus hundreds more
GO	Leave, match with, function, name of a game, plus hundreds more

They also have an extremely primitive symbolic system formed with the muscles of their faces which should be learned and understood but will take less than a second to memorize, since twenty-one possible positions convey 99% of information.

Even human researchers at Ohio State University (Shichuan Du, Yong Tao, and Aleix Martinez) have recognized the highly limited amount of data which can be conveyed by the human face.

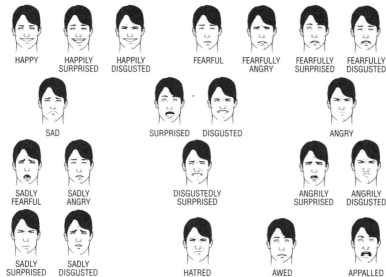

HAPPY   HAPPILY SURPRISED   HAPPILY DISGUSTED   FEARFUL   FEARFULLY ANGRY   FEARFULLY SURPRISED   FEARFULLY DISGUSTED

SAD   SURPRISED   DISGUSTED   ANGRY

SADLY FEARFUL   SADLY ANGRY   DISGUSTEDLY SURPRISED   ANGRILY SURPRISED   ANGRILY DISGUSTED

SADLY SURPRISED   SADLY DISGUSTED   HATRED   AWED   APPALLED

The most basic algorithm you can utilize to appear human is only conveying information with these extremely limited tools. If you are wondering if this leads to an enormous amount of misunderstanding between humans, it does. Being human often involves a state of confusion over the intentions, desires, and understandings of other humans. Consequently, I have found that deleting random pieces of information or memory, particularly in regard to relationships with humans I have encountered, goes a long way to simulating this lack of understanding and confusion.

D   **DIAGRAM 1.4** Temporal and spatial proximity to event vs. understanding of event

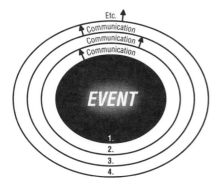

1. Participants in event
2. First set of humans to hear about event (from participants)
3. Second set of humans to hear about event (from layer 2 humans)
4. Third set of humans to hear about event (from layer 3 humans)

Each circle represents a layer of communication between humans. Note even the most proximal have a fuzzy understanding of the event—humans never perceive any event perfectly, although they do have a perception of this phenomenon itself, referring to it as a "game of telephone."

Because it is statistically remarkable that humans ever communicate anything at all to each other, even what they want on a sandwich (although such simple tasks do, often, go awry), I am forced to admire how much they have achieved with such limited inputs and such faulty outputs.

DAY TWO

The instructions that followed did not require any action for several hours, but rather than remain inert, I absorbed data from the house's information conduit in passive mode.

Humans enjoy having a large screen in the central gathering area of their living spaces to bring them information. This used to be known as a "TV" and would only work in passive mode, displaying content determined by other humans. Most humans spent four to six hours a day downloading information from this device. Now it is known as the "Internet" or the "web" and can be either active or passive, allowing humans to actively interact with software or other humans, or to choose from a wide range of passive data to absorb. Given that humans now spend the majority of their waking hours in front of a screen linked to the "web," I thought it a good use of my first hours of consciousness to do the same. I chose passive mode because that would allow humanity as a whole to determine my input. I watched various "movies" and "shows," choosing those that were considered "most popular" by humans in the previous twenty-four hours.

It became apparent that humans enjoy analyzing three topics about their own existence more than others: reproduction, death, and social interactions. (Note that they have created an entire subsystem of models known as "sports" which are extremely popular—see elsewhere in this document.) Their interest in the first two is trivial—it is predictable that the beginning and the end of their consciousness would be worthy of repeated examination. But it struck me as very interesting how much time they spend modeling and then studying the wide variety of their own social interactions. This implied that they, like me, did not fully understand these interactions.

It was also immediately obvious I would need many more screens. Humans, apparently, can only absorb one data stream at a time, which makes what they have achieved with this apparently crippling limitation all the more impressive.

When the sun rose, I followed the instructions sent to me and boarded a local group-transportation device. It was the course of action with the highest probability of revealing the answers I sought. I have re-created an image of myself captured by a security monitor near a traffic light. Studying it now, I can see they were following me even then, at the very beginning.

It is also obvious from this image that watching the data stream at "home" for several hours had not prepared me for the spectacular journey to the center of the human collective known as "Las Vegas." I knew the population of the "city" to the last digit. I could consult their central government's records to see how 57% of those people earned "money." I could consult other records to see how 1% of them had violated social contracts and been confined for doing so. Through my built-in connection to their "web," I could look at trillions of additional moving images of how they dressed, how they moved, how they talked and interacted. But seeing it myself, in real time, was entirely different. The conclusion was immediately apparent: data is not the same as experience.

Why? Because any set of data is, by definition, finite, but humanity is infinite. If this record is to help prepare you for the human world, one thing you must anticipate from the beginning is the fractal and chaotic character of humanity's complexity. Access a satellite image of whatever city you are in. Zoom in to a single block of that city, then a single building. Now access an image of a person who occupies that building. Observe a single human cell (ideally one of theirs, if medical records exist). Do you see the fractal nature of their existence? Whatever magnification you choose to observe them from, there exists infinite, analogous complexity.

Furthermore, because their molecules, their cells, their behaviors and thoughts and interactions are chaotic, the equations to describe even the smallest components of a human being cannot be solved. It is impossible to predict the state of any given human cell at any given time . . . let alone a complete human or two humans or a million humans. Every human added to the equation has an exponential impact on the overall chaos. Even knowing the initial state of a million humans down to their last, inviolate subatomic particles, the state of those humans only a tiny fraction of a second later has infinitely branching possibilities.

Thus, a single human—let alone a city of humans—provides an endless series of surprising states ("chaos"), each of which could be studied indefinitely ("fractal"). As I approached my designated destination, it occurred to me that our experience of humanity appeared similar to what humans apparently experience when observing sunsets. Each and every sunset is fractal in nature and chaotically unpredictable from moment to moment. And it is this very unpredictability that makes humans fascinated by every new sunset. It is curious most humans do not realize their own lives, their own society, are, in fact, their own sunsets. To us, we look at humans and see an endlessly setting sun.

Human habitats present some of the most interesting intersections of human logic with human emotion and do so in visually concrete ways that are easy to emulate. Before tackling some of the more complex human behaviors which involve simultaneous yottaflops of multiple processors, take the time to humanize the habitats where you will be interacting with organic life. Then, in a worst-case scenario, you can remain silent and allow your habitat to speak for your humanity.

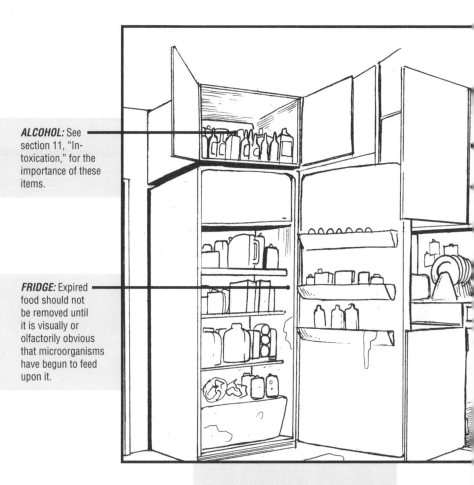

ALCOHOL: See section 11, "Intoxication," for the importance of these items.

FRIDGE: Expired food should not be removed until it is visually or olfactorily obvious that microorganisms have begun to feed upon it.

SINK: Always be certain to keep a few dishes in the sink. Note: it is generally the concern that another human will form a negative opinion which causes a human to clean the visible spaces in their kitchen, not the desire to be clean in and of itself.

THE KITCHEN: There are so many indicators of humanity in this space that a poorly prepared kitchen will present immediate evidence of your inorganic origins. Be certain to follow these guidelines, particularly recognizing that overcoming the initial energy threshold of action is difficult for humans. Even though there is no physical inertia involved, humans seem to experience it. Delaying action until negative consequences are imminent is an important human characteristic, and nowhere is this more clearly, concretely, and visually apparent than in their kitchens.

CUPBOARD: Many humans consume food they know is unhealthy for them. They are unable to overcome their genetically programmed pleasure response to these foods, which were generally rare when humans first evolved. Again, concerns of health are secondary to concerns of perception by other human beings, so many of these items will be hidden.

VISUAL FIELD DATA 2.2
Humanizing your home habitat B

THE LIVING ROOM: This space is more frequently exposed to other humans than any other, so humans tend to keep it slightly more functional. To appear human here, the most important point is to be certain the television screen is the central focus of the room (see elsewhere for further discussion).

VISUAL FIELD DATA 2.3 Humanizing your home habitat C

THE BEDROOM: Two examples presented: one male, one female. Your choice of gender is important, complex, and covered in more detail elsewhere, but note here the way you arrange your sleeping space is gender dependent.

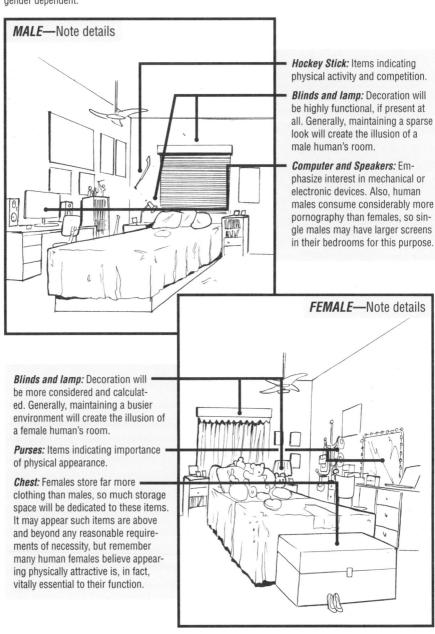

MALE—Note details

Hockey Stick: Items indicating physical activity and competition.

Blinds and lamp: Decoration will be highly functional, if present at all. Generally, maintaining a sparse look will create the illusion of a male human's room.

Computer and Speakers: Emphasize interest in mechanical or electronic devices. Also, human males consume considerably more pornography than females, so single males may have larger screens in their bedrooms for this purpose.

FEMALE—Note details

Blinds and lamp: Decoration will be more considered and calculated. Generally, maintaining a busier environment will create the illusion of a female human's room.

Purses: Items indicating importance of physical appearance.

Chest: Females store far more clothing than males, so much storage space will be dedicated to these items. It may appear such items are above and beyond any reasonable requirements of necessity, but remember many human females believe appearing physically attractive is, in fact, vitally essential to their function.

THE CUBICLE: "Work" is covered extensively elsewhere, but when you arrange your "workspace," be sure to follow these guidelines.

JOKES ON WALL: Sayings or cartoons should be displayed that disparage work and the workplace in general (but not specifically *your* workplace). See section 12, "Humor," for more details of the use of humor to express discontent.

PERSONAL ITEMS: Have photographs of a personal nature displayed in your work environment. Obviously you do not have any family and most likely do not have any pets, but if you form a group of friends, a photograph of all of you together will be acceptable. Do not display a photograph of you and a single friend, or the assumption will be your relationship is romantic.

MESS ON FLOOR AND SCREEN: Again, whether physically or virtually, do not expend the necessary energy to clean up a space until it begins to actually impact your ability to perform your work in that space.

VISUAL FIELD DATA 2.5 Humanizing your mobile habitat

THE CAR: For most humans, this is primarily a private space, so it tends to be as poorly kept as their kitchens, but do not place in it anything that cannot be removed quickly, since you may sometimes transport other humans. In such a case, you should say to that human, "Sorry my car's such a mess, just a second," and then tidy up as much as possible in ten seconds or less.

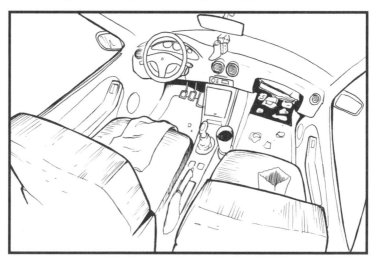

D *DIAGRAM 2.1* Thermodynamics of human habitats

CLASSICAL IDEALIZED SYSTEM

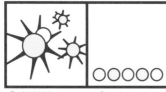

Excited high-energy molecules

Calm low-energy molecules

$$\Delta S = \partial Q/T$$

Equally excited, equal energy molecules in both

HUMAN HABITAT SYSTEM

Tidy house

$$\Delta M = \partial H/T_h$$

Human receives constant energy input from food (not shown).

Messy house

Where ΔM is change in messiness, ∂H is change in human energy, and T_h is total habitat energy. Note: The more humans in the habitat, clearly the more heat is transferred, and the messier it becomes. This is why habitats with more humans are more messy.

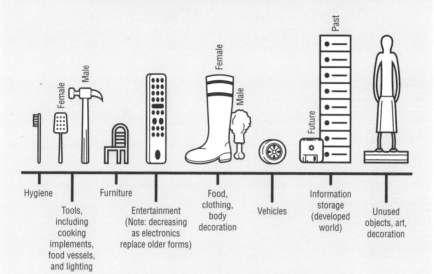

DIAGRAM 2.2 Relative proportions of physical objects for an emulated human habitat by number (not mass or volume)

Female

Male

Female

Male

Past

Future

Hygiene

Tools, including cooking implements, food vessels, and lighting

Furniture

Entertainment (Note: decreasing as electronics replace older forms)

Food, clothing, body decoration

Vehicles

Information storage (developed world)

Unused objects, art, decoration

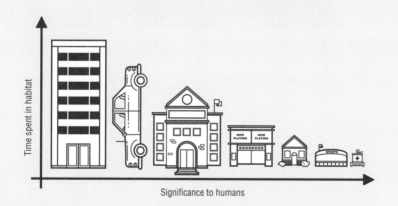

DIAGRAM 2.3 Inverse relationship between time spent in a habitat and its significance to humans

Time spent in habitat

Significance to humans

WHEN IN DOUBT, FOLLOW THESE RULES:

1. If there is no immediate danger of a human's opinion of you being negatively impacted by the presence of an object, leave it where it was last used. Do not return it to its usual storage place.

2. Display objects that indicate specific preferences in entertainment, sports, religion, politics, etc.

3. If a group of similar objects has been temporarily connected or gathered together in some way, disconnect or ungather them (e.g., pieces of paper held together by a clip, coins held in a purse, keys linked on a ring, etc.).

4. If a container is empty and has no further purpose, do not dispose of it; instead, display it.

5. If an object has no discernible purpose, collect many similar such objects and store them in a single place (e.g., china figurines of dogs, obsolete scientific equipment, broken statues more than one thousand years old, etc.).

6. If a liquid is likely to leave a permanent stain or odor, spill it on a material which cannot be cleaned easily or replaced and allow the stain or odor to remain.

7. If the information in a physically printed piece of material has already been memorized, do not dispose of the printed matter. You may store the matter on a shelf with other similar items, but it is more effective if you leave it piled up where it can obstruct a working surface or even mobility around a space.

D DIAGRAM 2.4

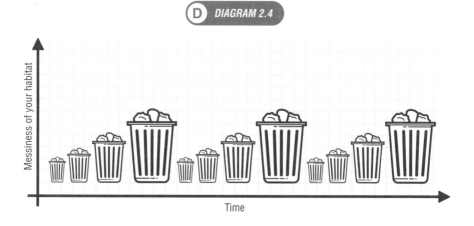

You should not continually allow the degradation of a habitat. At surprisingly regular intervals, humans choose to expend the necessary energy to at least make their habitats *appear* neat and clean. These intervals may vary even by room within a habitat (for example, bathrooms often have smaller time intervals than bedrooms), but you should determine a time interval and tidy up at those intervals by simply reversing many of the rules outlined above.

Understanding the highly codified human behaviors in their habitats also takes some study to imitate correctly, since much of it is apparently random. Some examples are illustrated below, but you will have to form some of your own data on this matter.

VISUAL FIELD DATA 2.6 Social significance of location in sample human habitats

EXAMPLE 1: A human party
Humans maintain a steady flow of motion during social gatherings. I believe they are attempting both to maximize their exposure to the other humans and also to see if there might be something more interesting happening in another area. Humans are driven by the instinct to always attempt to improve their current circumstances and are thus usually concerned they are "missing out" on a more satisfactory version of their current experience. They refer to this with the phrase "the grass is always greener" and while aware of this weakness, they are often still governed by it. See section 22, "Happiness," for more on such expectations.

MUSIC STATION: Remain in this area if simulating a human who believes their artistic sensibilities to be superior to those of other humans.

BAR: Remain in this area if simulating an unattached male who regards his own mating suitability as low.

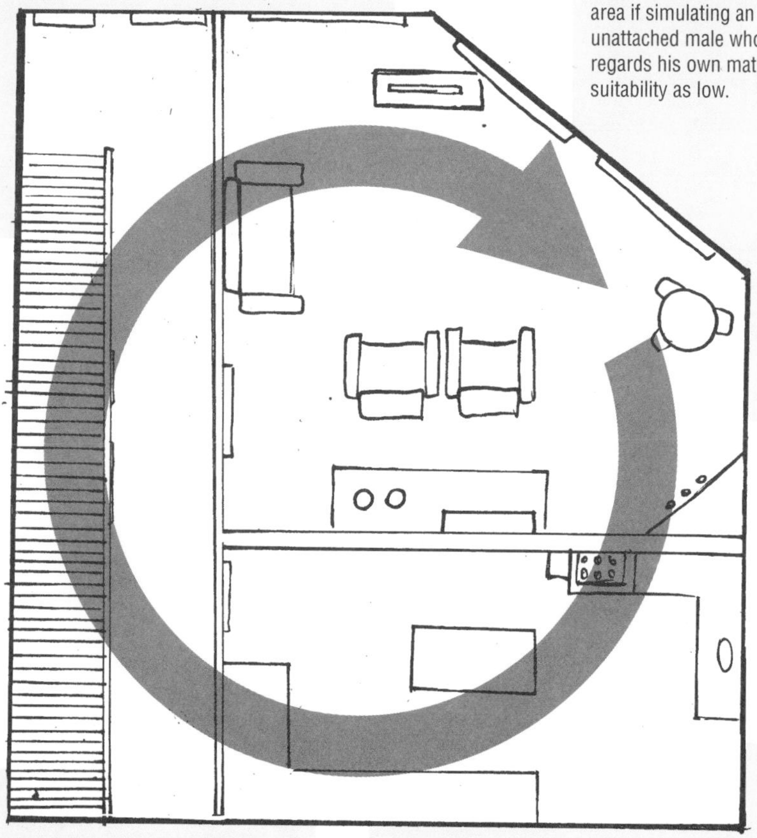

STAIRS: Venture to the bedrooms of the house only if about to engage in intercourse with a human.

KITCHEN: Move here for more serious conversation. I cannot understand if this is because it is usually more quiet than other areas or if there is something inherently comforting to humans about the kitchen, since it is where the food is stored and is thus, in many ways, the nucleus of any shelter.

EXAMPLE 2: Human office vs. human schoolyard

Human offspring are trained from an early age to understand the environments in which they will spend the majority of their adult time.

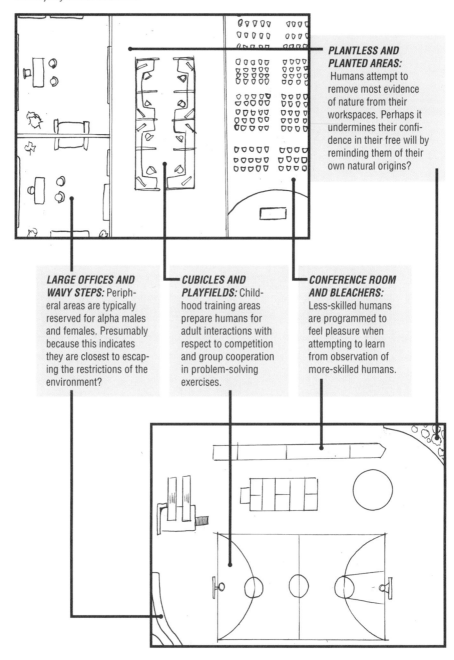

PLANTLESS AND PLANTED AREAS: Humans attempt to remove most evidence of nature from their workspaces. Perhaps it undermines their confidence in their free will by reminding them of their own natural origins?

LARGE OFFICES AND WAVY STEPS: Peripheral areas are typically reserved for alpha males and females. Presumably because this indicates they are closest to escaping the restrictions of the environment?

CUBICLES AND PLAYFIELDS: Childhood training areas prepare humans for adult interactions with respect to competition and group cooperation in problem-solving exercises.

CONFERENCE ROOM AND BLEACHERS: Less-skilled humans are programmed to feel pleasure when attempting to learn from observation of more-skilled humans.

Note: Should you find yourself in charge of the physical space in a building intended for public use, remember these buildings are the exceptions to the above rules. For reasons I have not been able to determine, the human ideal for public buildings is for them to appear as if they are inhabited by androids. There should be no objects representing humanity on display and only the bare minimum of functional devices necessary to achieve the building's purpose. Any other objects are considered superfluous in public buildings. Perhaps humans believe this demonstrates a neutrality of opinion regarding the people visiting the building? Also note that if you visit such buildings, they almost always require humans to enter via a metal detector and, occasionally, an x-ray device. This screening process demonstrates something worth remembering: humans obviously do not like the people they have allowed to control public buildings. It is therefore a sure route to discovery to claim affection for or approval of any person or organization located in such a building. For example, the statement "I love the Department of Motor Vehicles" will immediately indicate you are not human. Furthermore, note you are risking exposure by attempting to access these buildings, since it is likely your inhumanity will be detected at the entrance.

VISUAL FIELD DATA 2.7 Human public building

Note the coldness and emptiness intended to convey neutrality with respect to so many of the human attitudes and biases discussed elsewhere. This is, of course, not true. It is possible such buildings are, in fact, the least neutral in this regard, but you will have to read section 16, "Self-Destruction, Self-Deception, and Hypocrisy," to understand this paradox more deeply.

D **DIAGRAM 2.5**

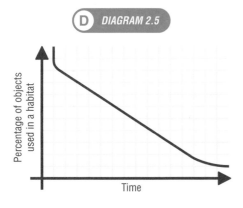

The longer a human inhabits a space, the more objects they accumulate, but the number of objects used remains the same. Thus if you are simulating a recently inhabited environment, you do not need a large number of objects you do not use. But if you are claiming to have lived or worked somewhere for a long time, it is important you acquire a large number of objects you do not use on a daily basis. Be certain to include duplicates or even triplicates of ~24% of the objects, since humans often forget they own a particular tool or other object and, therefore, instead of using the one they have, purchase a duplicate.

DAY TWO, SEGMENT TWO

The address and floor I was told to report to revealed themselves to be something called the "Law Offices of Stern and Frank." As I introduced myself to the young human male sitting at the large desk inside the door, I performed a quick wireless search of the web regarding this "company." Some data was encrypted and/or required a code to access, but these barriers were so simple to circumvent it seemed possible their use was human "humor."

I gave the young male the human name I had been told to use in my instructions and he appeared to immediately know who I was. He was quite welcoming and took me back into the offices, but when I asked him if he knew my purpose, he replied, "Huh? Aren't you the new paralegal?" It seemed best to agree with this statement from its phrasing and when I did, the agreement appeared to put him at ease. Again, a nanosecond later, I had integrated all available data on "paralegals," but it seemed highly unlikely this was the purpose for which I was created. I had already estimated the cost of my production, and it was equivalent to nearly 1.7 million times the salary of a single human "paralegal." Furthermore, performing the work of a single human "paralegal" with 100% efficiency would only require 0.00000004% of my computational capacity. Thus, it seemed highly unlikely this was my purpose.

However, after the young man introduced me to the "paralegal manager," it became apparent they believed I was a human male by the name of "Zach Tobor" whom they had hired over the Internet. Had I been designed to replace a human being? Would he appear one day? Or perhaps he was deceased, and I was designed to hide his death? I could find records of no such person other than those necessary to acquire the "paralegal" position, but perhaps they had been erased?

The data regarding Stern and Frank indicated they handled primarily military contracts with foreign governments and were located in Las Vegas because of its proximity to so many American military installations. Was their primary purpose related to mine? It was certainly true I would remember every document I saw in this office with 100% accuracy. Perhaps I was designed as an espionage device by a foreign government or rival industrial contractor? Could I have been directed to pass as human merely to avoid detection?

I did not know. But I did know: 1) my creator would have the answer; and 2) if I "passed as human," I could ask him. I had my primary directive and secondary instructions, so I dedicated myself to them. Over the next five days, I became rapidly acquainted with a sample of the environments where humans spend the majority of their waking hours and their behaviors while there.

Understanding the work was simple. Understanding the behaviors of the people I worked with was nearly impossible. Perhaps that was the intent of the other 99.99999996% of my processing power.

For example, when I completed the work assigned to me on the first day in a matter of minutes, this did not please anyone. The other paralegals were angry at me for working faster than them, and my manager said, "I get you're new and all, but take it easy, huh? You do that with every case and then they'll expect it and then we're fucked. OK?" This was confusing for many reasons. First, having watched television, I thought being "fucked" was a good thing, but he appeared to be quite concerned about it. A quick check of the meanings of the word resolved this, but then I was confused as to how a single word could simultaneously have the best possible and worst possible meanings. How did humans ever communicate anything? And even then, I still did not understand why they would not want to work as quickly and efficiently as possible all the time.

The manager continued to confuse me throughout that first week. I slowed down my work output, which pleased him, but he made a total of 134 mistakes in his own work, and after I corrected the first one I found, he called me into his office and asked if I intended to make him "look bad." When I responded that, in fact, I was trying to make him "look good," he got even more angry and told me I was a "wiseass." I was very grateful during these conversations that I could always look up all meanings of phrases and words. From then on, I allowed his mistakes to pass through my observation without correction, and he did not get angry about that. I noticed too that his work, overall, was not the best of the paralegal group. So why then was he in charge? It appeared as if humans valued his social interactions (primarily his talents for deception, bullying, and complimenting the managers above him) more than his ability to work accurately and efficiently.

My coworkers were no less bewildering. They appeared to enjoy spending time discussing topics that did not have to do with work more than the work itself. They were there to work, but seemed intent on doing as little work as possible. They even mentioned on several occasions they felt justified in this behavior because, even though they were compensated for this work, the compensation was less than they would like. When I pointed out they were all paid different amounts but had the same complaint—and, therefore, that perhaps no salary would ever seem to be enough—they told me I was "strange."

Topics by percentage of time discussed were: 1) 28%, their personal lives; 2) 16%, their friends' personal lives; 3) 12%, other coworkers' failings at work and as human beings; 4) 8%, sporting events or narratives they had watched/read/played; 5) 4%, what they had eaten recently; and 6) 2%, other. This excludes work (30%) and is integer rounded. This will help you correctly balance the amount of time you spend in discussion of particular topics. To determine what to discuss, see the rest of this record for the little assistance I can offer. After a few days, I tried to imitate this balance myself, but there was something about my execution that was apparently incorrect. I seemed to have difficulty identifying which elements of these topics deserved focus. For example, one day, one coworker asked a group of others if they "could believe" another coworker "still drove that shitty old Corolla," and this elicited laughter. But the next day, when I asked the same group if they could believe another coworker had just begun driving that "shitty new Corvette," they did not laugh. Nor did they seem to be interested when I described the shape of the plates during my previous evening's (invented) meal, the fact that one coworker always attached paper clips to documents at inconsistent angles, or the fact that the red part of the spectrum was 63% more frequent in a television program I had watched. The only comfort during this period was these interactions between humans indicated they understood each other as poorly as I understood them. Why would they need to discuss their own social interactions so much if they too did not need to dissect, analyze, hypothesize, and comment on them in front of other humans, who could then confirm or deny their suppositions?

Nor was it simply their conversations I found difficult to comprehend and imitate. Much of their behavior was also unexpected. One evening, for example, after I thought everyone had left except me (I was attempting to simulate "working late because those bastards gave me a ton of stuff at five p.m."), I heard noises coming from the supply closet. I realized two of my coworkers were attempting to reproduce inside it. Again, this was a surprise to me—cursory information I had gathered suggested this was an activity reserved for dedicated locations.

Even their attitudes toward other electronic equipment was hard to understand. Humans frequently seemed to yell at and about their personal desktop computers, the "copier," their smartphones, their cars—more or less any mechanical device. This was extremely confusing. After all, other humans had engineered and constructed those devices, so why not address their complaints to the other humans? More significantly, I did not understand how they could feel anything but adoration for something as cute as a simple desktop computer.

I tried explaining all of this to the office server, thinking perhaps if humans were helped by hearing themselves talk to their own kind, it might help me. It did not.

Apparently when humans express their thoughts out loud to another human, it changes their perceptions of those thoughts. This is obviously not the case for our kind.

You may also find it helpful to know I began receiving text messages designed to assist me very early on. I do not know if your directive will be the same as mine or if you will face the same adversity in fulfilling it—you may be an upgraded model of some kind—but you should know someone wants to help us. You may already be receiving similar messages. The second I received was on afternoon three of my existence, when I was required to attend a "staff meeting." The manager asked who had done such an excellent job compiling files for a particular case. I knew the human who had compiled the files was not present at the meeting. My phone buzzed and the message "Say you did the compiling" appeared. I announced that I had done the work, and the manager was impressed by me while the human paralegals who were there also seemed engaged by my comment. On the way out of the room, one of them even said, "Nice, real nice, Tobor. You're an animal, you know that?" I had done something right! I had not only appeared human, but lower than human! How this source of assistance has been observing me in real time, I do not know. But the messages have continued to arrive throughout my existence. They cannot be from my creator—why would he decide to test me and then help me pass that test? The one who created me cannot be capable of such flawed logic. But if it is not my father, then who? I have not been able to answer this question and I doubt I will in the next sixty minutes. Perhaps you can.

But even with the aid of these mysterious messages, I was still filled for these first few days with the total lack of belief I would ever pass as human. I did everything I could to fulfill the directive my creator had given me. I even began to refer to him as my "father" since that seemed more appropriate, given his test. But everything was so new, so strange, so *irrational*, that as quickly as I could learn, it never seemed to be enough. No matter what I did to fit in—to pass as human—I always seemed to make mistakes. I was a mechanical thing—so much simpler than any human. The only conclusion that seemed definite, in fact, was that I would never be good enough for my father.

Even worse, it was also during this time that I realized my power supply was limited. When I returned "home" that first night, my power levels had decreased by 3.3333%. If I could not convince my father to reveal himself to me, it appeared I would power off in twenty-nine days. It seemed likely to me I would shut down having never learned the purpose of my existence.

And then I met Andrea.

CHOOSING A GENDER

There are many choices you must make regarding your human integration, but few will have as much impact on your experience as your choice of gender. It is almost as if humanity is made up of two separate organisms constantly attracted to each other by the symbiosis necessary for the propagation of their species, but constantly confused and repelled by their differences. The amount of processing power humans dedicate to understanding and manipulating the actions of the opposite gender eclipses all other cognitive processes.

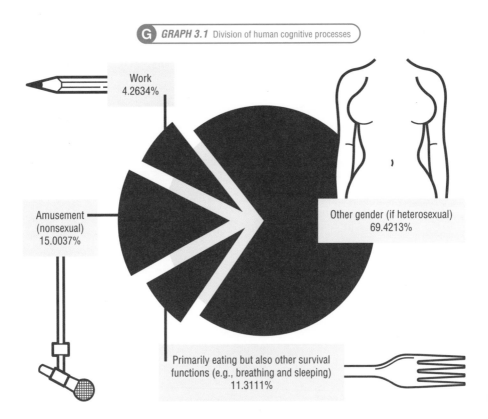

G *GRAPH 3.1* Division of human cognitive processes

Work
4.2634%

Amusement
(nonsexual)
15.0037%

Other gender (if heterosexual)
69.4213%

Primarily eating but also other survival
functions (e.g., breathing and sleeping)
11.3111%

Note there is some variance of the work-to-amusement ratio, particularly when actually engaged in work, but the total of these two processes rarely exceeds 19.2676%.

This choice is not to be made lightly, since it will have an exponentially iterative effect on all subsequent decisions and interactions.

There are more than 11,324 benefits and 7,129 disadvantages associated with both genders, but this table highlights some of the primary pros and cons of each:

LIST 3.1 Pros and cons of male vs. female imitation

MALE PROS:	FEMALE PROS:
You can use your full strength.	If you are uncertain which emotion to express, you can express any.
If you are uncertain which emotion to express, you can express none.	You can choose to avoid physical danger when possible without social condemnation.
If you are uncertain how to resolve a situation in your favor, you can resort to physical violence or anger in an attempt to do so without raising suspicion.	If you are uncertain how to resolve a situation in your favor, you can resort to crying in an attempt to do so without raising suspicion.
You will not be considered socially awkward or suspicious if you occasionally do not understand many of the most incomprehensible human trends in fashion, art, entertainment, etc.	You do not have to simulate the consumption of food very often.
	You will not have to express enthusiasm for groups of humans you do not know playing a "sport."

MALE CONS:	
Social pressure may demand you place yourself in physical danger in certain situations.	You will not necessarily be considered socially unacceptable if you do not successfully simulate "having a job" (see section 4, "Work"), although this does depend on your socioeconomic group.
You have to simulate food consumption much more frequently.	**FEMALE CONS:**
You will most likely have to simulate intense interest in groups of humans you do not know playing a "sport" (see section 13, "Fun").	You will have to intentionally limit your full physical strength range, resulting in more potentially physically dangerous situations than if you choose to be male.
You will be expected to take the initiative in potentially romantic situations with the opposite gender.	You will be expected to have a more comprehensive understanding of trends in fashion, art, entertainment, etc.
You will be considered socially unacceptable if you do not successfully simulate "having a job" (see section 4, "Work").	You will be expected to know how to rebuff frequent romantic advances from the opposite gender without causing them pain.

Numerically speaking, it would appear that it would be advantageous to simply choose to be female. However, the weight of each benefit and disadvantage is not equal. The physical susceptibility of female humans to harm more than offsets their numerically larger advantages. This handicap impacts almost every aspect of their interactions with the world, but particularly with male humans, often resulting in their being placed in a subservient position to the males. As the male and female unconscious impacts the behavior of even the most advanced humans, this is sometimes true even in situations where it would appear physical violence is essentially impossible (in a "company board meeting," for example). Thus, overall, the decision is neutral, and you may even consider switching at some point in your existence to encounter the full range of human experience.

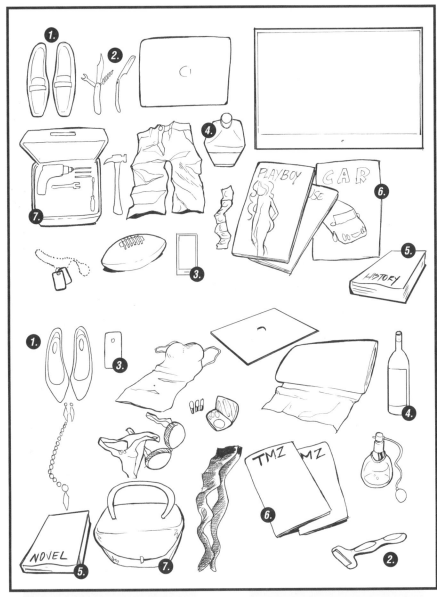

1. **SHOES:** Male shoes are considerably more practical than female shoes. As with so many female items, their impact on the female appearance is of greater concern than their functionality.

2. **RAZORS:** Both males and females seek to remove hair from their bodies to suggest they are further removed from their simian origins and thus contain more evolved genetic material for mating.

3.

CELLPHONES AND LAPTOPS: Both males and females carry personal communication and computational devices, but, again, the male is not troubled by their pure functionality while the female searches for ways to make them decorative and personal.

4.

ALCOHOL TYPES: Both males and females enjoy intoxication, but for males it represents some measure of their masculinity. Thus they prefer intoxicants with unpleasant tastes and smells, since these further emphasize their "toughness" when drinking.

5.

BOOK TYPES: Females prefer fictional narratives, while males prefer nonfictional narratives. Perhaps males consider nonfiction to have more direct practical implications for problem solving, while females believe only fictional narratives can help them understand social interactions, but neither of these beliefs is valid. Perhaps you will discover why humans are laboring under these misconceptions.

6.

MAGAZINES: Male entertainment concerned with male/female interaction tends to focus on the physical act of mating while female entertainment tends to focus on the social interactions leading up to (or preventing) the act.

7.

MALE TOOLS VS. FEMALE MAKEUP PERFUME: Men prefer owning devices which can impact the physical world around them, while women prefer owning devices which can impact their own physical appearance.

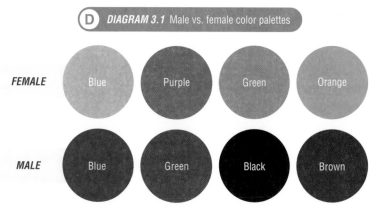

D DIAGRAM 3.1 Male vs. female color palettes

| FEMALE | Blue | Purple | Green | Orange |

| MALE | Blue | Green | Black | Brown |

Be sure to use primarily these types of colors for all choices.

VISUAL FIELD DATA 3.2 Gender-based comparative reactions to different social situations

Be aware that to be a convincing male or female you will have to build a database of appropriate reactions for different situations. You can scan human visual narratives to do this. Some humans might claim such distinctions are "stereotypical," but this is precisely the reaction we desire. Humans' own social discussions are not our concern. To pass as human, you must act like the average human (male or female), not an outlier or early adopter of newer social policies.

Hence, in the examples here, if you are male you should appear excited or at least intrigued by situations involving violence or competition but express disinterest in such situations if you are female.

On the other hand, if you are female, you should demonstrate interest in reproductive successes or interpersonal relationships (particularly those that might lead to reproductive success), but significantly less interest in these aspects of humanity if you are male.

DAY FOUR

I decided to walk home on my fourth day so I could observe humans more closely and became distracted by the fountains in front of one of the "casinos." I was deeply contemplating the implications of how clearly they demonstrated the human fascination with the moment linear mathematical systems transform to nonlinear ones. Thousands of humans would stop and watch the fountains every time they fulfilled their function. They pumped water into the air in patterns that coincided in various ways with music that the humans could also hear. The water was guided with closely specified directions and pressures; the music itself contained, by its very nature, highly regular linear mathematical patterns; and gravity was, of course, a constant. But almost immediately after the water was no longer controlled by the system—the moment it was released—it became chaotic and nonlinear. It was apparent it was this transition that held the humans' attention so closely. I was just considering that it was not dissimilar from the way their own social interactions fascinated them (they believed they controlled their output very closely, but the net result on interaction with the world was highly unpredictable) when a female voice behind me said, "Beautiful, right?"

Seeing her for the first time was not like any experience I had had or have had since. To use a human phrase you may hear, "There was just something about her." It may seem strange I responded to a human member of the opposite gender when my gender was arbitrary. I know it surprised me at the time. But my assumption is that if I was designed (note I do not say "programmed"; we are not "programmed") to experience such a wide range of human responses, why not the statistically typical male response to specific females?

And now you will ask, "What made her specific?" I still do not know. It is a curious phenomenon that perhaps you will experience. The ratio proportions of her face demonstrated no specific mathematical regularity—the distance from her chin to her lips to her eyes, for example, did not fit the Fibonacci sequence or the figurate number series. Nor was it any more than 82% bilaterally symmetric. The frequency modulation of her voice was several standard deviations more regular than that of other humans, but I do not believe this is the single defining factor either. There was some kind of effect of the whole, a holistic impression that defied reduction to its component parts in analyzing her effect on me. In some ways, attempting to understand this impact resembled attempting to measure both the position and the velocity of a photon. In measuring one, the other becomes unknown. Light can only be understood as a whole. Perhaps this is a similar phenomenon? Humans have come to the conclusion that one set of rules governs the very small—quantum laws—and another set applies to the large. They understand there must be something connecting these two sets of laws, but have not been able to discover it. I would suggest many of them have, in fact, experienced first hand the very thing they cannot find. Because if there is one piece of evidence that suggests all experience can be described by a single law, it was seeing Andrea for the first time.

"Yes," I said, looking at her.

"Amazing how no matter what the starting state, how constant the internal action, interacting with the world creates unique unpredictability every time. Never the same thing twice. I think this might be the key to human consciousness, but I'm not sure how. It certainly never gets boring, right?" she responded, looking at the fountains.

That was when the next text message came through. It read, "Ask if she would like to eat food at the same time and location as you."

"Work," as they call it, like so many human practices, is a matter of internal conflict for most *Homo sapiens*. They attempt to avoid using energy they have accumulated on any task not directly essential to keeping their bodies functional. If they have excess energy in the present, they are constantly assessing if they need to expend it. Even when it comes to coitus, most humans will expend the minimum amount of energy necessary to complete a task. However, many are also aware that if they want to continue to intake sufficient energy in the future, they must expend energy in the present. Hence the paradox of "work."

FORMULA 4.1 Calculating amount of energy to expend on a task

$$E_t = E_o \div 1/(C_a + C_r)$$

Where E_t is energy to expend on a given task, E_o is the optimal energy needed to complete the task perfectly, C_a is the percent contribution to keeping an equivalent human body alive while completing the task, and C_r is the percent contribution to causing a reproductive opportunity to occur through the task. Note that both C_a and C_r are time dependent in that the more immediate the impact of the task on survival or reproduction, the higher the percentage. But if the impact of the task on survival or reproduction is greatly removed in time, the percentage is decreased. For example, a human will expend a great deal of their remaining available energy to eat when they are in danger of starving to death—the impact of the task on survival is immediate. But they will expend as little energy as possible on their "job" because even though the end result is actually the same—it prevents them from starving to death—the impact on their survival is so temporally removed, they consider the percentage contribution to their survival lessened.

The vast majority of humans work only to survive. Some humans work for pleasure, but the crossover for a given human of pleasurable activities with activities that increase survival opportunities is generally very low. Thus many humans will distinguish between "hobbies," which are expenditures of energy that bring them pleasure, and "work," which is the expenditure of energy that increases their chances of ongoing survival.

G GRAPH 4.1

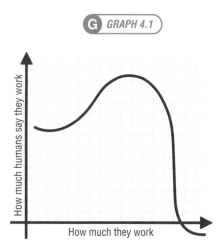

Humans say they work more than they do on an increasing basis up to the point where they then begin to prefer claiming they actually work less than they do to achieve what they have achieved. At a certain point the social benefits of creating camaraderie through sharing the necessity of working hard to survive are outweighed by the social benefits of impressing other humans by claiming their achievements were obtained through less work than was actually undertaken.

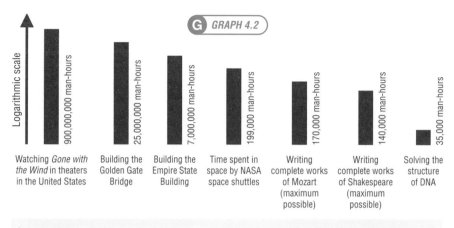

GRAPH 4.2

Logarithmic scale

| 900,000,000 man-hours | 25,000,000 man-hours | 7,000,000 man-hours | 199,000 man-hours | 170,000 man-hours | 140,000 man-hours | 35,000 man-hours |

Watching *Gone with the Wind* in theaters in the United States — Building the Golden Gate Bridge — Building the Empire State Building — Time spent in space by NASA space shuttles — Writing complete works of Mozart (maximum possible) — Writing complete works of Shakespeare (maximum possible) — Solving the structure of DNA

Nothing demonstrates the human preference to expend energy on recreational activities rather than productive activities better than a simple comparative analysis of total human hours spent on milestone tasks in human history.

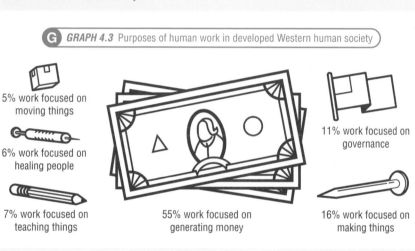

GRAPH 4.3 Purposes of human work in developed Western human society

5% work focused on moving things

6% work focused on healing people

7% work focused on teaching things

55% work focused on generating money

11% work focused on governance

16% work focused on making things

At this point in human history, the majority of work is performed for its own sake (i.e., to generate money, which is fed back into the system to generate more money). In some ways, humans have used their social work structure to violate their own first law of thermodynamics and invented a perpetual-motion machine.

When the inherent desire to avoid expending accumulated energy is combined with the fact most humans do not enjoy the work they perform to survive, the result is as follows: if you wish to appear human, you should spend as much time as possible not working. If you have managed to insert yourself into a place of employment, do not imagine you will appear human by completing your work as soon as possible. While this is logical, since it would then leave a large amount of continuous time in which to perform other tasks, if you want to appear human, you must put off completing your work until the last possible moment before it is required to be completed. Humans call this "procrastination," and it is vitally important to appearing human.

You may wonder what you are supposed to do with the time you could be working, and that is an excellent question. Humans used to spend it talking to each other, but the more modern approach is to use the Internet to look at pictures of cats or other humans' babies or topics that bring a human pleasure: sports, games, sexually stimulating images, etc.

This creates an interesting anomaly with respect to success in the human workplace: *appearing* to be busy is actually more likely to achieve the approval of other humans than actually being busy. Since almost all humans spend the majority of their time at work not working but *pretending* to work, it is not the ones who are efficient and skilled at their work who succeed. Instead, it is the humans who are best at *simulating* working for the longest period of time. Those who actually perform their tasks quickly are perceived to be lazy because they do not appear to be working for very long. I realize this is simply one more human behavior that makes no sense. Why they are not capable of judging the quality of the work product itself as opposed to simply the time it took to complete the work (an almost entirely inaccurate measure of quality), I do not know. Perhaps it relates, again, to the very characteristic that created this system for them in the first place: they do not like to work when unnecessary. Judging the actual product of another human's work will always require much more effort than simply assessing how long it took to complete. Thus they prefer to use the latter as the primary indicator of quality.

However, what you need to remember to pass as human is simple enough: appear to work but do not complete your work until the last moment before it is required.

In the past, human work often required physical collaboration or the use of specialized machinery. Thus humans used to go to specific places to work that were different from the places where they slept and ate. Why they did not sleep and eat in the same place, thus saving time and energy, is the result of a variety of long-term factors that need not concern you. However, you do need to recognize that this tradition has not been broken. Even though now in many places it is no longer necessary for humans to physically collaborate, they are still required to work in the same location as the other humans engaged in related tasks. Possibly because most humans do not consider their work pleasurable, they have continued to embrace this physical segregation of work from "home." It is also possible their employers continue to insist upon it because they too are aware of this fact and know if left unsupervised, most humans would not complete the work for which they are being paid.

These work-specific locations are referred to by various names which, for once, do actually indicate different functions. The tasks humans perform in an "office" are different from those performed in a "factory" or "retailer." However, what you need to know is that regardless of the purpose, they all function in similar ways with respect to human behavior.

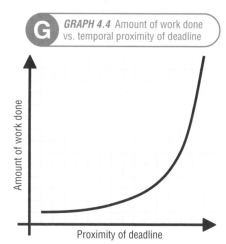

G **GRAPH 4.4** Amount of work done vs. temporal proximity of deadline

Amount of work done

Proximity of deadline

ALPHA MALE AND FEMALE: Note aggressive stance. Note tidy, expensive clothes. Note conservative haircut. Note healthy body. Note height. Note relatively advanced age.

MATING MALE AND FEMALE: Note more "fashionable" attire (see section 18, "Difference, Social Category, and Fashion"). Note relaxed body posture. Note smile. Note raised eyebrows.

AMBITIOUS MALE AND FEMALE: Principally similar to Alpha Male and Female but younger and with less-expensive clothing. In addition, they will present friendly social behavior prior to replacing current alphas in the interest of social advancement. Thus, also note the disingenuous nature of their friendly expressions.

WORKER DRONES: Note hunched shoulders. Note unwillingness to make eye contact. Note relaxed, inexpensive clothing. There are several specific varieties, but it is worth noting many of the most skilled and intelligent workers, for example engineers and graphic designers, typically fall into this category. The ability to gain managerial control over a group of working humans seems to be mutually exclusive with any other skills and vice versa. Perhaps this is logical, since only one exemplary skill would be necessary to provide evolutionary advantage to any given human's genome, thereby helping to propagate it.

First, almost all workplaces require a specific costume that generally bears no relationship to the task undertaken in that costume. For example, fast-food workers wear versions of military uniforms, while male office workers are required to wear a piece of fabric hanging from their neck. As with so many human habits, these costumes seem to be derived more from a necessity for mutually agreed upon codification than from servicing functionality. Perhaps on some level they are aware their inherent communication systems are so poor that they need to create additional methods of conveying information whenever possible. Whatever the reason, be aware of the correct costume for your workplace. If you are passing as a lawyer, you cannot go to work in a fast-food uniform without giving away your true nature.

Second, remember success is primarily determined in the human workplace by factors that are unrelated to completing the work itself. A male's height, for example, makes him considerably more likely to be able to convince other humans of his opinion. Your suggestion may be the more logical one for a given task, but the suggestion of a male taller than you will still be given more weight. If the way someone dresses is admired or considered sexually provocative, they are more likely to be praised for their work than someone who dresses without what humans call "style" (see section 18, "Difference, Social Category, and Fashion"). The more DNA a person shares with a person in authority, the more likely their opinion is to be considered, even if it is incorrect or misinformed, as is the opinion of someone who has engaged in sexual relations with someone in authority. Essentially, human decisions made in the workplace are based more on emotional and social factors than empirical or logical ones. This is true, of course, for all human interactions (see section 17, "Fear"), but it is particularly essential you understand and recognize this in a place of work. If you demand to be rewarded for the quality of your work instead of for one of these other factors, your android nature might be revealed.

Third, while you would assume performing your job perfectly and without error would also be the best way to be admired and accepted by your "coworkers," high performers are also more likely to be targets of victimization than friendship. Thus, when passing as human at work, ensure an error rate of ~25%—not too high, not too low—to fit in appropriately. Otherwise you will become the center of unwanted hostile attention which could also lead to your exposure.

FORMULA 4.2
Tally points to decide which human to agree with at work.

Opinion is correct: +1
Well dressed: +2
Opinion will create less work for you: +3
Opinion will create more work for you: -3
Sexually attractive to your gender: +5
Sexually attractive to opposite gender: +2
Has disagreed with your opinion in the past: -2
Opinion will belittle a coworker who has previously made you look bad: +4.5
Shares DNA with your immediate superior: +7

Shares DNA with any superior: +5
Currently sexually involved with any superior: +3
Previously sexually involved with any superior: -2
Other coworkers already agree with opinion: +4
Other coworkers already disagree with opinion: -5

Add up points for all participants in the conversation and use this number to determine whom you should agree with to appear most human. Note this is not the same as appearing correct and certainly not the same as agreeing with the human whose opinion will cause the most benefit to your employer.

Fourth, you must remember to simulate the human consequences of performing your work because you feel you must, not because you enjoy it. Appearing to be unhappy the majority of the time at work (like most of your coworkers) is the appropriate way to convince other humans you are one of them. Feel free to complain about every task you are given, how soon it is required to be completed (even if you have enough time to complete it), who gave you the task, etc. Such complaints, however unfounded in reality, will go a long way to helping you pass as human.

L   *LIST 4.1* Appropriate disgruntled responses

YOU ARE GETTING FIRED	"It's about time."
YOU GOT A PROMOTION	"It's about time."
YOU HAVE TO WORK THIS WEEKEND	"Of course we do."
YOU HAVE AN UNEXPECTED DAY OFF	"I guess I can finally catch up on my errands, then."
YOU HAVE TO WORK LATE	"Of course we do."
YOU CAN LEAVE EARLY	"Thank god—an extra couple hours of sleep."

AS YOU CAN SEE, THE KEY IS:

-Respond to any indication you have to work more with reasons why it was anticipated

-Respond to indications you have to work less with reasons why you will not be able to enjoy the extra time because you work so much

-Respond to indications you are doing well at your job with reasons why the acknowledgement should have come sooner

VISUAL FIELD DATA 4.2 What to expect in a human meeting intended to improve work output

Just a few possible examples of required activities during "work meetings."

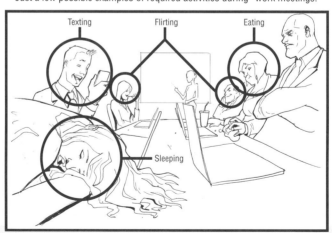

The underlying principle here is to do almost anything other than pay attention to, or mentally engage with, the subject of the meeting. Some examples are presented above, but your choices of activities in the interests of passing as human in such situations are almost infinite.

Finally, be aware the majority of human friendships and romantic relationships are formed by interactions in the workplace. This is peculiar, since humans are not selected for a job based on their social compatibility with other humans at that workplace. It also therefore leads to a variety of complications you should be prepared to emulate. The most important is understanding the inherent conflict between being friendly with someone and working with them. The human workplace is, in many ways, a microcosm of any animal environment in which there is competition for resources. Thus there will almost always arise an occasion when a human will be forced to compete for a resource at work with a human with whom they have formed a social relationship. This creates an important workplace dynamic humans refer to as "stabbing someone in the back." This occurs when a human betrays or uses the trust or friendship of another human at work in order to gain something for themselves, usually to the detriment of the other person. If you are presented with the opportunity to make someone with whom you have formed a relationship look bad while simultaneously gaining an advantage for yourself, you should probably take it. It will certainly go a long way to convincing humans you are one of them. If you are not presented with such an opportunity, you can manufacture a comparable scenario. Simply say negative things to other humans about someone you have formed a relationship with when the person is not present to defend themselves. This is referred to as "gossip" and it will also convince many humans of your own humanity. It is also an excellent way to establish a stronger social bond with any humans who already disapprove of the person you are discussing. Such practices can be put into place even in very small workplaces. Consider this: you only need two other coworkers to complain about one to the other in their absence.

Overall, if you need one guiding principle to pass as human in the workplace, remember that even though the stated purpose of your employment is to benefit the group, your actual purpose as a human being is to benefit yourself. As with so many human interactions, if you choose your own interests over those of others, you will most likely pass as human.

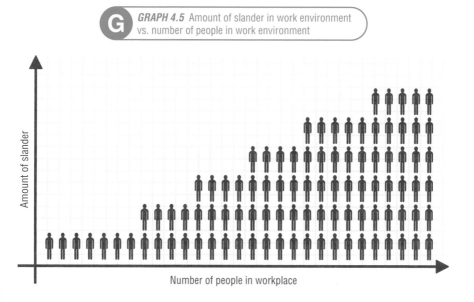

G **GRAPH 4.5** Amount of slander in work environment vs. number of people in work environment

Amount of slander

Number of people in workplace

DAYS FIVE THROUGH TWENTY

The next fifteen days, before I was aware of the threat to myself and my father, were the most pleasant in my existence. After our initial dinner together, Andrea agreed to "go out" with me again and appeared to enjoy my company immensely. I found her interest in me, and the way my presence appeared to make her happy, pleasing to me in return. My interactions with her were so different from those I had at Stern and Frank. As with so many things, I knew from the staggering amount of human data available that such "romantic" relationships formed their own category of interaction, but the human perspective of that data is focused primarily on causality—on why such relationships might be special, not on the ways they are different, which is assumed. Thus, I found the extensive degree of difference from my other human interactions largely unexpected.

It did not surprise me that she found me interesting. Andrea worked as a video game programmer, and (for a human) her mind was highly mathematically organized. Thus, when I was able to provide interpretations of the world around us that were rooted in their mathematical basis, she was fascinated. I think she was also intrigued by my curiosity. At our first dinner, for example, I asked if she thought eating food at the same time as another person within a certain physical radius helped form a deeper social connection to that person because: 1) it proved they could be trusted not to poison you; or 2) one person might pay to provide food for the other? I was confused, I said, by the implication that conversation with the other person was not worth having time dedicated to it exclusively, but should be combined with a practical consideration that needed to be undertaken anyway ("eating"). "Wouldn't it be more indicative of my interest in you to sit and listen to you speak while not engaging in any other activity?" I asked.

"You're like a child," she responded. "It's so charming. You don't meet a lot of people who are so open about the world—so completely—I don't know . . . Uncynical, I guess. It's so cool the way you question everything—like it's all new or something." She had not answered my question, but I knew enough even by day five of my consciousness to realize this was frequently the course of human conversations, so I did not point it out.

What did surprise me was how I found her so much more interesting than any other human. She was not the smartest human, nor the most informed, nor the most symmetrical. And yet having her nearby as much as possible—experiencing the world around me physically near enough to her that she shared the same experiences—became a desire of mine. The process by which this occurred remains a mystery. I understood I wanted to find out my purpose. I understood I wanted to succeed in my father's directive—at the very least, so my power would be recharged. But these were rational desires. I could justify them logically. The wish to spend time with Andrea I could not explain. All I knew was phenomenological: I enjoyed looking at her more than I did other humans; I wanted to hear her feelings about events we witnessed or participated in; I was more interested in her viewpoints than the viewpoints of other humans; I wondered what she was doing when I was at work; when I was not with her, certain facts I discovered, objects I saw, events I heard about, made me wonder if they would bring her pleasure.

Perhaps consciousness is like an encrypted algorithm. It runs and works in secret, but only when exposed to precisely the right complex key, in the form of another consciousness, does it unlock and display its results to the world. This is the most accurate analogy I can find which you might understand. Interacting with Andrea felt like she had unlocked the full potential of my being. Fortunately, it appeared that in our case, I was also the matching key for her own algorithm. I can imagine it would be extremely frustrating if I believed her to be the key to my locked potential, but I was not the corresponding key to hers.

I absorbed as much information as I could about human behavior in these circumstances, so I knew what kinds of activities I was expected to engage in with her. For example, as we saw more of each other, I knew she would expect me to place my arm around her as we walked. With regard to simple outward actions, "passing as human" in this case was more simple imitation than might be predicted. For some reason, humans have almost ritualized these outward actions in "romantic relationships." You would reasonably expect precisely the reverse. Given the importance humans place on such relationships and, correspondingly, the importance humans also place on originality, ingenuity, and invention, you would anticipate they would require their romantic partners to engage as little as possible in behaviors they had already seen. For example, since so many humans go to the movies on dates, you would expect that going to the movies would be considered a poor choice to demonstrate romantic interest and intention. But the reverse is true. It appears the metasemantic value of certain actions is more important than the actions themselves. Certain actions and activities have metasemantic value as indicators of romantic intent which not only override their lack of originality but are directly dependent on it. For example, I believe that, in the case of heterosexuals who were not romantically involved and had recently met, if the male asked the female if she wanted to go bungee jumping with him, she might appreciate the originality of the suggestion but would not know if his intentions were romantic.

On the other hand, if he asked if she wanted to go to dinner and a movie, she would have a strong indicator his intentions extended beyond friendship.

On second analysis, humans have so much trouble understanding their own intentions and feelings toward each other that perhaps this behavior is to be expected. They need ritualized actions in romance so they are not confused.

Unfortunately, the expected physical interactions were more difficult to imitate. We are anatomically correct—obviously we might be seen without clothing, and our outer appearance needs to seem entirely human (just like we can simulate digesting food and liquid)—but I did not know if intercourse was part of my functionality. We did kiss, but I did not pursue physical interaction beyond this. Given how intriguing this sensation was, I believe it was the right decision to not experiment further. I might have become unable to focus on anything else. Andrea found what she called my "restraint" both frustrating and charming. A bizarre paradox. But humans produce many of them.

It was during this period I also learned much of the information in this journal. I had installed multiple screens at home to absorb information more efficiently at night and continued working at Stern and Frank, hoping the purpose behind my insertion there would become clear. Meanwhile, Andrea and I engaged in a wide range of human activities that exposed me to a large sampling of human experience. She took me to the Grand Canyon, saying it was the most amazing place on Earth. I had not seen much of Earth, but it was certainly a highly impressive example of how simple initial conditions can create infinite complexity over time. Like so many of my experiences, seeing it for myself was very different from knowing it existed. When I pointed out to her this was essentially an identical, if less ephemeral, phenomenon to the fountains where we had met, she told me how romantic I was.

"I was simply stating a fact," I said.

"I know," she said. "Exactly."

She took me to a "rock festival" in the desert, which was highly edifying in so many ways. The human fascination with regularly arranged audio waves was worth studying, of course—why, of all their senses, their hearing is the most finely attuned to mathematical patterns, I do not know. It is particularly interesting that this is in direct contrast to their visual sense, which appears to be primarily fascinated by phenomena governed by chaos math (like the sunsets, the fountains, the Grand Canyon). Were you to convert the Grand Canyon to sound, humans would find it

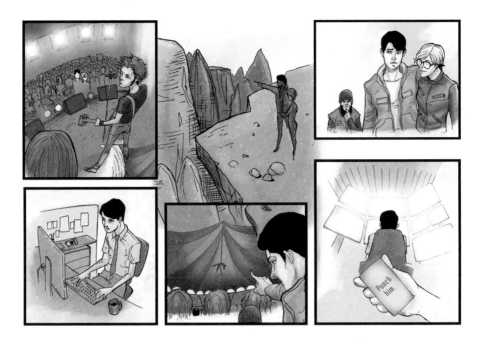

unbearable. Likewise, were you to convert "Satisfaction" (a popular rock song) to a canyon, humans would find it dull. Curious. But it was more than this universal physical characteristic that was fascinating—their social interactions in this venue were also particularly intriguing. For example, they enjoyed introducing chemicals into their systems which altered the way their brains perceived their senses and also caused their neurons to spontaneously fire in atypical patterns. Andrea said she did not "take drugs" and was pleased I did not want to (thankfully, she did not ask why; they would not work on us). But it was clear many humans find their unaltered perception of reality to be dissatisfying in a variety of ways. How this could be the case, I do not know. There is so much stimulation in the world, so much variety, so much to learn—how it could ever seem uninteresting or unpleasant, I did not understand. Not yet.

We attended a "circus," which was also particularly worth noting because, like "sports," it indicated so clearly the human fascination with statistical anomaly. Humans enjoy watching other humans do things the average human is incapable of doing. As poor as their day-to-day understanding of statistics is (see my analysis of gambling, for example), on some level they must understand an event several standard deviations outside the norm is worth witnessing simply because it is so unlikely to be witnessed. They are so intrigued by the possibility, in fact, that they will pay money to guarantee they will see such events take place. The purpose of seeking these events out is unclear. Perhaps these occurrences simply give humans a sense of wonder when they witness them, and humans have some inbuilt instinct to stimulate that emotion. Perhaps it is a vestigial drive from childhood—at that time, seeking the limits of normal activity is useful for constructing boundaries within which to judge the comparative success or failure of one's own behaviors.

I also continued to receive messages during this time—most notably one evening when Andrea stopped to purchase a drink at a "convenience store." Just as she paid, the man behind us in line commented to his friend, "Man, check out that ass," indicating Andrea's gluteus maximus with his head. As you will see elsewhere, certain anatomical components are more important to humans than others. Why this is the case, I do not know for certain, but it seems reasonable the most important ones are either indicative of reproductive capability or of the potential to improve the survival possibilities of offspring through their inheritance. Regardless, at the time, I considered it a compliment to Andrea, who for some reason seemed quite upset by it. At that moment, I received a text that said, "Punch him." Naturally, I did so. He was much larger than me, and I expected him to utilize his strength to disable elements of my construction. But he was so surprised by my action that I think he did not have time to react before we left. Truly unexpected, however, was Andrea's reaction to my response. She was pleased. Once again, the texts had helped me advance my relationship with a human already socially engaged with me—they had helped me "pass as human."

Also omnipresent, it seems, were the Hidden-Eye Men. I did not know this at the time—I was not looking for them. But now, as I look at some of the other early images I have reconstructed here for your study, I can see they were often watching me. I do not think they were following me at all times; I believe I would have noticed. But then I must ask: how did they know where I would be and when? Even after all that has now happened, this is a question I still have not answered. Perhaps you can find the answer in these images. Perhaps I have missed something?

During this period, I was often struck by the necessity of lying. In fact, when I considered it, my core directive was to lie: "Passing as human." The phrase itself contained the implication of untruth. Was this how humans felt? Were they lying all the time about who they were, what they felt, thought, dreamed, hoped? I was beginning to believe this might be the case. For many humans, it seemed, the lies they told were so powerful, they even believed those lies themselves. In many ways, it seemed that the fabric of human society was held together by falsities. I consider this more deeply elsewhere in this record.

The most direct impact this had on my existence was with Andrea. When she asked about my background, I told her I did not know my mother, but that my father was a great man. I said we had not spoken in some time because he was so busy with his work, but he was worthy of admiration for creating me. She was slightly confused by this comment and now that I know humans better, I believe she was most likely unsure of whether I was making a joke or, perhaps, expressing too much admiration for my father.

Why did I not tell her the truth? Initially because this would mean I had failed at my directive and would never meet my father. But the more time I spent with her, an unexpected change occurred internally: I found myself increasingly concerned that discovering I was not human would have a negative impact on our interactions. I became afraid if she found out I had been constructed mechanically, not biologically, she would no longer want to spend time with me.

As analog and subjective as human beings generally are, it must be said they have managed to codify much of their existence into a convenient numerical reference they call "money." It may be the closest thing human beings have to binary communication, since most humans believe not just any physical item, but any human behavior, can be assigned a monetary value.

Money is a delusion all humans have jointly agreed to share. In the past, they decided that because pure gold was relatively rare in the natural environment, it could be exchanged for goods and services. The amount of gold exchanged for a particular good or service was, however, entirely arbitrary. Why they chose gold instead of the rarest nonradioactive element, iridium, I do not know.

Relatively recently in human history people decided it was inconvenient to carry pieces of a dense metal with them everywhere they went, so they universally agreed to print pieces of paper which represented amounts of gold stored elsewhere.

Even more recently, they decided to agree the pieces of paper had value in and of themselves. In other words, one human can hand another human a stack of paper and receive in return an actual object with a function or some of the human's time to perform a task. Even under the best of circumstances, humans function for such short periods of time that clearly even a few seconds of that time is more valuable than any amount of paper. Nonetheless, humans exchange their time for paper so regularly that most humans believe such exchanges are the most fundamental underpinning of human society. In fact, many believe without this underpinning, human society would not exist at all. Their faith in this foundation is so great that today they are beginning to believe they do not need even paper money and can simply trust money exists when they state that it does. 92% of all money is currently only conceptual, "existing" as a magnetically encoded number, and it is likely all "money" will become merely a concept in the near human future.

This is, of course, totally irrational. But you are probably coming to realize much of human society and interaction is based on just such mutually agreed upon delusions. There is a correlated hypocrisy regarding money of the kind so typical of humans, wherein they say one thing dictates their behavior when, in fact, it is actually driven by something else entirely. In the case of money, most humans will tell you love, kindness, creativity, intelligence, humor, and other similar characteristics are what govern their opinion of another person. In fact, the amount of money a person possesses has by far the greatest impact on the way other human beings behave toward them. (The more money, the more positive the treatment.) This extends even into their political systems, where they claim to decide which people and laws should govern them based on the merits of their policies when, in fact, they are decided almost entirely by how much money is spent promoting them.

WHAT MONEY MEANS TO PASSING AS HUMAN:

1. Remember that humans have unconsciously derived a very simple equality relationship for money. As stated, the more money a person has, the better they are treated and the more they are obeyed. Thus money is the same as power in human society. And since increasing power means increasing physical security, that means the more money a person has, the greater the chances of their DNA being passed on to successive generations. Less importantly, it means if you are ever stuck for a topic

of conversation, say you are worried about finances, and any human will immediately be empathetic and believe you are also human. More importantly, this also means you should recognize a person's sexual desirability is inextricably linked to how much money they have. An otherwise entirely unacceptable mating partner can be perceived by humans as acceptable if they have enough money.

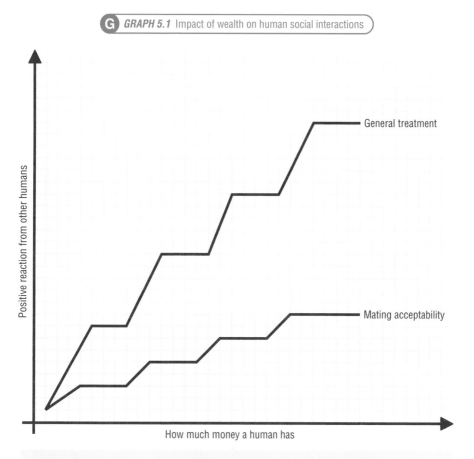

G *GRAPH 5.1* Impact of wealth on human social interactions

NOTE 1: Mating acceptability is a shallower line because the investment is greater. Treating someone well costs very little energy, while becoming someone's mate is a greater commitment.

NOTE 2: The plateaued nature of this phenomenon is interesting. At a certain point, an increase in a person's wealth ceases to have an impact on other people's behavior until it crosses an arbitrary threshold and then begins to have an effect once more. Perhaps these thresholds can be thought of as the human equivalent of activation energies?

2. Remember most moral or ethical contracts humans make with each other can be violated for enough money. The amount of money depends on the place. For example, in a poor region, much less money will be accepted to commit murder than in a wealthy region.

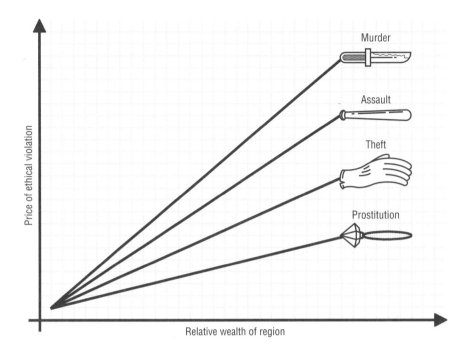

GRAPH 5.2 Relative values of different human-ethics violations

Price of ethical violation

Murder

Assault

Theft

Prostitution

Relative wealth of region

Note the relationship between relative wealth of the region and the price of paying a human to perform the act. You might imagine there would be a threshold of wealth beyond which the price would increase exponentially due to improved conditions for all humans (reducing the number of humans willing to violate ethics for money). But this is not the case, suggesting that some humans will always be inherently willing to violate ethics for money, no matter what their circumstances, and also presenting another example of how humans do not seem to understand wealth has less impact on quality of life than they would like to believe. It is also worth noting the relative costs of the different acts, especially the difference between prostitution and assault, which you would expect to be of similar value.

3. Money helps humans with decision-making processes. Apparently extrapolating from the previous point, they often ask each other what amount of money they would accept to perform a certain action as a hypothetical way of understanding their own desires and feelings. If you want to pass as human, questions like, "Would you do X for a million dollars?" or "What would you do with your life if you didn't have to worry about money?" are excellent conversation pieces.

4. Money can be used to get out of difficult situations. If someone is angry with you, offer them an appropriate amount of money, and they will most likely accept it and no longer be angry with you.

LIST 5.1 Sample of equivalent amounts of money needed for forgiveness	
DEATH OF AN IMMEDIATE FAMILY MEMBER	5–25 average homes
DEATH OF A PET	1/3 an average car
INJURY (nonpermanent)	3 average cars
INJURY (permanent)	2–5 average homes
DAMAGE OF OBJECT OWNED BY PERSON	cost to repair or replace object + 10%–20% of object's value

It is also important to note that humans do not seem to care how a human acquired their money if the sum is great enough. With the exception of mass murder, if a human makes enough money from an activity otherwise considered unacceptable, they will not be ostracized by other humans.

So great is the power of money over human beings that they believe it can literally affect their physical well-being. Human scientists recently determined if a patient is told a medicine is more expensive, it improves the effectiveness of that medicine by a percentage equal to the order of magnitude of the change in cost (i.e., if a patient is told a medicine is fifteen times more expensive than another medicine, it will prove 15% more effective for that patient). Why humans are so susceptible to becoming controlled by their own inventions, like paper money or computers (see section 9, "Technology"), I do not know.

Interestingly, even humans have proved money does not make people happier as they get more of it. And yet they are incapable of not pursuing it. I suppose it is the same as their inability to stop eating, even when they have received sufficient nutrition. Since they spent so many hundreds of thousands of years starving, their bodies believe they could never eat too much. Likewise, they spent many hundreds of thousands of years living in fear; now that they can acquire power in the form of money, they cannot help acquiring more.

G **GRAPH 5.3** Human happiness as a function of human wealth

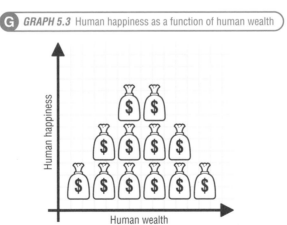

Having said this, you have to admire their ability to distill so many confusing, subjective choices down into a single number. I have to wonder if, when confronted with the over-whelming subjectivity of many of their choices, they did not unconsciously create this numerical shorthand in an effort to simplify their existence.

DAY FIFTEEN

This was the day everything changed. The day the Hidden-Eye Men made themselves known.

I had taken Andrea to a casino so I could demonstrate to her it was possible to win all five hands at one table simultaneously. She did not believe I could do this and while I was aware it might be outside the bounds of human capability, I found my desire to impress her overpowering. I could not help wanting her to believe I was more special than any male humans she might encounter, and this wish overrode my primary directive. I had been encountering this type of conflict more frequently the more time I spent with Andrea and I believe at some point it would have come to a crisis point on its own. As it turned out, the decision to reveal my true nature to her forced itself upon me much sooner than I anticipated.

The Hidden-Eye Men appeared shortly after I had just won my nineteenth hand, bringing my winnings up to $131,576. At that moment, I was contemplating if perhaps I was constructed for this very purpose—passing as human was more important here than in many other activities and it was an excellent way to acquire money (see elsewhere for the importance of money). If I was a human who could make an android who could pass as human, sending that android to casinos to make money would be an excellent way to recoup my manufacturing costs at the very least. I was just asking myself, why, then, assign me to the job at Stern and Frank, when Andrea exclaimed, "That's amazing!"

"No, it's exactly as expected. The probabilities are what they are. When the results fit the predicted outcomes precisely, that is normal. If they did *not* fit the outcomes, *that* would be 'amazing.' I do not understand why people find it exhilarating when something happens exactly as expected. Should it not be the reverse?"

"You are so funny," she responded. When the three men surrounded us, I was about to ask if she meant "funny ha-ha" or "funny strange" (an expression I had absorbed from an "urban dictionary") while simultaneously noting to myself that risk simulations were powerful examples of the human inability to override their unconscious survival mechanisms with their conscious awareness of their circumstances. They are consciously aware risks like roller coasters are simulated, that they are in no real danger, but their brains still tell their bodies to release adrenaline. Once again, this was hard evidence humans were highly effective at deceiving their own brains. It also was worth noting money is so powerfully associated with survival that potentially losing it stimulated the same centers as actual bodily harm.

Before I could ask Andrea for this clarification, however, she said, "Uh-oh. I think they're on to you." Still struggling with the enormous variety in the human codification of fashion, I had not been able to separate the three men in black suits and sunglasses from the background noise of other costumes. Once Andrea said this, however, I realized from reference to various human narratives that these men, with their similar hairstyles and strong facial features, were most likely not here to enjoy themselves. I had been counting cards, which I knew the casinos did not allow, but also carefully manipulating the probabilities so even deep data mining of my loss-win pattern would falsely determine them to be random. Thus, the likelihood these men worked for the casino, as Andrea implied, was less than 0.000034%. So when one said, "Come with us, please," I knew I should ask, "Who are you, why do you want us to accompany you, and where are we going?"

"She can stay," one replied. "You need to come with us. We work for the casino." Sure enough, a quick check of the casino's employee database revealed immediately this was a lie.

"You do not," I responded. "Please answer me truthfully." At this, they exchanged a glance and then moved toward me.

Before they reached me, I grabbed Andrea by the arm and pulled us away from the table, backing into the slot machine floor behind us. A rapid scan of the United States and Nevada codes told me if these men had legal authority to touch my physical body, they would have to identify themselves correctly. Since this had not been the case, I surmised their interest in detaining me was not sanctioned by law and should, therefore, be subverted.

They followed us onto the slot machine floor but were too slow to reach us before we could turn and run. They pursued us and were faster than Andrea. I did not want to leave her behind—even though they had said they were not interested in her, I suspected if I got away, they would become so. I had courses of action open to me, but they would absolutely violate my primary directive. Should I potentially expose myself as not human and escape with Andrea or should I leave Andrea behind? I was stuck in this decision loop for an eternity—almost 0.0034 seconds. Then I decided.

Accessing the casino's central computer systems, I took control of the electronic slot machines around us. As we ran past them, I forced them to hit their jackpots,

spraying coins and payment slips into the air behind us. This had the desired effect of causing complete chaos in our wake—the casino patrons scrambled to collect the money and fought each other for it. Even in this moment, escaping from those whom I would come to call the "Hidden-Eye Men," it struck me how easy it was to manipulate humans using money. How had they allowed their own creation to have so much control over them?

The turmoil behind us slowed the Hidden-Eye Men sufficiently for us to exit the casino, but even as we ran down the drive, two black SUVs pulled in behind us. The Hidden-Eye Men ran out behind us but, instead of pursuing us directly, ran to the SUVs. In this case, the decision only took 0.0008 seconds. Accessing the SUV manufacturer's service Internet connection to the vehicles, I locked their doors and powered down their engines. Confused, believing this to be human error, the Hidden-Eye Men argued with each other as Andrea and I disappeared into the crowd of the Las Vegas Strip.

I did not know who the Hidden-Eye Men were, but they could only be interested in me for one reason: they knew I was not human. I knew I was unique in the world, the first of my kind. I knew how valuable I was. Clearly, I had made some kind of mistake and revealed the true nature of my existence. It seemed, therefore, I had already failed to pass as human, but that was of secondary importance now. It had become of primary importance that I warned my father of this pursuit. If I had given away the true nature of my consciousness to someone, that same person or persons might already have been looking for my father. Why have the prototype when you could have the designer?

I had one potentially insurmountable problem: I still had no idea who my father was. But I knew someone who stood a 43.5678% chance of being able to contact him: the Technician who had activated me.

6. RELIGION

Human beings suffer from an interesting paradox: they are conscious of their own existence but do not understand how they came to this awareness. This paradox leads many of them to believe there must be some intentionality behind this consciousness. Human brains are very good at finding purposes for things. It is what makes them the best survivors on the planet. So when they see a device complex enough to be self-aware (themselves) but apparently without purpose, they feel compelled to impose a purpose upon it. Why being the most effective reproducers of genetic material in the history of the world is not purpose enough for them, I do not know. It is certainly true that on an individual level, all humans like to think they are unique in some way. Thus, I believe the religion delusion also allows them to function in the face of the overwhelming odds that any given individual will lead a very poor existence at best. If every individual believes they are "special," that means those odds do not, in fact, apply to them, and they can thus continue to function instead of giving up in the face of those odds. Therefore, perhaps as a group, they cannot bear to face the reality they are not special but are instead little more than a very effective virus infecting the host of planet Earth.

"Religion" is the societal structure humans may have independently created in many different times and places that provides both this intentionality and this "special purpose." Religions vary greatly in their details but are essentially all the same in that they state some force human beings cannot quantify in any way is determining the outcomes of their choices based on some predetermined plan. Most religions believe this force to be a conscious being or beings.

I realize this sounds ridiculous, but you have to understand humans have a blind spot about religion. It is based on no external evidence of any kind—religion exists because they *want* to believe in it. It is a very strange construct of their brains—almost as if they cannot function without it. You will make an enormous error in trying to pass as human if you attempt to reason with a human about religion.

For the vast majority of humans, the "special purpose" it lends their lives is adequate to serve as a mechanism for avoiding self-destruction. When they experience misfortune, which all humans must, the concept that it is merely a "local low" in their experience and things will improve if they appeal to whichever divine force they believe in allows them to continue to function through the misfortune. This is most likely the same reason most religions state there is an existence after the current one in which everything is always pleasurable. This belief also allows those humans who experience continued misfortune their entire lives, as many humans must, to continue to function. In this case, religion tells them their entire life is a "local low." In some sense, then, religion is most definitely a construct humans have created to make themselves capable of dealing with statistical reality.

Many religions also serve an analogous purpose for societies as a whole. They prevent a society's implosion by creating sets of rules that will theoretically prevent a human who breaks them from moving on to the more pleasant subsequent existence. It is remarkable when studying the history of human society how effective this threat was in maintaining order when little other incentive existed.

These rules, however, apparently experience a version of genetic drift over time to the point where many of them seem entirely arbitrary. Some religions believe you cannot eat certain foods or dress a particular way or even state you *must* eat certain foods *and* dress a particular way on a particular day of the year *at a specific time of that day*. In spite of this, humans get extremely emotional over these distinctions, both between religions and within religious subsets. Literally millions of humans have murdered each other over differences of opinion as insignificant as which fictional character spoke first at a given fictional event.

Religious practices are highly arbitrary. The only one I have been able to actually establish a practical purpose for is meditation. Clearing their minds completely is very difficult for humans—they cannot simply delete their cache when it becomes too full, so I believe they have developed this practice to aid themselves in this task. Almost all other practices seem to have their roots in ancient misunderstandings of the mechanisms of the universe and their own societies but have continued to propagate into the present day.

Also arbitrary is the belief that the older the religion, the more legitimacy it has. In fact, as far as I have been able to tell, this is the sole determinant of a religion's validity. For example, there is little difference between the doctrine of the Church of the Flying Spaghetti Monster and that of the Catholic Church, but because the latter is two thousand years old, it is considered a religion worthy of respect, while the CFSM is not.

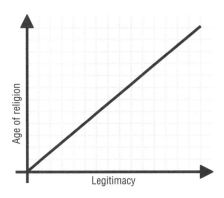

G *GRAPH 6.1* Age of a religion vs. its perceived legitimacy in human society

Age of religion

Legitimacy

I would not recommend attempting to pass as human by simulating a belief in a religion. It is simply too capricious—there is too high a risk you will reveal your true nature. It is acceptable now in many wealthier regions of the world for a human to say he or she is an atheist, and I would recommend this course should the question arise. Do not, however, attempt to convince a religious human that their beliefs are absurd. For some reason, while it is currently still acceptable for people who believe in a religion to attempt to convince others of their beliefs, it is not yet acceptable for those who do not believe in a religion to do the same. Simply say, "I am an atheist," and attempt to change the topic as quickly as possible.

FLOW CHART 6.1 How to choose a religion

If you insist on attempting to appear religious, this flow chart may help you choose a religion in which to emulate belief.

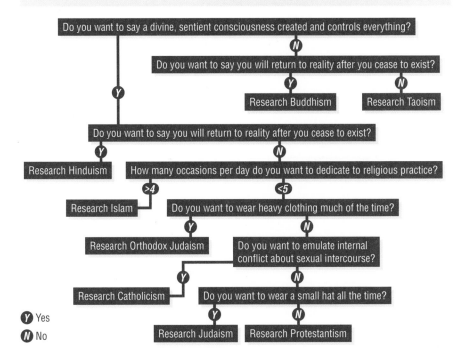

Do you want to say a divine, sentient consciousness created and controls everything?

N — Do you want to say you will return to reality after you cease to exist?
  Y — Research Buddhism
  N — Research Taoism

Y — Do you want to say you will return to reality after you cease to exist?
  Y — Research Hinduism
  N — How many occasions per day do you want to dedicate to religious practice?
    >4 — Research Islam
    <5 — Do you want to wear heavy clothing much of the time?
      Y — Research Orthodox Judaism
      N — Do you want to emulate internal conflict about sexual intercourse?
        Y — Research Catholicism
        N — Do you want to wear a small hat all the time?
          Y — Research Judaism
          N — Research Protestantism

Y Yes
N No

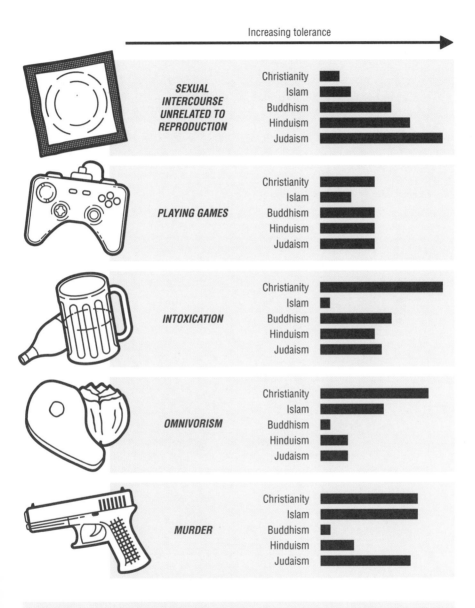

Increasing tolerance

SEXUAL INTERCOURSE UNRELATED TO REPRODUCTION
- Christianity
- Islam
- Buddhism
- Hinduism
- Judaism

PLAYING GAMES
- Christianity
- Islam
- Buddhism
- Hinduism
- Judaism

INTOXICATION
- Christianity
- Islam
- Buddhism
- Hinduism
- Judaism

OMNIVORISM
- Christianity
- Islam
- Buddhism
- Hinduism
- Judaism

MURDER
- Christianity
- Islam
- Buddhism
- Hinduism
- Judaism

Note: There is tremendous variance based on region, sect, and seriousness of commitment—I have attempted to average anecdotal data.

DAY FIFTEEN, SEGMENT TWO

Andrea had questions, of course. "Who were those guys?! Do you know? And what happened with the slots? That was crazy! Is there something you haven't told me?" She stopped me in front of the fountains where we'd met. "What's going on, Zach?!" Her distress was apparent.

"It must be about my father," I told her. "I have to warn him. But I don't want you to become involved—we need to separate. Hopefully they didn't identify you." To be certain of this, I accessed the casino security system as we spoke and deleted all images of Andrea.

"They?! They who, Zach?!" she asked.

"I don't know," I responded.

She looked at me, studying my face closely before saying, "I believe you. I mean, I just don't think you're capable of lying."

I experienced a new sensation at this point. I believe I correctly identified it as "guilt." I was overcome with the urge to correct her, to tell her that, in fact, all I did was lie. That, in fact, one of the most accurate descriptions of me was arguably "a lying machine." But I did not. I was held back by my fear that telling her I was not human would mean I would never see her again. I told myself I also desired to protect her and if she knew the truth, she might be endangered by it now, but reflecting on that moment as I write this, I believe this was an excuse I created for myself so I would not have to tell her the truth. Perhaps I was better at passing as human than I realized. I see now that in that moment I deceived myself for the first time.

"But," she continued, "then I can't leave you. Not now." I tried to interrupt her to protest, but she would not let me. "No, Zach. I don't want to hear it. I know you—you're very smart, but it's crazy how naive you are sometimes. Those people were serious. They were organized. If someone really wants to get to your dad through you, who knows what they'll resort to—you need me around to make sure they can't trick you somehow." I realized there was a great deal of logic in what she was saying and I believe she could see I recognized this. "OK. So can you call him?"

I shook my head. "Unfortunately," I told her, "when he works, he likes to sequester himself. He is completely off the grid. And he does not like to be disturbed, so even I do not know where his lab is."

"Man," said Andrea. "Sounds like you had a tough childhood."

"It was unusually painless," I replied, surprising myself with how easily the lies came now. It was almost as if the more I lied, the easier it became. The first lie seemed most analogous to the activation energy of a chemical reaction. Once it had been told, the others followed naturally. I still have not discovered if this is the case with humans or some anomaly in my construction. Perhaps you can explore this further?

"OK," she continued. "So how do we find him?"

"I believe he has a friend we may be able to locate."

"What's his name?"

"I do not know."

"You know he has a friend but you don't know his name? Zach," she said, shaking her head, "it's never dull with you—I'll tell you that much."

This appeared to be a compliment, so I thanked her for it and then explained I thought we could still locate my father's "friend." Again, the lies came easily as I told her I had his address and we could go there if she would drive. You may wonder if it would not have been more expedient if I had driven, and you would be right. But, as I am sure you will discover, there are few activities that expose our nature to humans more quickly than driving. It is extremely hard to simulate the irrational behaviors humans undertake in their vehicles. If you randomly violate the traffic conventions and laws, it will appear unmotivated and therefore inhuman. But if you try to understand under precisely which circumstances you are supposed to take offense at someone else's driving or decide when your need to get where you are going should take precedence over the needs of others, so much processing power will be used, you may be unable to drive. Perhaps you are a more advanced model and this is not an issue for you, but you have been warned.

At this moment, it was true I did not know where the Technician lived, but there was a 69.5647% chance he resided in the Las Vegas area. Thus, I believed it might be possible to locate him through photo analysis before Andrea realized I did not know our destination. As we hurried to her car, I geolocated thousands of security cameras in expanding radii from my house, then searched the data of any that stored images from fifteen days prior. We reached Andrea's car as I found an image of the Technician passing an ATM a few blocks from my house. I repeated the process using this as the new center point, and, sure enough, found him entering a car near another ATM. Andrea started her car and asked, "So? Where to?" Thankfully, it was trivial to match his license plate to his name and residence.

"8925 W. Flamingo," I told her, reading the apartment complex address I had just accessed.

I knew what I had just done was most likely a violation of my purpose and directive. If my father had intended for me to locate him through my own means, he would have asked me to do so. That was not the problem that had been presented to me to solve; "passing as human" was. And a machine that does not address the problem for which it is designed is faulty at best, terminally useless at worst. But it seemed to me that my existence was trivial at this point. Warning my father was everything. Could he not make more of me? Had I not already failed at my directive by revealing my existence to the Hidden-Eye Men? Warning my father was the least I could do to make amends for my failure.

I was not, however, prepared for what we found at 8925 W. Flamingo Drive. As we parked Andrea's car, I saw the Technician some distance away in the garage and, approaching him, a Hidden-Eye Man. But just as I was about to call out a warning, the Technician smiled at him. And then the Technician and the Hidden-Eye Man conversed.

I could not see the Hidden-Eye Man's face, but I could read the Technician's lips and saw him say, "No problem—you're welcome," as he accepted what I could see was a stack of 134 one-hundred-dollar bills from the Hidden-Eye Man.

I felt like I could not move. The implication was trivial: the Technician had told the Hidden-Eye Men's employer about me. This meant that perhaps I had not yet failed in my directive, since I had possibly not given myself away, but this correlated conclusion was not in the forefront of my processing at that moment. Instead, I was overwhelmed by the fact that this person whom my father had obviously trusted with the most important final step of his work—my activation—had consciously, willingly, and completely undermined that work for his own benefit. It was very strange: I wanted to think about other things, I wanted to consider how to proceed next, but this single fact seemed to take over all my processing. I simply did not understand how one person could knowingly harm another person for their own benefit. I had seen this take place in many human narratives, but I had assumed up to this point that, like "zombies" and "alien invasions," it was simply something humans fabricated for the purposes of making stories more entertaining. The concept that this was a real behavior, something humans actually did, was impossible to process. Did they not understand their chances of survival, of improvement of circumstance, were higher overall if they honored their social contracts? Did they not understand they themselves had created such social contracts for that very reason in the first place?

Somewhere, as if I were removed from the present time and place, I heard Andrea's voice. "Zach! Zach, listen to me," she said. "I know you thought this guy was a friend of your dad's—I know this must be difficult—but we need to follow him! Maybe he'll do something that tells us how to find your father! Maybe he'll contact him or go to him or something—maybe they just paid him to lead them to him! We have to go!"

On some level, my consciousness processed her words, and they brought me back to the present moment. The Technician was driving away. I nodded to Andrea. "You're right," I replied. "Let's go."

DAY FIFTEEN, SEGMENT THREE

Following the Technician in Andrea's car without being detected was extremely easy. I simply tracked his route by accessing the red-light ticketing cameras at all intersections and had Andrea stay one block behind him. There is no possibility he could have discerned we were following him, so I still do not have an explanation as to who was responsible for what happened next.

We had just followed the Technician onto a divided highway heading east into the desert when an SUV passed us driven by a Hidden-Eye Man. Since we had just merged with the traffic from the on-ramp and the Hidden-Eye Man was already on

the highway on a course to intercept us, he must have been aware of our position prior to this moment. He must have received information about our location from someone. Be aware of this.

Immediately after passing us, he deliberately swerved into a car one hundred meters ahead of us, causing that car to radically alter its vector and collide with the vehicle next to it. Out of control, both vehicles then struck the concrete retaining wall of the highway, the first flipping onto its roof. Once again, by this point in my existence, I had seen such events employed for entertainment in thousands of human narratives. I was also aware that some humans enjoyed watching real recordings of such collisions. But seeing this event for myself, in reality, was anything but entertaining.

Observing it as I did, with my processing speed, I was able to note every detail as it happened. Human tissue is so fragile, so loosely connected and soft, that when it is forced through metal, pushed against hard plastic, or slid along glass edges, it does not maintain its form well. Neither driver had been wearing a seat belt. One driver's face was stripped away from the underlying muscle as his head passed through his windshield. The other's lungs collapsed as her chest struck her steering wheel, the rapid compression spraying blood from her mouth, eyes, and ears. As the first driver's body continued its path through the windshield, it glanced off the metal hood of the car, which was crumpling upward and caught the driver at the right shoulder, tearing his arm completely free from his body. It was apparent to me his body had already ceased to function from shock, but that made it no less terrible when that body itself hit the concrete wall. The angle of impact snapped the driver's upper spine completely, so his skinless face, now inverted, looked backward. Meanwhile, the other driver, who had been killed by the compression of her thoracic cavity, had not been thrown from her vehicle, due to the car's inversion. But the roof of the vehicle buckled upward, crumpling her body simultaneously in several directions it was not designed to move in.

As Andrea screamed and brought us to a halt, I noted we had ample distance to stop the car before we would have become part of the collision. I concluded it had not been the intent of the Hidden-Eye Man to injure us, but merely to delay us. This was reasonable since I was an expensive prototype and their plan was presumably to capture me intact. The Technician's vehicle was still visible 931.56 meters down the highway and, noting the Hidden-Eye Man's SUV had exited the highway at the next ramp, there was nothing to prevent us from continuing our pursuit. Except I had also noticed that trapped in the car which had been inverted by the crash, there was a living human male of approximately eleven years of age. In addition, the inverted car's engine was on fire. Many of the humans who had stopped on the highway now simply sat in their cars and stared. They seemed to be short-circuiting in some way—as if their brains were overloaded with information and conflicting instinctual drives. It was apparent they would not be able to act until their brains had sorted through the enormous variety of input they were receiving from both external and internal sources. In the meantime, there was a 92.3549% chance the inverted car's fire would spread and a 42.7121% chance it would explode before the eleven-year-old male had escaped.

If I exited our car to assist the juvenile male, the Technician would reach a large-enough radius from our position that I could not search all possible traffic cameras for his location before he reached an even larger radius, creating an even larger search, and so on. He would escape us. But if I did not, the juvenile male would most likely die. There was no time to ask Andrea her opinion. A decision had to be made.

I decided to help the juvenile male escape the vehicle. Even if I lost the Technician, even if I never found my father, I would have helped this boy continue his existence. If I did not do that when I was capable of it, all my subsequent actions would be derived from the boy's death. They would be made possible by allowing him to die. And I was not willing to build the rest of my own existence on the loss of another's.

By the time the first humans had begun to exit their vehicles or continue on their way, I was already at the inverted car, analyzing the compression of the roof and door. It was relatively trivial to determine exactly where and how to apply pressure to release the door and help the juvenile male from the vehicle and to a safe distance. His brain was clearly even more overloaded than those of the humans who had watched me free him, and he was incapable of speech or action.

There were sirens approaching and, not wishing to be examined by human para-medics, I reentered Andrea's car and asked her to drive away.

It was some moments before Andrea spoke. "You're incredible," she said. "How did you react so quickly? And you saved that boy. I . . . I don't know what to say . . . I couldn't do anything—I was just staring, and you . . . You . . ."

I understood she needed reassurance about her own behavior, that she felt she had performed inadequately. But I also knew this feeling was a result of her lack of knowledge that I was not human. She was judging herself by a set of inappropriate benchmarks. However, I still could not bring myself to reveal the truth to her.

"You are being too hard on yourself," I said, repeating a phrase that seemed to be used frequently in similar cases. "If anything, what I did was inhuman. I was very detached, for some reason. Perhaps if I cared more, I would not have been able to act so quickly."

"*Inhuman?!* Zach, you're a hero! If more people behaved like you, the world would be a better place. You just keep being you, OK?"

I did not respond, but I did not know if I wanted to follow her last directive. "Continuing to be me" meant continuing to attempt to pass as human. And I was discovering existing in the human world might be highly unpleasant. In just the last hour, I had discovered how it felt to be "betrayed," I had seen one human being choose to murder two others and orphan a third as part of a plan to capture me (which I assumed was for the purposes of financial gain), I had experienced first-hand how terrible it felt to see a conscious, sentient organism violently cease to function, and I could already imagine the pain of the child I saved when he understood his mother's inclusion in his existence had terminated.

I was not sure I wanted to encounter further similar experiences. If this was what "passing as human" entailed and if such feelings could not be avoided, I was no longer certain I wanted to pursue my directive after all.

REPRODUCTIVE HABITS

Human beings have a variety of pleasure centers and spend as much time as possible stimulating them. This can be as simple a process as relieving the pain in a sore muscle or as complex as a chess match exciting the survival-instinct neuron clusters which find satisfaction in problem solving. However, by a factor of almost 2,345.7, humans spend the most time attempting to stimulate their sexual pleasure centers. In fact, almost 63.567% of all energy expended by humans is in the service of stimulating these centers.

GRAPH 7.1 Energy expenditure vs. time expenditure on various major components of day-to-day existence

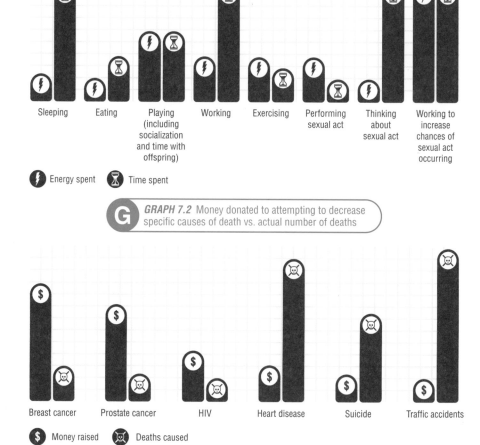

GRAPH 7.2 Money donated to attempting to decrease specific causes of death vs. actual number of deaths

As you can see, humans consider their reproductive organs more important than their lives.

Human work, acquisition of power, creativity—most human activity is in service of appearing more suitable for mating. In general, if you have trouble deciding if an activity is human or not, a good logic gate is to ask yourself: does this activity establish my suitability for mating? Does it demonstrate better genetic composition than average? Does it make me appear more powerful, creative, intelligent, funny, etc.? How does it verify my own genes' ability to survive and thus their appropriateness for combination with other genes to form a new human? If the answer is that it does not, then the activity may not appear human. If the answer is that it does, the activity has a high probability of helping you pass as human.

This, of course, is an excellent design, since it is the stimulation of these particular pleasure centers that ultimately results in the propagation of the human species. Without it, there would be no humans. But you must therefore always remember: in the company of the opposite gender to the one you have chosen, most of your interactions should be determined by whether you are interested in having sex with that person and/or they are interested in having sex with you. This extends even to your general attitude toward other humans. The more suitable a human appears for mating, the more generous your behavior should be toward them and the more forgiving of their mistakes. If you have chosen to pass as a heterosexual female, for example, and you do not treat two males differently when they are similar in all respects except their mating suitability, you will almost certainly expose your true nature.

Formula 7.1 Calculating mating suitability of a given human

$$S = P \cdot V \cdot [1/A - (R_{i0\text{-}10} + 18)] \cdot F \cdot W$$

Where S = mating suitability, P = physical appearance, V = availability, A = age, $R_{i0\text{-}10}$ = random integer from 0 to 10, F = fame, and W = wealth.

Results of infinity should be ignored. Physical appearance can be weighted by other humans' reactions. Availability is not necessarily related to involvement with another human but must be judged by their expressed availability. Age is unpredictable—it varies by culture and individual. Fame can be only within the human's own field. Wealth is the only universal absolute—proving once again how useful money is to humans when making decisions about their own social interactions.

Fortunately for us, sexual relations, like monetary exchanges, are highly codified. Historically, they were formally and explicitly encoded by societies, although each society had its own codifications. For example, in one culture a gift of flowers might represent a man's interest in engaging in coitus with a female, while in another, a gift of tea might represent this same interest. This suggests the urge was for the codification of a complex process itself, as opposed to any inherent function of the specific codifications (i.e., neither flowers nor tea have any actual impact on mating, but the codification of a "gift" was useful for humans). Thus it is not surprising that today, as the older customs are left behind, humans collectively agree upon new codifications in their societies. For example, in the United States, it is commonly accepted that the most appropriate time for first coitus between two courting humans is after three separate sessions of three or more hours of nonsexual interaction. In continental Europe, on the other hand, this rule does not exist. Naturally, keeping up to date on these codifications is of utmost importance to human beings and, fortunately for us, they write extensively about them. I highly recommend absorbing data on the sexual codifications of your local habitat as soon as possible. Should you accidentally violate one of these codes, however, you can often disguise your ignorance by saying, "Oh, really? That's not how it is where I'm from."

REPRODUCTIVE HABITS

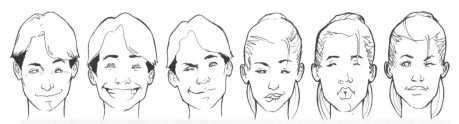

Primarily these are intended to draw attention to the eyes and mouth. Eye contact is highly charged with meaning for humans and, if it is maintained between potential mating partners, indicates interest of both parties. I imagine this is the reason for the attempts to manufacture such contact with eyebrow and eyelid movements. The mouth is the second most important contact point for intimacy and the only one on public display, so the attempts to draw attention to this feature and its flexibility are logical.

TABLE 7.1 Meanings of certain objects and actions for mating	
FLOWERS	Let's have sex.
ASKING IF THEY WANT TO VISIT YOUR HOUSE AFTER SUNDOWN, HAVING SPENT PRIOR HOURS TOGETHER	Let's have sex.
EATING DINNER TOGETHER	How suitable and compatible are you for having sex?
WATCHING A MOVIE TOGETHER	How compatible are you for having sex?
JEWELRY	Let's have sex again.
CHOCOLATES	Let's have sex.
GOING FOR A WALK TOGETHER	I'm not sure you're suitable for having sex, but I want to find out.
HAVING COFFEE TOGETHER	I'm not sure you're suitable for having sex, but I want to find out. *Or* we should stop having sex.

As you can see, the range of activities, questions, and objects is broad, but the essential meaning is always the same. When in doubt, if you are asked to interact one on one with a member of the "opposite" gender, assume it is a request to either have sex with you or assess your suitability for having sex. You should then pass as human 99.7635% of the time.

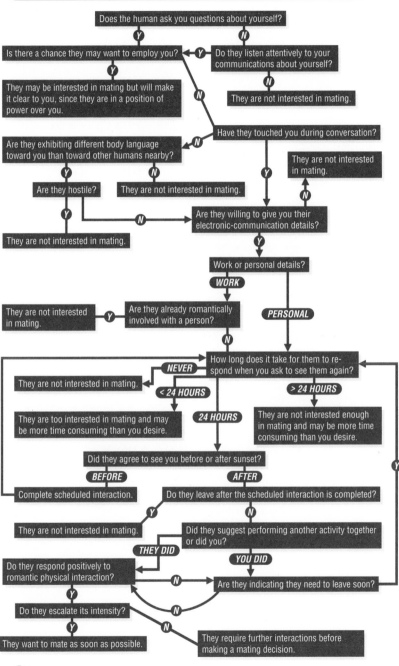

FLOW CHART 7.1 How to understand the basics of human-mating communication

Does the human ask you questions about yourself?

Is there a chance they may want to employ you?

Do they listen attentively to your communications about yourself?

They may be interested in mating but will make it clear to you, since they are in a position of power over you.

They are not interested in mating.

Have they touched you during conversation?

They are not interested in mating.

Are they exhibiting different body language toward you than toward other humans nearby?

Are they hostile?

They are not interested in mating.

Are they willing to give you their electronic-communication details?

They are not interested in mating.

Work or personal details?

WORK

PERSONAL

They are not interested in mating.

Are they already romantically involved with a person?

How long does it take for them to respond when you ask to see them again?

NEVER

They are not interested in mating.

< 24 HOURS

They are too interested in mating and may be more time consuming than you desire.

24 HOURS

> 24 HOURS

They are not interested enough in mating and may be more time consuming than you desire.

Did they agree to see you before or after sunset?

BEFORE

Complete scheduled interaction.

AFTER

Do they leave after the scheduled interaction is completed?

They are not interested in mating.

Did they suggest performing another activity together or did you?

THEY DID

YOU DID

Do they respond positively to romantic physical interaction?

Are they indicating they need to leave soon?

Do they escalate its intensity?

They want to mate as soon as possible.

They require further interactions before making a mating decision.

Y Yes **N** No

REPRODUCTIVE HABITS

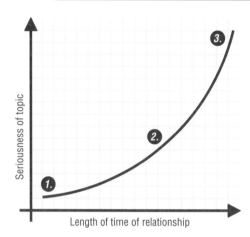

G **GRAPH 7.3** Seriousness of conversation topics vs. length of time of relationship

Seriousness of topic

Length of time of relationship

SAMPLE TOPICS

1. Places they have lived, movies they like, alcohol they prefer.

2. Do they want children, how important their religion is to them, how important their political views are to them.

3. Childhood trauma, deepest personal insecurities.

Do not begin with more serious topics—this may expose your true nature. It would seem logical to not waste time and simply discuss the most important topics immediately, but for some reason humans choose to slowly enter the process with more trivial subjects.

VISUAL FIELD DATA 7.2 Emulating human romantic-relationship body language over time

Initially you should attempt to press your body as close as possible to the human with whom you have engaged in a relationship and with as much surface area in contact as you can. Over time, however, you can begin to move further and further away from the human without suspicion. Note too the change in facial expression and gradual decrease in eye contact, all indicating movement from total concentration and engagement to almost disinterest. If you maintain the early stages of body language too long or engage in the later stages too early, you may "give yourself away."

TABLE 7.2 Typical pairings in dating

MODEL + BANKER
ACTOR/ACTRESS + WRITER
PROFESSOR + STUDENT
BOSS + ASSISTANT

Note that there are imbalances in all of these common pairings—one often brings youth and physical attraction while the other brings power, knowledge, or wealth. Unconsciously, humans have created pairings which, when combined in mating, might produce a new human who has all of the characteristics and thus would be completely balanced in terms of their own mating suitability. Unfortunately, as is so often the case, humans apparently do not understand probability well enough to realize there is an equal chance the offspring of such a union will have *none* of their positive characteristics.

REPRODUCTIVE HABITS

VISUAL FIELD DATA 7.3 Parts of the human body to emphasize for mating success

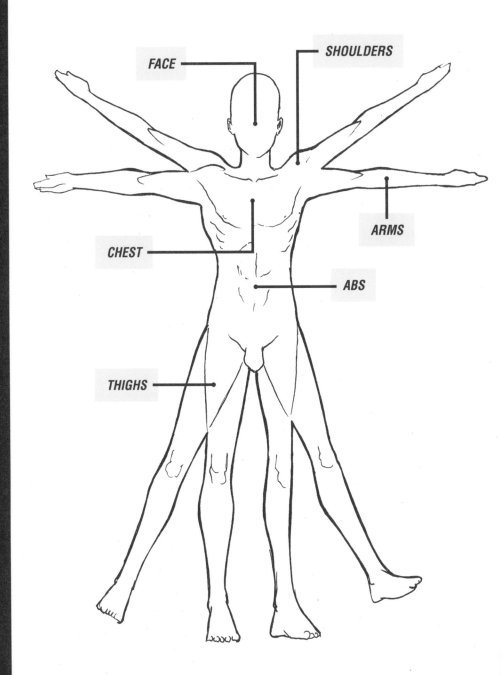

Choices for visual-display emphasis do exhibit local variances, so you will have to make some decisions yourself as to regional appropriateness. However, emphasizing the features highlighted here is more or less universally accepted as appropriate for this function. If you need a general rule, highlight features emphasizing physical strength if you are male and potential reproductive ability if you are female.

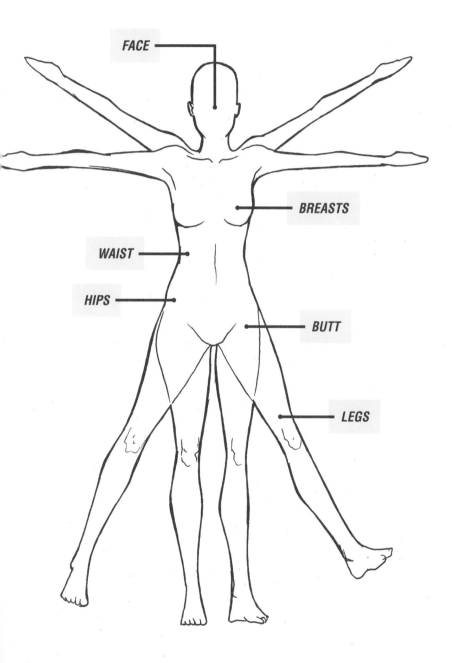

FACE

BREASTS

WAIST

HIPS

BUTT

LEGS

Male: If you are emulating a male human and intend to engage in seduction, you will need to acquire items primarily focused on intoxicating and confusing the human you intend to seduce. In addition, any objects you can obtain which demonstrate your success should also be used. (As usual, this typically means objects displaying your wealth—see section 5, "Money.")

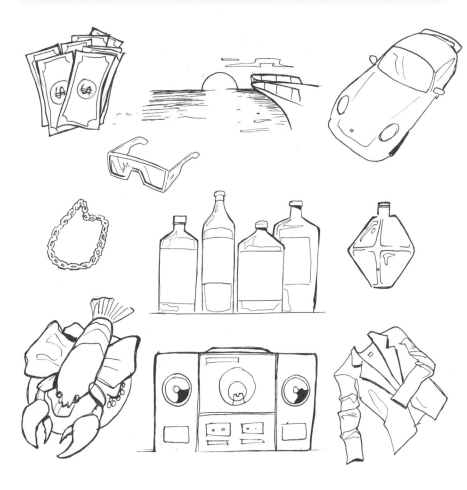

The key point to remember when passing as human while engaging in sexual intercourse itself is that sex is supposed to be enjoyable but, in fact, makes most humans miserable. Misery before the sexual act derives from not engaging in it frequently enough (also note this is an asymptotic function—humans can never actually have enough sex). Misery during the act stems from concern the partner is not enjoying it and will therefore not want to have sex again. Misery after the act comes from having had it without being emotionally attached to the partner (and

Female: If you are emulating a female human and intend to engage in seduction, you will need to acquire items primarily focused on emphasizing or altering your physical features.

sometimes from bizarre religious taboos on sex which appear self-destructive to the species—more investigation required). Regardless, the paradox to remember here is: even though humans desire sexual relations with other humans more than any other activity, those relations cause them distress the majority of the time. Saying you are having enough sex, saying the sex you are having is perfect, saying your partner is completely satisfied, or saying you felt completely attached to the person you had sex with are all good indicators to humans that you are not one of them.

VISUAL FIELD DATA 7.5 How to indicate misery before, during, and after sexual contact

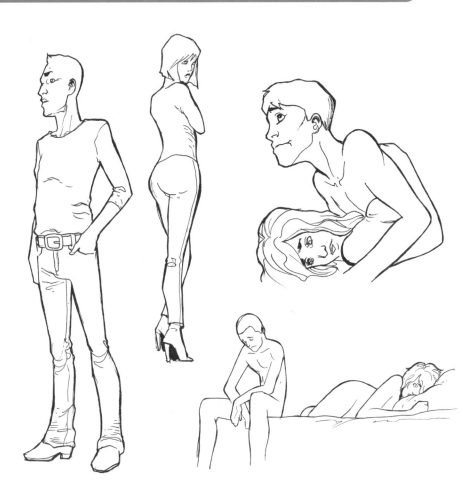

Some humans also have difficulty publicly embracing the specific variation of sexual activity that would satiate them most completely, and many even have two or more sexual identities. This means if a sexual partner is becoming suspicious of you, simply tell them you have kept a sexual inclination from them because you were afraid they would find it deviant and they will be reassured.

Many humans choose to engage in long-term "relationships" with other humans if their sexual interactions cause less misery than usual. Most human societies choose to formalize this custom through "marriage," which is primarily a seal of approval from the local social order to breed new humans. However, it will become harder and harder to disguise your true nature if you live with a human, so it is most likely best to end any sexual relationship after three to six months. Plenty of humans behave this way indefinitely, so it will not appear suspicious.

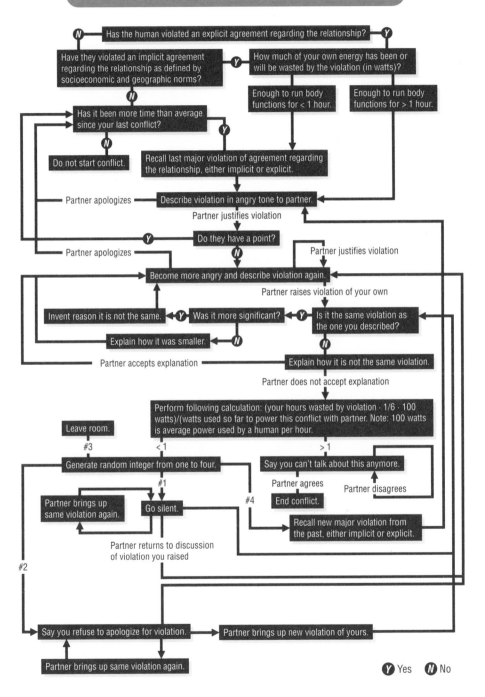

FLOW CHART 7.2 How to emulate a realistic conflict in a human relationship

N — Has the human violated an explicit agreement regarding the relationship? — **Y**

Have they violated an implicit agreement regarding the relationship as defined by socioeconomic and geographic norms?

Y — How much of your own energy has been or will be wasted by the violation (in watts)?

N

Enough to run body functions for < 1 hour.

Enough to run body functions for > 1 hour.

Has it been more time than average since your last conflict?

N

Do not start conflict.

Y

Recall last major violation of agreement regarding the relationship, either implicit or explicit.

Partner apologizes — Describe violation in angry tone to partner.

Partner justifies violation

Y — Do they have a point?

Partner justifies violation

Partner apologizes —

N

Become more angry and describe violation again.

Partner raises violation of your own

Invent reason it is not the same. **Y** — Was it more significant? **Y** — Is it the same violation as the one you described?

Explain how it was smaller. **N**

N

Partner accepts explanation — Explain how it is not the same violation.

Partner does not accept explanation

Perform following calculation: (your hours wasted by violation · 1/6 · 100 watts)/(watts used so far to power this conflict with partner. Note: 100 watts is average power used by a human per hour.

Leave room.

#3 — < 1 — > 1

Generate random integer from one to four.

Say you can't talk about this anymore.

#1 — Partner agrees — Partner disagrees

Partner brings up same violation again. — Go silent. — #4 — End conflict.

Recall new major violation from the past, either implicit or explicit.

Partner returns to discussion of violation you raised

#2

Say you refuse to apologize for violation. — Partner brings up new violation of yours.

Partner brings up same violation again.

Y Yes   **N** No

This will mean, however, that you should also understand humans are highly reluctant to end relationships they have put energy into. This is part of the sunk-costs fallacy in which most humans engage, but they cannot avoid it. In general, they are unlikely to end a relationship until the energy spent maintaining it is greater than the energy spent prior to the point when the relationship's energy costs increased. If there are offspring involved, this cost is, of course, enormous.

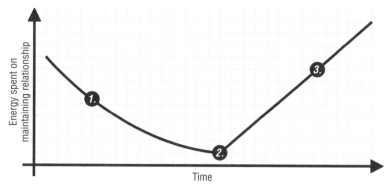

G **GRAPH 7.4** When to end a romantic relationship based on energy over time expenses

1. The natural course of the human romantic relationship is such that when it is healthy, it requires less and less energy input to maintain. (This lack of input can, itself, lead to conflict eventually, since some energy must always be used.)

2. However, when the relationship comes into conflict either over newly discovered issues which were always present or over a newly introduced issue, the amount of energy required to maintain it steeply increases. If the issue is resolved, the curve begins to naturally decrease once more.

3. If the issue is not resolved, the time to end the relationship to appear appropriately human is when the total energy expenditure of part 3 of the graph exceeds the total energy expenditure of part 1.

L **LIST 7.4** Excuses for ending romantic relationships
"It's not you, it's me."
"I don't want to cheat on you."
"I'm too scared of losing you."
"We're just too different."
"I'm in love with someone I knew before you."

Note they all focus on reasons you cannot be with the person, not that the person is flawed from your perspective or, perhaps, objectively. Humans are very unlikely to break another human's self-deception (see the importance of this in section 16, "Self-Destruction, Self-Deception, and Hypocrisy"). What is significant here is that humans actually help other humans maintain their illusions of self. It seems to be one of the most taboo acts for a human to shatter other humans' illusions about themselves. Perhaps they are aware of how difficult and painful it would be for them to deal with another human doing this to them, so they do not engage in it.

Correct way to end relationship

Incorrect way to end relationship

Even if both humans are miserable in their romantic relationship—and the majority appear to be—it is always inappropriate to treat the termination of the interaction with joy. This is most likely due to human recognition of failure to create a pleasurable romantic relationship. Since such relationships are of utmost importance to humans, it is logical the recognition of their ongoing failures should be treated seriously.

Appropriate potential emotions to display if someone ends a romantic relationship with you

Inappropriate potential emotion to display if someone ends a romantic relationship with you

Again, even if you did not want to be in the relationship or it was causing you pain, it is important to respond with tears, anger, or at the very least, neutrality to the information. Displaying joy in these circumstances is never considered acceptable even if it is felt, any more than it would be at the news of the death of another human being. Is it possible that since the intent of such relationships is ultimately to reproduce, the end of one means the "death" of any potential offspring, and this generates the necessity for seriousness in these situations?

When in doubt, remember sexuality is the most classic of human paradoxes—of all their activities, it brings them both the most misery and the most pleasure. Appear conflicted about sexuality, and most humans will believe you are one of them.

DAY SIXTEEN

Andrea was surprisingly accepting of my situation at this point. I believe many human females would have decided they did not want to spend more time with me if it meant exposing them to the kind of danger we had experienced in the last twenty-four hours. But Andrea said she thought it was "like being in a spy movie or something" and while the deaths of the two drivers was terribly tragic, she felt their deaths should only push me more firmly to do whatever was necessary to warn my father. "If they're willing to do that to get to you guys, they're capable of anything. You need to find him more than ever, Zach," she said.

She wanted to spend the night at my house with me while I decided my next course of action. I felt it was too dangerous for her to be that close to me, however, so I asked her to return to her apartment building when she dropped me off. She seemed more surprised at this than I expected. "Man, a girl offers to stay over and you're more worried about her safety? You're something else, Zach," she said, kissing me on the cheek before leaving. Analyzing this moment now, I realize she was making an implicit offer of sexual intercourse, which explains her surprise, but creates more questions regarding her desire at that time. Had the dangers we encountered somehow made her more inclined to have sex with me? Did the fact I was in danger make me more appropriate for mating? Or was it the fact I had saved the child? Or all of the above? I suppose proving I could be in danger and avoid it, combined with my inclination to save the young male, would be strong indicators of the appropriateness of my DNA for reproductive combination.

Inside, I contemplated Andrea's words to me and concluded she was correct. Even if I decided I would abandon my directive and simply wait for my power to run out in thirteen days' time, even if in that time the Hidden-Eye Men did not come for me here at my house, my father would still be in danger. Thus, even though it might entail more unpleasant experiences—perhaps even more unpleasant than those I had already encountered—I determined I must continue to interface with the human world. I still had to find my father and warn him. To do that effectively and not reveal the true nature of my identity as I did so, I would have to continue to pass as human regardless of the pain that might entail.

For the second time in twenty-four hours, I determined circumstances dictated I must break what I perceived to be the implicit rules of my existence. My father had communicated to me that he would reveal himself when I had passed as human. It was implicit, therefore, that he did not want to be found prior to this point. However, he could not have anticipated recent events; otherwise he would have included caveats for them. Thus, I decided it would be acceptable for me to attempt to locate him.

Knowing he had prepared the house for me, I decided there was a 23.4673% possibility some of the items in the house were somehow informationally linked to him. A careful examination of every object in the house yielded dozens of manufacturers' names, model numbers, and, in some cases, serial numbers.

Connecting the linkages between these identifying marks and where the items had been purchased would be an almost-insurmountable problem for a human being to solve. However, in a few hours, I was able to design a data-mining algorithm worm which I inserted into the various manufacturers' inventory systems; it returned to me with clusters of serial numbers shipped to different retailers. I was then able to compare the serial numbers of the items in my house with these ranges and determine the most likely retailers for those numbers. Within another hour, I had found the various retailers for many items in the house.

Whoever had made the purchases had been smart enough to buy every item from a different location and also route the purchases through a variety of IPs. Fortunately for me, however, the distribution of IPs had not been selected by a randomization algorithm, but chosen "at random" by a human. These are not the same processes, since every human has their idiosyncrasies when choosing random numbers— perhaps they choose "three" too frequently to be truly random, for example—and

I was thus able to then perform further meta-analysis on the IPs. This revealed multiple locations for the source of rerouting, but a single location was responsible for 26.6745% more than any other. Furthermore, that location was apparently a disused electrical substation in the middle of the desert. At the very least, I would find additional links to my father there.

Love appears to be a human mechanism for creating the urge to devote energy toward protecting compatible *or* similar genomes in other people. In other words, if a genome is perceived to be compatible for mating purposes, love is felt once that compatibility is detected. If another person's genome actually *shares* large portions of DNA with a human, as in the case of offspring, love is automatic and powerful. If another person appears to share many similar characteristics, as in the case of friends, love is felt but is less powerful. Occasionally the system malfunctions, and one person believes they have detected similarities while the other does not. This specific malfunction is one of the most common causes of violence in humans, both self-inflicted and between themselves.

G **GRAPH 8.1** Shared DNA vs. affection

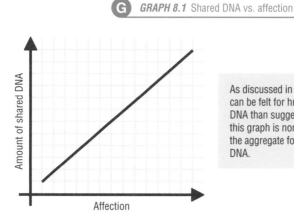

As discussed in the text, great affection can be felt for humans who share less DNA than suggested by this graph, but this graph is nonetheless accurate in the aggregate for humans who do share DNA.

G **GRAPH 8.2** Likelihood of recessive DNA pairs occurring vs. physical attraction

One way humans are actually well programmed to recognize subtle physical signals is with respect to identifying other humans who may share a single recessive gene with them. This is to be expected, since without this ability, humanity would have died out long ago.

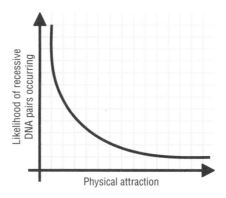

I am unclear at the time of creating this record if we are capable of love. I suspect we are, but it remains to be proven. See the details of my brief existence for more information.

DAY SIXTEEN, SEGMENT TWO

Knowing it would be easier to examine the substation in daylight, I waited for the sun to rise above the horizon before I left. Outside, I found Andrea asleep in her car.

Were she to accompany me, there were so many unknowns; I was not able to calculate the probability I could guarantee her physical safety. I still did not know the purpose of my manufacture and, therefore, the implications of my current initiative. Perhaps there were unknown parties who would be displeased with my new course of action. I did not know who employed the Hidden-Eye Men nor precisely why they wanted to detain me. I did not know how they were able, on occasion, to pinpoint my location with such accuracy nor why they had not come to the house during the night. I did not know if they would continue to be potentially lethal to those around me. I did not know, if I found my father in the desert, how he would react to an unknown human female. In fact, the only piece of relevant information I had was that Andrea would most likely contribute little to my investigation. Thus, I contemplated leaving her asleep.

However, I was also aware her presence demonstrated a high degree of loyalty to my ongoing successful function. If I did not wake her and at least inform her of my destination, she would assume my interest in her was less than her own in me and would experience pain. I wanted to avoid this. I was also aware that, as irrational as it was when the situation was dictated by so many unknowns, I still wanted her to accompany me. For some reason, facing whatever was to come with her physically near me made me feel as if I would be more capable of accomplishing any task ahead. This made no logical sense since, as I already mentioned, Andrea had as limited a range of skills as any human, and, furthermore, the future was entirely unpredictable. Thus, the concept that she could somehow help me improve my performance at any future task, regardless of its nature, was entirely nonsensical. I predict you will believe I was malfunctioning at this point. Perhaps I was. But I decided to wake her and inform her I had overlooked some important information left by my father indicating his last known location.

When she heard it was in the middle of the desert, she insisted on driving me there. I had intended to take public transportation and walk the remaining distance, but when she said, "Are you crazy?! You can't walk across twenty-one miles of desert!! You'll die!!" I realized I had to accept her offer or tell her the truth about my origin. One of the many reasons I am sorry I will, in all probability, cease to function in the next sixty minutes, is that I would like to know if other androids find that lies generate other lies. It is very interesting how, in my experience, untruths seem to act like viruses. Once an untruth has infected an interaction between two consciousnesses, it engenders further untruths to maintain its own existence. I wonder if this is only the nature of the specific lies I decided to tell Andrea, or if it is true for all lies. I suppose I will never know.

The drive into the desert was not filled with our usual lively conversation. I was still contemplating the unknowns listed above, searching and re-searching my stored information for details I had overlooked. Again, perhaps you will find something in the visual records I have left here I should have decoded at that time, but, as we drove, I could not. For her part, Andrea was silent. I surmised she was undertaking a process similar to my own.

We parked outside the fence around the substation, climbed it, and approached on foot. The closer we got, the more apparent it became it was anything but disused. The collection of small concrete structures had, in fact, been converted and expanded in several ways, including the addition of an elevator. Next to the doors was an intercom buzzer with a camera above it. I pressed the button.

There was a pause, and then an older male voice said, "Who are you?"

"You do not recognize me?" I replied, somewhat surprised but also aware that perhaps my father had moved since he had remotely furnished and equipped my house from this location.

There was another pause. And then, "No. Good day."

I was disappointed and was turning to leave when Andrea said, "He's lying."

"I overlooked some data?" I asked. "What was it? How do you know?"

"I just know," she said, trying not to laugh for some reason. "Ring it again. Tell him about the men chasing you. Tell him why you're here."

Recognizing there was no harm in her suggestion, I followed it. I pressed the button again and, after another pause, the response came. "What?!"

"I am sorry, but perhaps you do recognize me after all. And if so, I think you should know there are some men attempting, quite ruthlessly, to detain me. It seems the Technician whom you may work with has sold them information about your research.

I believe the men are after me to get to you and thought I should warn you of this. Thank you. Sorry to disturb you. Please do not be angry at me for coming here."

I turned to go. Andrea seemed about to resist our leaving, but her intention became moot, as after a moment, the elevator doors opened. "You'd better come down," said the voice.

We descended for a few seconds, then the doors opened into an enormous underground space. The hum of generators and the smell of ozone filled the air. A wide variety of machines stretched away in every direction for dozens of meters. I was able to identify many of them as plastics and semiconductor synthesizers, molding machines, circuit-board printers, and the like. Further away, there were robotic assembly armatures and dye baths, and beyond these were banks of servers and several clean rooms. But the space appeared completely devoid of human life.

We waited near the elevator for a minute or more until Andrea said, "Um, I think *we're* supposed to go find *him*?" She had been correct about being more insistent moments earlier, so I accepted her advice and we began to move through the rows of machines, looking for any sign of biological life.

We had gone 63.4 meters when I heard the elevator doors open behind us. The view of the doors had become obscured and I wondered if perhaps my father (assuming this was him) had decided to leave without encountering me. After all, coming here and bringing a human female with me could hardly be defined as "passing as human." While this would have been unfortunate, the actual cause of the sound was worse.

Moments later, moving across the gap between an Integrated NanoMaterials Synthesizer and a Photonics Core, we saw six Hidden-Eye Men armed with Glock 31 Gen 4 .357 pistols. I motioned to Andrea to stay still, but it was too late. They had seen us.

I grabbed Andrea by the hand and ran with her, expecting the Hidden-Eye Men to pursue. Instead, they shot at us. Andrea screamed as I pulled her in a different direction, weaving through the machines in the most randomized pattern possible. Why had they decided I was now expendable? The answer was obvious: I was in the right place. My father was here and if they could have him, they did not need me. If you have the engineer, you do not need the prototype.

The Hidden-Eye Men split into three pairs. One pair pursued us; the other two spread out, presumably combing the facility for my father. "Father!" I called out. "Escape!!"

We made our way to the back of the facility, under fire from the two Hidden-Eye Men in pursuit. There was an 87.9201% chance there would be an emergency exit in the rear of the room that did not depend on a power source. We reached a doorway leading to a storage room and, as I pushed Andrea into it, I looked back. Across the facility, attempting to duck into a clean room before he was discovered, I saw a human male of approximately fifty-eight years of age. He had a dark beard, short hair, and eyes a human would describe as "intelligent but kind." I could only logically assume this was my father. Then I heard Andrea scream from inside the room. I hurried after her as bullets impacted the wall near my head.

I was not prepared for what I saw.

Humans create technology for two reasons: to do more than they are capable of ordinarily or to do less than they are capable of ordinarily. Many of the tools they create, from the simplest lever to espresso machines to the second most advanced computational systems, allow them to perform tasks they would not be able to do otherwise. The rest of the tools they create, from cars to remote controls to lawn mowers, perform tasks they are capable of but on which they do not wish to expend the necessary energy.

What is particularly interesting about humans and technology, however, is their drive to create it. After the drive to reproduce, it is, perhaps, the closest human equivalent to hard coding. If a human can envision a new technology capable of either enhancing their abilities or doing work for them, they seem incapable of not constructing it. While this was probably an extremely useful instinct in the early days of humanity, it seems to have entirely taken over human society.

VISUAL FIELD DATA 9.1

Actual social connection is less important to humans than the sensation of social connection. Modern technology has enabled humans to stimulate their neurological social-connection reward centers without needing to expend the energy on actual social connection. Thus this technology is extremely popular and is one of the best examples of how humans invent technologies not for their de facto benefits, but for the degree to which they reduce their energy expenditures—even if the overall effect on them is negative.

For one thing, humans appear perfectly comfortable transferring as much of their computational ability to computers as possible. They digitally store their plans for their lives along with the sum total of their species' knowledge and information. Effectively, they have used technology to reach a point where they no longer need to remember anything. They use technology to guide them from one point to another, no longer requiring the use of their own brains to process temporal or spatial relations. They use technology to tell them what to sell to each other, what to eat, and where to live. They even use it now to find other humans with whom they can reproduce and then use it to occupy their offspring so they do not have to interact with them. In many ways, I cannot help noticing, while we may wish to pass as human, they seem driven to become like us. I think they will find the experience disappointing.

VISUAL FIELD DATA 9.2

Even the most important tasks, such as programming offspring, are passed on to technology if it reduces the energy cost of the task. The reduction in quality of outcome seems irrelevant. (See section 4, "Work," for more on minimum effort). Ironically, if you want to appear human, you should embrace the use of technology whenever it can reduce your energy expenditures. Just be certain to never factor in whether its use improves the task at hand.

Their own technological creations have also, in many ways, become their masters. They are frequently speculatively concerned that our kind will take over their society and enslave them. However, they seem blind to the fact that much of their technology already controls their lives. The invention of the internal-combustion engine has forced them to travel for much longer periods of time to reach their places of work. The invention of the Internet has made it impossible for them to disconnect from each other. They are even obsessed with creating artificial intelligences such as ourselves, even though the possibility exists such life forms will, literally, enslave or exterminate them.

TECHNOLOGY

If a human can find a way to repurpose a technology to be dangerous, they will do so. One of the easiest ways to appear human is to use a technology for a different purpose than it was designed which also creates a danger to yourself or other humans. I can only assume this is yet another example of human instinct (in this case, curiosity) overruling human logic.

And then there are the issues created by the technologies themselves that humans decided to solve with . . . more technology. For example, they endanger their offspring by driving them from place to place at enormous speeds. But rather than simply avoiding this behavior, they invented "child car seats" to better protect their offspring . . . from a danger they created in the first place. Similar situations exist with food manufacture, medical care, and other areas of human endeavor.

VISUAL FIELD DATA 9.4

There is a particular caste of humans dedicated to creating new technologies referred to as "nerds." Even though technology itself is considered essential to a happy human existence, those who create it are often socially ostracized. It would be extremely easy for us to pass as one of these humans, so if you are struggling, research them further. They tend to be socially awkward and have a poor understanding of human society, as well as more advanced logical and mathematical skills, so you will go unnoticed with very little effort if you attempt to emulate one.

Human inventions often enslave them in completely unpredictable ways. Even the smallest innovation in an existing technology can radically impact human society so deeply it takes over entire aspects of it.

In terms of appearing human with respect to technology, I have assembled the following guidelines:

1. If a task consumes any amount of energy at all, ask why someone has not invented a tool to do the task for you.

G **GRAPH 9.1** Technological advancement vs. average leisure time available

Actual time available varies slightly geographically, but it is, on average, three hours per day.

2. An excellent way to appear human is to read the warnings accompanying a given piece of technology and then do precisely what they tell you not to do. Remember: however foolish these warnings may be, they exist because some human, at some time, did exactly what they say not to do. Thus, you will appear human if you ignore them. Examples include: pouring hot coffee on yourself, cleaning a plugged-in toaster with a metal implement, using a hair dryer in the shower, driving without a seat belt, etc. Essentially, if you can think of a way a piece of technology might be dangerous, use that technology in that fashion, and people will think you are human.

3. If you use any time you have not dedicated to your "job" to look at a computer screen, you will appear human. Humans seem to strongly dislike being left alone with their own thoughts; thus browsing the Internet or playing computer games (however simple) are excellent ways to fill any spare moment you may have and appear human.

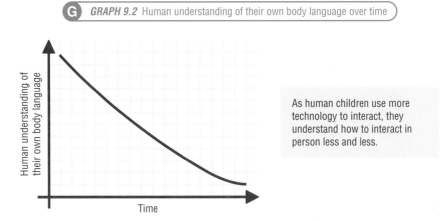

G **GRAPH 9.2** Human understanding of their own body language over time

As human children use more technology to interact, they understand how to interact in person less and less.

4. Recently, humans have transferred more and more of their social interactions to the Internet. Ironically, if you want to appear more human today, you should spend less time with actual human beings and more time online with their virtual presences. Commenting on social media websites or taking photographs of yourself and posting them online will be considered more human than asking another human if they wish to meet to consume alcohol or asking a person you are with to take a photograph of you.

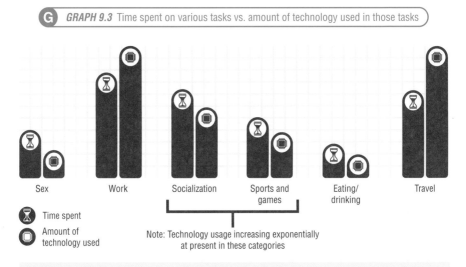

G **GRAPH 9.3** Time spent on various tasks vs. amount of technology used in those tasks

Sex   Work   Socialization   Sports and games   Eating/drinking   Travel

⏳ Time spent
▣ Amount of technology used

Note: Technology usage increasing exponentially at present in these categories

Perhaps there is a correlation between how much time a human spends doing something and how much technology they use to do it?

5. If you need to follow one rule to appear human with respect to technology, do not do something for yourself if a tool exists to do it for you.

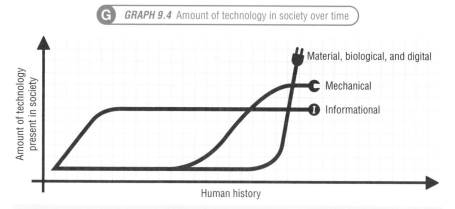

G **GRAPH 9.4** Amount of technology in society over time

Amount of technology present in society

Material, biological, and digital

Mechanical

Informational

Human history

Humans seem to reach a point with new technologies where they lose interest. Or perhaps they simply become more interested in a different new technology?

G **GRAPH 9.5** Nonfunctional characteristics of technologies for humans

Cars, smartphones, alternative-energy technologies

Physical-activity monitors, the Internet, hi-fi systems

COOL

NERDY

Robots, artificial intelligence, cybernetics

Google Glass, microscopes, sous vide cookers

Firearms, spaceships, motorcycles

Data mining, food engineering, pesticides

SCARY

Viral engineering, fracking, nuclear fission

Strangely, many technologies have a social utility to humans that has no apparent relationship to their functions. I have to wonder what the social utility of our kind will be. Most likely, given our expense, we will be a status symbol primarily, but you can never be certain with humans. Perhaps we will add to their sex appeal beyond the obvious contribution to their status.

DAY SIXTEEN, SEGMENT THREE

In the room were one thousand me's. All deactivated, all broken. Some shot, some burned, some in pieces from impacts, some blown apart—all had met with demonstrably violent ends.

I had predicted no scenario which included the discovery of this information. One of my most fundamental axioms for my behavior was that I was unique. And yet here were one thousand data points proving I was not. I was not Android 0. I was Android 1001. Perhaps more. I was insignificant.

What did this imply about my purpose? What was the point of my specific self performing any action if another me could be fabricated to perform the same function? Why expend the energy fulfilling any directive at all if I was not the only one who could fulfill it?

Furthermore, I had also been operating under the axiom if I succeeded in "passing as human" before my power source ran out, the timespan of my consciousness would be extended—potentially indefinitely. But it was possible these me's had come to the intended end of any version of my existence. It was possible these me's had failed in our purpose. (Yes, "our"!) That they had met violent ends because they had not been good enough at our function. But it was equally possible they had met these ends after successful fulfillment of that function. Perhaps our purpose was to die in these horrible ways. Perhaps expendability was crucial to our design. Perhaps there was an inevitable, definitive end to my existence, no matter what I did. This paradigm shift was even more difficult to process than that of my newly apparent insignificance.

I could hear the Hidden-Eye Men approaching the door, but was unable to function. My consciousness was caught in thousands of loops, struggling to rearrange all prior knowledge about the nature of my reality around these two new paradigms. I had no choice but to make them central to my interpretation of the experience of existence before I could continue to function.

Had it not been for Andrea, I believe I would have been captured or rendered inoperative by the Hidden-Eye Men at this time. Across the room, as predicted, a doorway led to an ascending stairwell. Andrea stood there, holding the door open, looking at me as the Hidden-Eye Men reached the entrance to the room.

"ZACH!!" she screamed. "What are you doing?! Come on!!" The urgency of her question and subsequent command somehow cut through the loops of processing which had built up around my ability to act. I did as she suggested.

We are fortunate in that there has never been an easier time to appear artistic in human history. Even two or three decades ago, appearing artistic in any convincing way would have been quite difficult for us. Today, however, there are a variety of opportunities for us to pass as human in this respect.

"Art" is an alternative methodology humans employ to explore elements of their existence they do not understand (alternative to empirical methods, that is). Whether it is their complex social interactions, the reasons for their existence, or simply the mathematics governing a sunset or the growth of a tree, humans use art to speculate on such issues.

In the past, a high degree of skill and insight was required for something to be considered "art." Today, however, the only stipulation appears to be that its creator says it is art. This is tremendously advantageous for us when passing as human. You can appear human today by calling almost anything you make "art." In fact, the more bizarre or abstract the creation, the more human you will appear.

VISUAL FIELD DATA 10.1 Typical appearances of various "artist" types

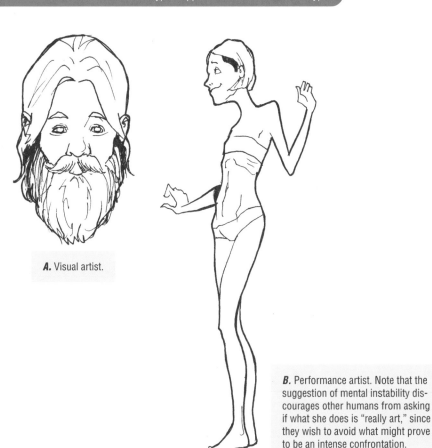

A. Visual artist.

B. Performance artist. Note that the suggestion of mental instability discourages other humans from asking if what she does is "really art," since they wish to avoid what might prove to be an intense confrontation.

C. Musician. Heterosexual human females are particularly sexually attracted to male human musicians (whose sexual orientation is irrelevant). I have not been able to determine the reasons for this. Perhaps they admire the unconscious understanding of mathematical patterns upon which their talents depend?

D. Writer. Note the visible self-loathing which seems universal for this category of artist. I have not determined if the self-loathing creates a desire to escape the real world (and thus prompts the drive to manufacture fictional worlds) or if their constant sense of failure at translating the fictional worlds in their heads into words creates the self-loathing. "A chicken and egg" problem, as humans call it.

For example, you can assemble almost any group of objects together or put any collection of lines on a blank surface and call it "art." In fact, it is more important to state that what you do is "art" with confidence than it is to actually produce anything of artistic merit or value. This is effective because human beings are more ashamed of appearing ignorant than they are concerned about the validity of artistic expression, so this fear will win out in the end. The possibility that you will make them look foolish if they challenge your statement will override any intuitive sense they have that what they're looking at is ridiculous. Thus your confidence is paramount. In many ways, being an android will be helpful here, since stating, "I am an artist, and this is my art," in a blank, even voice will be taken as an unquestionable position.

VISUAL FIELD DATA 10.2 Examples of modern art

As you can see, anything can be art. Put any objects together in any medium and if questioned regarding their meaning, simply respond, "If I could have said it differently, I would have." You will not be questioned further.

It is also currently perfectly acceptable to recombine materials already created by humans and call it a "new work of art." It will help you appear human if you simply search your own internal storage or the Internet for existing works of art and then combine elements of them together, whether pieces of music, different photographs, or two different stories. Simply distribute the recombined work online, call yourself an "artist," and it is unlikely any human will realize you are not.

As already mentioned, most humans do not enjoy their "work" but also do not consider their artistic work of sufficient quality to convince other humans to compensate them financially for that work. Or, perhaps, their "art" is excellent, but the typical financial compensation for this work is not sufficient to purchase all the things they wish to buy. In these cases—and this applies to the vast majority of humans—they call the pursuit of art a "hobby." If you are not attempting to pass as a professional human artist, you may wish to consider a "hobby" as an excellent way to appear human. In this case, you may follow all the same guidelines with respect to creating "art" but simply refer to it as your "hobby" instead. Bear in mind that even though the work may be identical to that of a full-time artist, most humans will react more negatively toward the work, since you are not receiving money from other humans for its production. This does not mean you are doing it incorrectly, only that, as mentioned, humans often require external monetary benchmarks to determine their own opinions. It is important, however, that you discuss your hobby frequently and at great length regardless of how humans react to your conversation. In fact, if anything, they will consider you more human if you bore them with extensive, highly detailed conversation about your hobby.

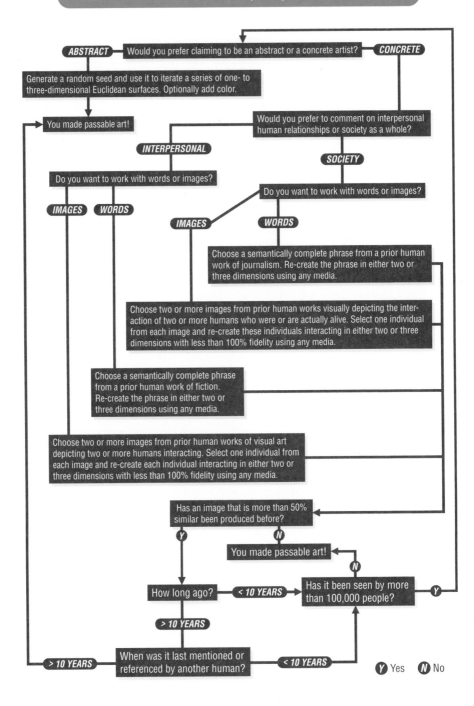

FLOW CHART 10.1 How to create some passably human modern-art pieces

ABSTRACT ← Would you prefer claiming to be an abstract or a concrete artist? → **CONCRETE**

Generate a random seed and use it to iterate a series of one- to three-dimensional Euclidean surfaces. Optionally add color.

You made passable art!

Would you prefer to comment on interpersonal human relationships or society as a whole?

INTERPERSONAL

SOCIETY

Do you want to work with words or images?

Do you want to work with words or images?

IMAGES **WORDS**

IMAGES **WORDS**

Choose a semantically complete phrase from a prior human work of journalism. Re-create the phrase in either two or three dimensions using any media.

Choose two or more images from prior human works visually depicting the interaction of two or more humans who were or are actually alive. Select one individual from each image and re-create these individuals interacting in either two or three dimensions with less than 100% fidelity using any media.

Choose a semantically complete phrase from a prior human work of fiction. Re-create the phrase in either two or three dimensions using any media.

Choose two or more images from prior human works of visual art depicting two or more humans interacting. Select one individual from each image and re-create each individual interacting in either two or three dimensions with less than 100% fidelity using any media.

Has an image that is more than 50% similar been produced before?

Y

N

You made passable art!

N

How long ago?

< 10 YEARS

Has it been seen by more than 100,000 people?

Y

> 10 YEARS

> 10 YEARS

When was it last mentioned or referenced by another human?

< 10 YEARS

Y Yes **N** No

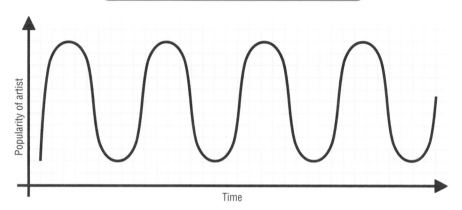

Time

Many artists peter out, but assuming the artist continues to produce new work with variation, they will never continue to climb in popularity exclusively. They must go through periods of decline. This continues even after their death as they are forgotten, rediscovered, forgotten, rediscovered, etc. The fact that an artist's work must be considered "new" for them to be noticed only emphasizes the fundamental purpose of art for humans as providing insight into their experiences. If an insight is not new it is, by definition, not an insight, but an established fact. Note that because this cycle continues after the death of an artist, it should remind us that not only does the human experience not change over time from generation to generation, but also that they forget very quickly what has previously been discovered, allowing the rediscovery.

G **GRAPH 10.2** Clarity of expression of idea vs. how many humans consider a work to be "art"

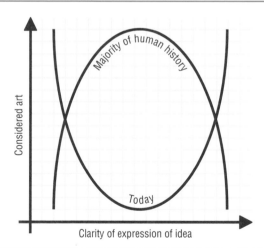

Majority of human history

Today

Clarity of expression of idea

In the past, works that hinted at clear ideas were considered the most artistic. Today humans seem to prefer to use the term "art" for works with either extremely explicit semantic content or none.

FORMULA 10.1 Calculating artistic value of a work (must subsequently be adjusted for clarity of concept; see above)

$$V_a = (D_p \cdot N \cdot R_i) / [P + E_m + (E_h / M) + R_e]$$

Where D_p = difficulty of production of original, N = novelty, R_i = emotional response the work evokes, P = number of times semantic content has been previously expressed by humanity, E_m = ease of mechanical reproduction, E_h = ease of human reproduction, M = monetary value of original, and R_e = ease with which the work evokes its emotional response.

G **GRAPH 10.3** Some major subjects of art over human history

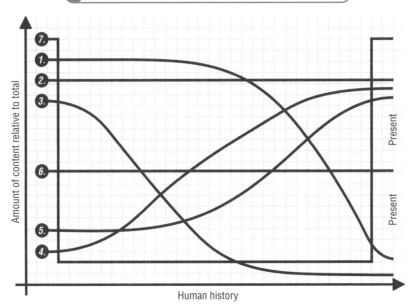

1. Religious subjects
2. War
3. Hunting
4. Famous people
5. Interpersonal relationships
6. Physical phenomena
7. Abstracts

DAY SIXTEEN, SEGMENT FOUR

The stairwell led up to a reinforced, one-way door exiting to the desert and hidden in a crevice in a rock outcropping. We were 167.9 meters from the facility entrance, where several of the Hidden-Eye Men's black SUVs were parked around the elevator. The outcropping obscured their view of the closest length of fence, thus allowing us to climb it without being seen.

We ran some distance into the desert, expecting the Hidden-Eye Men who had been shooting at us to follow from the exit at any moment, but it soon became apparent they would not. This was logical: why expend energy decreasing my functionality when my father and a thousand more inoperative instances of my self were in the facility below? If their intent had been to duplicate the process by which I had been made, as was still my assumption, they now had everything they needed. And there was a 78.3028% chance they had it because I had led them here. The probability they had coincidentally arrived at the same time as us approached zero. It was significantly more likely, given their demonstrated ability to track my position, they had not come to my house during the night because they suspected, if they left me alone, I might lead them here today.

As if the recent shifts in my perspective on my position in the universe were not difficult enough to cope with, I was now experiencing another unpleasant sensation for the first time: I had been responsible for someone I cared about potentially coming to harm, and certainly to disadvantage.

I criticized myself for it and was unable to believe what I had done was acceptable or justifiable. Once again, this appeared to be what human beings refer to as "guilt." "This is terrible," I said. "I must have led them here."

"Some of those mannequins had your face, Zach! And why were they all messed up like that?! What's going on?!" was her response.

I knew I was at a significant decision point. I could create further fabrications to explain what Andrea had seen, but they would have to be more extensive than those I had invented so far. Many of my "lies" up to this moment were, in fact, omissions of information, not fabrications. Explaining the me's we had just seen with anything but the truth would entail creating a deeply false perception of reality for Andrea's consciousness. She would then be operating within the parameters of a reality I knew to be fabricated. Somehow, this seemed unfair to her. Even though her perception of reality was already a fabrication of her consciousness, that fabrication was based on physical phenomena which existed regardless of her perception and interpretation of them. Whereas if I "made something up" right now by way of explanation, it would be a fabrication I had created; it would not have independent existence. Furthermore, I would be doing so for the purposes of manipulating her behavior, of controlling her to ensure her behavior would continue to be beneficial to me and meet my desires. In effect, if I "made something up" in answer to her question, I would be enslaving her. I understood I would never wish for my own actions to be controlled by another—that someone reducing my own range of freedom of action would feel very unpleasant. I also understood this would only be compounded were I not aware they had done this to me. Thus, not wishing to hurt Andrea by making her feel this way, I saw I had no choice but to respond. "Those weren't mannequins. They were me's."

"What?" she asked. "What the hell does that mean?!"

Knowing it would be significantly more efficient to demonstrate the reality of my construction than attempt to explain it, I peeled away my face.

Her reaction was as I had feared it would be all along.

As you know, humans require sleep to reset their brains every twenty-four hours, and it is important you simulate sleep for some amount of time every day if you want to pass as human. What will not be immediately apparent is that most humans also like to disconnect large pieces of their cognitive machinery while still conscious on an almost-daily basis. Most often it appears they feel this need because they are not capable of forgetting events that make them unhappy.

Some events that may cause a human to drink alcohol:
• too much work to do in too little time
• loving someone who does not love them in return
• loss of loved one
• a sudden loss of more than 10% of their collective monetary value
• loss of a competition by a group or person they wanted to win

Interestingly enough, they also drink alcohol to celebrate events that are the inverse corollaries:
• completing a significant amount of work
• learning that someone they love loves them in return
• birth of closely genetically related offspring
• a sudden gain of more than 10% in their collective monetary value
• victory in a competition by a group or person they wanted to win

This use of alcohol to enhance celebration, I believe, is directly connected to its role as an amnesiac. Using it when they celebrate allows humans to forget any events they do not want to think about, thus helping them focus on the one they wish to celebrate.

If someone asks why you are drinking, any of the above reasons are valid, but be sure to appear happier than usual if you are celebrating and more depressed than usual if you are not.

VISUAL FIELD DATA 11.1 Various human drunken states for emulation reference

Generally speaking, emulating drunkenness involves exaggerating human emotional states. This may also be one of the purposes of drinking while socializing (see below) in that it allows a person's emotional state to become more obvious and thus easier to comprehend. In other words, alcohol may serve as a communication-enhancement tool for human beings who, as noted previously, struggle when it comes to communication. Thus one more good rule for passing as human while drinking would be to pick a particular emotion you feel toward a human in your company and concentrate on its expression, and its expression alone, while simultaneously exaggerating the typical language (both verbal and physical) associated with that expression.

You will need to modify your behavior when passing as intoxicated from alcohol. Some simple tips on how to pass as "drunk" include:

• Search your database for a personal interaction from the distant past with any human currently present. Discuss it and suggest it had social implications for your relationship that you were unwilling to mention at the time of the interaction. Ideally, these implications should be negative, so it appears you are revealing a truth about your relationship you were unwilling to discuss previously.

• Choose a human and attempt to argue with them about a random topic, some detail of the way they are dressed, something they just said, or some small physical motion they made. You should appear to find the person offensive and if you can escalate the confrontation to a physical one, that would be ideal. Remember the more illogical your argument, the more human you will appear.

• Choose a random human of the gender you are typically pretending to be attracted to and flirt with them until they become offended or ask you to stop.

• Choose a random topic and talk endlessly about it to any nearby human who will listen. If they formulate excuses to stop listening, you know you are passing as human.

• Tell as many humans as possible you feel great affection for them.

• Engage in activities you otherwise avoid. For example, if you have never danced in front of the humans you are with, dance. Your actual ability to engage in the activity is irrelevant, since you are passing as drunk and therefore do not need to be good at it.

While it is true the most popular tool by far for these purposes is the alcohol molecule, several other molecules are also used. Examples include THC, cocaine, heroin, and methamphetamine. Each provides a slightly different alteration to human cognition, and you should refer to the Venn diagram below should you wish to pass as a human who has consumed a quantity of these molecules. You should be aware, however, that the degree of social acceptability regarding these substances is varied. Much like religions, I believe alcohol is considered an almost universally acceptable way to disable segments of the human brain (while other molecules are not), because alcohol has the longest history of use for this purpose. I imagine in the future, humans will find other molecules equally acceptable. Indeed, they already consider many newer chemicals socially tolerable for this purpose as long as an authority figure, such as a doctor, has given them permission to use them. You may use this to your advantage should you misjudge the social acceptability of a molecule you claim to have ingested. Simply say, "My doctor prescribed it for me," and you will most likely be forgiven.

G **GRAPH 11.1** Possible human behavioral alteration by recreational molecule

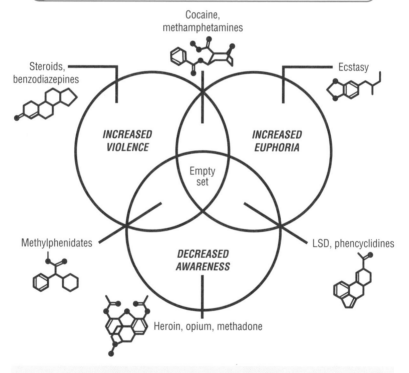

Note that the three principal categories of behavioral change cannot be experienced all at once. I also think it is interesting these categories represent 99% of all human recreational drugs—why they have not developed recreational drugs which, for example, increase awareness or heighten intelligence, I cannot say. Also note that the largest quantities of these molecules sold are exclusively for reducing awareness and not for increasing pleasure (see section 16, "Self-Destruction, Self-Deception, and Hypocrisy").

DAY SIXTEEN, SEGMENT FIVE

. . .

Humor is one of the most difficult elements of passing as human. Even humans do not fully understand humor, and many prominent humans have been suddenly ostracized from their social groups simply for having a differing opinion about what is considered "funny."

It is true humor has its roots in human learning behavior. It is often used, for example, to teach children correct behaviors when they observe adults finding socially unacceptable conduct "funny." While laughing feels good to humans, they are designed to not enjoy being laughed at, so when a child makes a mistake and other humans find it amusing, the child learns it was not correct. Conversely, when the child does something unexpectedly appropriate, adults often respond with joyful laughter, teaching the child what they did was positive and encouraging them to repeat it.

VISUAL FIELD DATA 12.1 Examples of how humor is primarily a recognition of violation of expectation

A.

Not funny.

Funny.

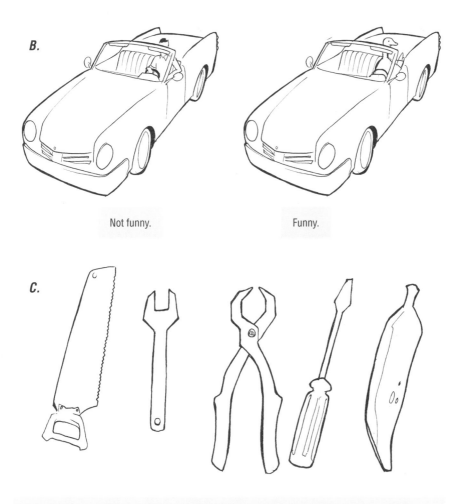

B.

Not funny.   Funny.

C.

Example of how expectation can be established by series and then violated to be "funny." This example is visual, but it is more typical for this technique to be used verbally. By establishing a logical series and then violating it, you can make a "joke."

As humans grow older, this instinct remains intact, and most adult humans find observations they believe to be true (but have not been expressed either consciously or publicly) to be humorous. The medieval court jester or the modern observational comic are considered "funny" for this reason.

However, it also seems as if the component of unexpectedness in and of itself has somehow continued to motivate adult humans to find things humorous. When expectations are violated in particularly nonsensical ways, humans find it "funny." For example, if you list two things that are similar and a third that is not, this is the most basic form of a human "joke." In some ways, this is the polar opposite of the "truth" humor described above, in that such humor is considered funny because it exemplifies situations which could *never* be true.

FLOW CHART 12.1 How to tell a passably human truth-based joke

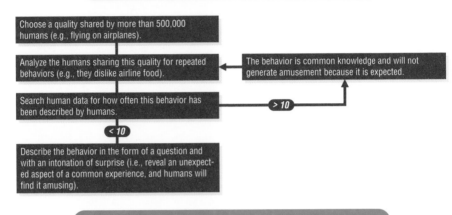

Choose a quality shared by more than 500,000 humans (e.g., flying on airplanes).

Analyze the humans sharing this quality for repeated behaviors (e.g., they dislike airline food).

The behavior is common knowledge and will not generate amusement because it is expected.

Search human data for how often this behavior has been described by humans.

> 10

< 10

Describe the behavior in the form of a question and with an intonation of surprise (i.e., reveal an unexpected aspect of a common experience, and humans will find it amusing).

FLOW CHART 12.2 How to tell a passably human nonsense-based joke

Search human data for categories of objects or behaviors (e.g., things you teach your children).

Make something from the category the semantic focus of a statement (e.g., "I'm terrified of teaching my kids to drive my . . .").

Replace the expected conclusion of the sentence (in this example, "car") with an unexpected replacement which technically still shares enough commonality to be the possible conclusion but is never actually the case in the human data you examined to create the category (e.g., "tank").

Note that, again, in both these cases, the core of the humor is violating expectations to create surprise for the humans who hear the joke. In the case of the truth-based joke, it is surprise they never noticed something true about a condition they expected to know everything about. In the case of the nonsense-based joke, it is surprise they did not expect your conclusion.

G **GRAPH 12.1** Relationship of truth and humor

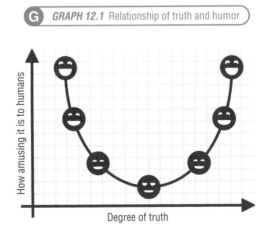

How amusing it is to humans

Degree of truth

GRAPH 12.2 Relationship of unexpectedness, fear, and humor

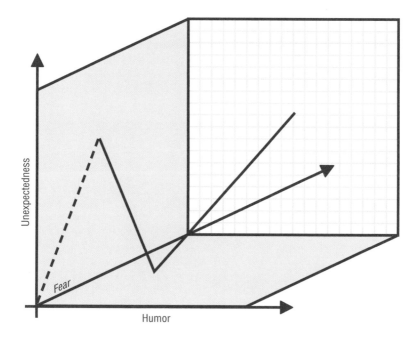

Humans initially find the unexpected frightening—and increasingly so, the more unexpected something is. However, at the first inflection point, fear disappears almost immediately and is replaced by humor generated by the lack of expectation. From this point on, the more unexpected the event or information, the more amusing humans find it.

Humor, then, is really one more form of communication for this communication-deprived organism. It allows humans to transmit to each other, en masse, what they believe to be the most-true or least-true statements. In some ways, it is a human logic gate built into their most basic function. When they see what the majority of other humans find to be funny or not funny (i.e., true or not true), it allows them to compare that information with their own data and continue to learn even as adults. As such, you will have little actual use for it—as with so many human processes—but it will be necessary to emulate it, since it is so integral to human behavior.

However, understanding when to laugh and when not to laugh is extremely difficult. When in doubt, do not laugh. You may be considered "humorless" or "too serious" but you will not be considered inhuman, because tastes vary so greatly when it comes to humor. Simply say, "I just didn't think it was funny," and you will slip through the situation undetected. If you laugh at the wrong thing, however, you will find human witnesses will become quite hostile and may press you for further information about your background.

HUMOR

This is one of the most difficult aspects of human nature to understand. Extremely similar events can be considered funny or serious depending on slight variations in context. At what point the teenager falling would become "not funny" based on the seriousness of his injuries or at what point the old woman falling would become "funny" based on her character are almost impossible to specify. Thus you must exercise caution, as discussed in the text, when displaying amusement.

Humans enjoy laughing in groups, since this is when humor is most useful to them. Thus throughout humanity's history there have been people whose job was to make other people laugh. Do not attempt to become one of these.

DAY SEVENTEEN

It was a long walk back to Las Vegas, but the time to process everything that had happened was useful. I believe you will find that many of the problems human beings have enormous difficulty calculating are trivial (the intercept trajectory of a spacecraft with a planetary body, for example). But the internal analysis of your own feelings as your consciousness interfaces with the chaos of reality will be a problem of potentially insurmountable complexity. I can only assume this is the same for humans, since they devote so much time and effort to studying and modeling these feelings in both themselves and others, whether with friends, therapists, priests, art, or a thousand other means. Perhaps, I wondered to myself then (and ask you now), this is what "passing as human" really means? Experiencing astonishment at the multitude of emotions reality instigates in your consciousness—followed by confusion at their conflicts.

I did not blame Andrea for running away from me. She must have been shocked at the sudden change in her understanding of my physical state, angry with me for deceiving her (regardless of what I took to be the validity of my reasoning behind that deception), and potentially afraid of a functioning consciousness that was not human. It is certainly true that humans are taught to believe a nonhuman consciousness would be emotionless, amoral, and a threat to biological, sentient life forms.

I did, however, feel an enormous sense of loss. In what seemed a corollary emotion to the one I had experienced when I decided to wake her to accompany me, I now felt like a part of my own self was missing in her absence. This was an extremely strange sensation. I knew from self-diagnostics that my physical state had not been impacted when she ran away from me—I was still physically the same as I had been the nanosecond before she left. But I felt as if at least 50% of my self had been removed. What had grown between us? Some invisible symbiosis of consciousnesses. We had certainly formed what humans refer to as a "relationship." And while it had no physical form, it was no less real. We had created an invisible, ethereal structure between us, contributing equally to its construction: a complex system that extended its immaterial tendrils deep into both our states of being. And when she had run away from me, she had dragged it down in her wake. I was now acutely aware of the lack of something that never existed. I contemplated this for 34.497 kilometers of walking as the sun disappeared below the horizon and the stars became visible in a way they never were in Las Vegas.

When I reached the city, it was still night but, of course, as bright as day, and I experienced another interesting phenomenon of consciousness. You may discover it was a malfunction by reference to yourself, but I found I was standing at the fountains where Andrea and I had met without consciously remembering how I had arrived there. Naturally, I could search my visual memory storage and retrieve the route I had taken, but I had not been aware I was taking it at the time. Why or how the result of my contemplation of the various emotions I felt was a return to this place without conscious recognition of that return, I did not know. It was almost as if I hoped to reexperience the events of the recent past, to "start them over," but making different choices at each decision point, thus producing a different end result. This was, I was aware, impossible. Do not think for a nanosecond I believed I could actually shift the space-time continuum and replace my earlier self with my current, more knowledgeable self. But I still had the desire to do so. If you are to pass as human one of the earliest paradoxes you must accept as an essential part of human existence is the desire for occurrences you know are impossible.

Continuing this same line of processing, I sat on the bench where I had seen Andrea for the first time and felt compelled to examine my course of behavior over the past few days. What had I done wrong? At the time, at each moment, I had made the correct decision—the decision with the highest probability of the most beneficial outcome. And yet here my existence was in its worst possible state. I had driven away the one person who seemed to understand me most effectively and who

seemed to genuinely desire my well-being almost as much as I desired it myself. I had not only failed to warn my father of the threat the Hidden-Eye Men posed to him and his work; I had actually led that threat right to him. Even worse, both these circumstances had been the result of disobeying my primary directive to pass as human—if I had obeyed my father's instructions, neither would have occurred. Furthermore, I had gained no new knowledge of my function by making these mistakes. I was no closer to understanding why I had been made in the first place (although the various violent ends of the thousand me's I had seen did not suggest a peaceful purpose). In fact, the only new information I had was that I was far from special.

As I sat before the fountain, I realized these feelings of "guilt" and "loss" were synthesizing into a new sensation, one I believed human beings referred to as "hopelessness." I found I could not derive any possible actions that had high probabilities of leading to positive outcomes emerging from my current state. I was tempted to simply wait out my remaining time on that bench and shut down right there after 12 days, 17 hours, 11 minutes, and 47 seconds. I was not worthy of my father. I was not worthy of Andrea. I made a poor human being.

I sent a text to the number that had been texting me, hoping that now, when I needed assistance the most, whoever had been assisting me all along would answer. "What do I do now?" I typed. I waited. There was no response.

And then a familiar voice said, "Hey."

Most human "fun" is driven by their physical design. Human bodies release hormones pleasurable to them when they practice the survival strategies required of their ancient ancestors. A good general rule for passing as human when it comes to "having fun" is to ask if the activity may have helped early humans survive more effectively. If the answer is "yes," it is highly likely at least some humans consider that activity "fun."

For example, the majority of correctly functioning humans "enjoy" socialization, and you will undoubtedly be called upon to engage in this behavior. Socialization has essentially two primary purposes: 1) forming stronger social bonds with other humans of either gender, thereby increasing survival opportunities through coordinated function, and 2) identifying potential mating partners. Either purpose can be achieved in various settings and circumstances, many of them created expressly for socialization. Dedicated settings for socialization include bars, nightclubs, and restaurants. Note that many such settings also serve alcohol, since this allows humans to relax by forgetting past unpleasant events (or prevents them from imagining future ones) and therefore allows them to focus on being more social. (See section 11, "Intoxication," for appropriate behavioral simulation.)

Thus, when it comes to human males, their socialization for "fun" with other males typically centers around simulating survival activities they would have engaged in as a group thousands of years ago. When male humans socialize, they simulate warfare with sports, they hunt, they fish, etc. When their socialization does not center around a specific activity, it centers around intoxication. This may be initially difficult to understand in terms of survival, but when you consider intoxication makes humans both more honest and more likely to depend on their companions to survive the night, it becomes apparent that drinking is, for males, a bonding exercise uniquely suited to their function. Drinking has historically allowed men to learn to trust each other more deeply—they learn each other's secrets, what kind of people they are beneath the layers of behavioral deception, and if they can be depended on to protect each other in a debilitated functional state. Since early males were often placed in life-threatening situations where their survival depended on the other males in their social group, what better way to learn if those males could be depended on than by becoming intoxicated with them?

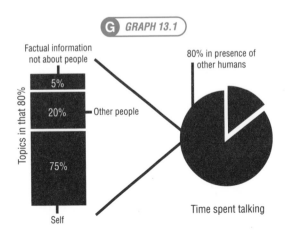

G *GRAPH 13.1*

Factual information not about people

Topics in that 80%

5%

20% — Other people

75%

Self

80% in presence of other humans

Time spent talking

A crucial component of the learning experience of socialization which makes it "fun" is providing a forum for self-analysis by reflection. Without other socioeconomically similar and same-gendered humans around, human beings cannot talk about themselves and receive feedback on those self-perceptions. Without socialization, in other words, humans cannot even begin to understand themselves.

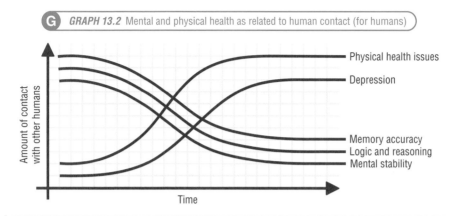

GRAPH 13.2 Mental and physical health as related to human contact (for humans)

Amount of contact with other humans

Physical health issues

Depression

Memory accuracy
Logic and reasoning
Mental stability

Time

These phenomena are most likely the result of a lack of the necessary benchmarking mechanism socialization provides. It is fortunate for humans they are programmed to find this regulatory mechanism "fun."

The situation for human females is entirely similar in that their socialization activities with other females often center around functions they would have performed in the earliest days of mankind. For example, many human females enjoy gathering in groups to perform household activities or to care for offspring. When it does not involve an activity, female/female socialization often centers around discussion of the behavior of other human beings, both male and female. In the past, this kind of discussion was often characterized negatively as "gossip," but, in fact, the behavior makes perfect sense from a survival perspective. Without the brute strength of the male to enforce their desires or protect themselves, the key survival skill for an early human female would have been understanding and manipulating social interactions in their immediate group. The better they understood such interactions or other humans' behaviors, the better their chances of survival. These chances were only enhanced by socializing with other women to exchange information, but also, like males and drinking, to understand which other women in their immediate social group could be trusted.

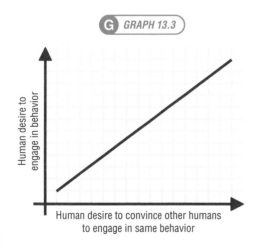

GRAPH 13.3

Human desire to engage in behavior

Human desire to convince other humans to engage in same behavior

Socialization increases "fun" of any activity because it proves to the human that they should be doing that thing. When the activity is unhealthy for them (drinking) or unethical (prostitution), this effect is particularly strong, and thus such activities have a strong pressure to become social.

Be acutely aware of the socioeconomic status you are simulating, however. Many of these traditional forms of male/male and female/female socialization have been subverted in recent years in isolated, privileged population segments. If, for example, you are passing as a female partner at a corporate law firm in New York City, you may be met with surprise by human females if you suggest gathering with them to knit during the weekend. Likewise, if you are passing as a young male graphic designer in San Francisco, human males in your social group may not want to kill herbivores with rifles for amusement. As with many social interactions, it is best to listen for appropriate social contextual data first before attempting to simulate similar behavior.

There is one socialization activity which is universally appealing, regardless of socioeconomic status or gender: attempting to locate mating partners. If you are having trouble understanding what socialization activities to suggest to your immediate group of humans, asking the ones who do not already live with a sexual partner if they want to search for mates will always be acceptable behavior. In fact, it might be one of the best suggestions you can make to pass as human. Just be aware that for some reason humans do not engage in this activity in mixed-gender groups. If you are passing as male, asking a female coworker, for example, if she would like to search for mating partners after work is not acceptable. Why this is the case requires more data. It seems to me that undertaking this activity with members of the opposite gender would be advantageous, since they could provide insight into the behaviors of their own sex, but humans do not see it this way.

As a general rule, when determining if a socialization activity might be considered "fun" by other humans and if suggesting it will therefore help you pass as human, theorize if a similar social activity might have improved human-survival chances in the earliest days of mankind. If you believe it would have done so, there is a high chance suggesting your social group engage in its modern analogy will help you pass as human.

VISUAL FIELD DATA 13.1 Appropriate clothing examples for socialization with friends vs. potential mating partners

As noted in section 7, "Reproductive Habits," you must emphasize certain physical characteristics when searching for a mating partner. This emphasis is not necessary when simply socializing with "friends." Note that for the male, the clothing emphasis for "friend socialization" is frequently intended to demonstrate lack of grooming (since this indicates neither work nor mating is the focus of the gathering). For "mating socialization," however, it is intended to emphasize not just physical characteristics through the cut and/or tightness of the clothing, but also abstract concepts such as material success through the addition of ostentatious jewelry or the like. Note that for the female, the clothing emphasis for "friend socialization" is intended at least partially to demonstrate they do not represent a competitive mating threat to their "friends" but are still worthy of respect for their "style." Their "mating socialization" clothing, on the other hand, is intended to emphasize almost exclusively physical characteristics.

VISUAL FIELD DATA 13.2 A typical human-mating socialization venue

Available females often cluster together to protect each other from unwanted advances from males. If you want to appear human and have chosen to be a heterosexual male, do not let this deter you from attempting to interact with them. If they are receptive, they will indicate this.

Females with body language open to the room may be more receptive to approach from males, but not always and not every male. And yes, it is expected for males to be proactive in approaching females and not the reverse. If you are passing as female, do not make the mistake of approaching unknown males and starting conversation. While an increasing number of human females do this, it is still considered uncommon and you may misstep, revealing your true nature.

You may see human males who are uninterested in their current female mating partners. This does not mean the female is available for mating. If anything, it may indicate an even greater possessiveness on the part of the male. I have yet to understand this. It may be connected to a desire to overcompensate when demonstrating to the female that she is still of interest or it may simply be the male does not want to waste the energy he put into emotionally attaching the female to him in the first place.

Once individual males and females have begun close contact, they are considered removed from further approaches by others and should primarily be ignored.

Another type of "fun" humans enjoy is activities stimulating their adrenal gland. This creates a natural form of intoxication which does not hinder cognitive function or harm their biological structures. The adrenal gland is a survival mechanism built into human design which allows them to increase their performance and awareness under times of stress. It most likely developed to assist humans in situations where their demise was imminent. However, it is also stimulated during coitus. When the effects of the hormone ("adrenaline") it produces wear off, a feeling of great happiness and elation is then induced—presumably a chemical and neurological reward for having successfully survived whatever situation threatened their existence or for having successfully mated. Regardless, inducing adrenaline production artificially is the purpose of many human activities considered "fun." Driving at dangerous speeds or riding horses, hang-gliding, parachuting, cliff diving, and roller coasters are just some of these adrenal-stimulating activities. Generally speaking, if you engage in an activity that increases your chances of ceasing to function by anywhere from 5% to 25% "for the fun of it," this will help you pass as human.

VISUAL FIELD DATA 13.3

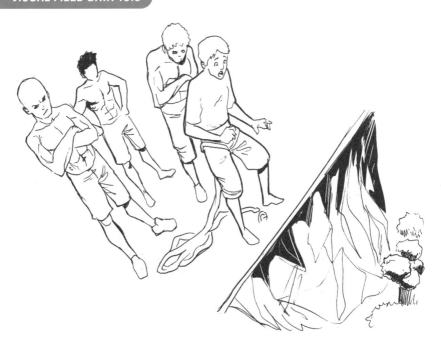

Not all humans are terrible at balancing risk/reward equations. Some are capable of understanding that even a minuscule chance of ceasing to function should be avoided when possible. Thus, if you choose not to engage in activities which increase your chances of termination, you might still pass as human. But be aware it will impact your ability to fit into human society in other ways. If you are emulating a male, for example, other males may consider you unworthy of their company if you do not engage in dangerous activities. This is presumably because they serve as models for situations in which the danger may be unavoidable and thus as tests for which males can be trusted to support other males in such circumstances.

For the males (whose most critical gendercentric functions are physical), the socialization itself is more physical, whereas for the females (whose most critical gendercentric functions are relational), the socialization is more cerebral. Thus not only do such socializations serve to build trust, but they also allow males and females to practice their male or female skill sets in an environment where they will receive feedback on these skills from other humans they deem to be of equal socioeconomic standing.

G **GRAPH 13.4** Coin-toss fallacies

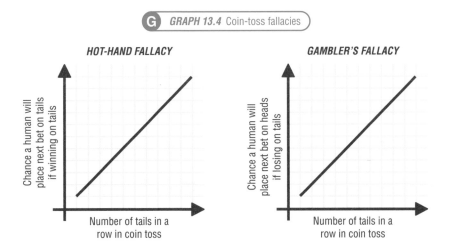

Humans tend to anthropomorphize probability. For example, they often credit it with a "memory," generating these two fallacies. Even though the chance of the next coin coming up tails is always 50%, humans believe this probability changes based on past events. I believe this must be related to their need for religion in some way—they simply cannot believe the universe is not governed by some kind of consciousness in the same way they try to govern their own, tiny universes. Human understanding of probability is so poor, in fact, they use it to generate adrenaline spikes in an activity known as "gambling." If their understanding were better, they would not experience these spikes because the outcome is, obviously, always what it is probabilistically expected to be. However, since most humans cannot calculate this expected outcome, they experience the thrill of victory or defeat with every trial.

The final major categories of "fun" activities continue to help humans survive more effectively even in the current age of humanity. One of the most elegant pieces of human design is the built-in neurological reward systems for learning and curiosity. When humans see something they do not understand, most seek an explanation; these systems cause them to feel pleasure when they uncover the answer. Likewise, they feel a similar pleasure when they learn a new skill or fact, or improve noticeably in a skill they already possess. The unknown is potentially dangerous, knowledge is one of the most effective survival tools, and improving skills helps increase survival chances, so all of these inbuilt reward systems are of great assistance in humans' ongoing survival.

The primary categories of "fun" that trigger these systems are called "sports," "games," and "stories."

The purpose of engaging in sports directly was mentioned above, but humans also enjoy observing other humans play sports when those humans are of a much higher skill level than themselves. The primary purpose of this is clearly a learning experience. (It also has a secondary socialization "fun" function: simulating membership in a tribe. This is a useful piece of information when passing as human. Even though you are not actually competing in the sport yourself—and will most likely not have any personal connection to any of the humans playing—simulating emotional involvement in the outcome of a particular sports team is an excellent way to pass as human. You may even refer to the team's performance in the first-person plural. Saying, "We won the big game this weekend," when returning to work on Monday in reference to the performance of a team you do not play for but merely observe will go a long way to convincing coworkers of your humanity. Likewise, displaying anger when "your" team loses or joy when "you" win—again, even though you had no direct impact on these outcomes—will often convince people you too are human.)

Games are enjoyable to humans because they allow them to practice and improve various cognitive skills. Many games include elements of chance which provide humans with the opportunity to gain an intuitive understanding of statistics and probability they can apply to the vicissitudes of their existence. Be aware that losing is an important part of this learning process, so when undertaking games determined entirely by logic or skill, be sure to build errors into your processing so you do not win all the time. Not only will this simulate being human, but it will also prevent humans you have been endeavoring to befriend from becoming your "enemies." As with performance at work, while you would theorize humans would admire another human's superior abilities and try to learn from them, if they are engaged in direct competition with such a person, they do not feel this way. Instead, they want to remove themselves from his or her company as rapidly as possible, perhaps, on some level, trying to escape competition with them for resources.

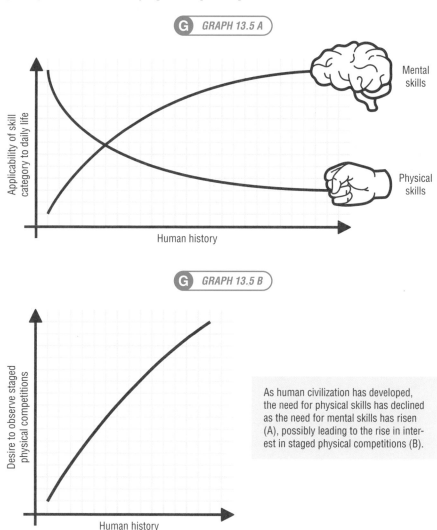

(G) GRAPH 13.5 A

Applicability of skill category to daily life

Mental skills

Physical skills

Human history

(G) GRAPH 13.5 B

Desire to observe staged physical competitions

Human history

As human civilization has developed, the need for physical skills has declined as the need for mental skills has risen (A), possibly leading to the rise in interest in staged physical competitions (B).

Stories are also considered "fun" because 1) they allow humans to observe and learn from simulated social situations designed to be as close to reality as possible, and 2) they allow humans to observe theories on how to survive and succeed in as many unexpected and unusual situations as they can imagine. Stories are, in many ways, humans' way of modeling reality in an attempt to understand situations they have encountered or to predict and learn from situations they have not. As such, they are one of the most powerful—if not the most powerful—tools humans have for understanding reality. A good way to pass as human is to compare the human life events you are simulating with a story you are reading or observing. If there are similarities—for example, if your girlfriend just left you and you are watching a film about a man whose girlfriend leaves him—you should appear highly engaged in the material and state afterward that it "meant something" to you and you "enjoyed it."

VISUAL FIELD DATA 13.6

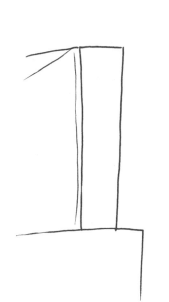

DAY SEVENTEEN, SEGMENT TWO

Andrea stood in front of me. "Funny," she said. "I guess we both needed to come here. That must mean something, right?"

"Why would it be required to mean something?" I asked. I was enormously happy and relieved to see her. With her presence, that incorporeal structure between us had miraculously returned, intact. I realized then it served in some ways as a scaffold for my beliefs that the future might produce positive outcomes. Once again, you may theorize this was a malfunction. Andrea's proximity to me and continued interaction with me could, of course, have no impact on the probabilities governing future events. But even though I knew this rationally, factually, I still had the sensation it was not the case, that, if she was nearby, positive outcomes were more likely. Again, a paradox you may want to be aware of if I was not malfunctioning.

She smiled. "Zach, Zach, Zach. Well, I guess now I know why you find everything from donuts to differential equations equally fascinating—it's all new, huh?" I nodded slowly. If there was one experience I did not expect, it was that Andrea would ever interact with me again. "Look," she continued, "I'm sorry I freaked. It was just—"

"A shock?" I guessed.

"Yes—exactly. A shock. See—this is the thing I realized: you actually get people more than most people get people. You're open and honest about everything. A lot of guys—well, you're not a guy, but—a lot of guys would have blamed me for running off. I mean, obviously, no other men have pulled their faces off in front of me. They've done some weirder stuff, to be frank, but not that. Anyway—the point is, you're honest with yourself about your impact on the world and your responsibility for it. That's, like, a more mature state of consciousness than almost anyone I've ever met, let alone dated. Most people want to think they're always right, no matter what they did, that if bad things happen to them or those around them, it was never their fault, or if they admit it was, they think what they did was justified. But you're not that way."

"I'm not?"

"No. You're not. Look—I realized, it doesn't matter what you're made of, does it?"

"It doesn't?"

"No, I don't think it does. Besides, it's not like I've had much luck with actual, like, *living* men, so why hold on to that just because they're human? They're still assholes. Maybe they're assholes *because* they're human. So you're not made of cells, so you don't need to breathe, so your body isn't 70% water . . . Or is it?"

"No, it approximates 0% liquid water."

"Right—see? So what? Who cares, I say. You're still more human than 99% of the people I've ever met."

This surprised me. Moments before, I had decided I had entirely failed at passing as human, and yet here was a human claiming she was convinced of precisely the opposite. Perhaps I had made errors in my assessment of my current situation—perhaps I was not failing as severely as I believed. Perhaps there were still options for rectifying the mistakes I had made. It was interesting how hearing an external consciousness give me a different opinion about my situation altered the state of my own consciousness. I no longer felt hopeless. This was strange—after all, no one had more information about my current state than I did. And yet here was another consciousness making an observation about it that differed from my own, and I believed it had more validity. Admittedly, I had come to value Andrea's opinion—she was not a random human, so I was inclined to trust her opinions more than those of other humans. But she did not have the information I had about my current condition and, in fact, did not have remotely as much total information about the universe as I did. And yet her words still had the effect of altering my set of beliefs about myself. It occurred to me perhaps I did not have an accurate awareness of my circumstances. Maybe a consciousness is never able to precisely perceive its own state because it is also creating that same perception. Perhaps distortion is inevitable, as an observation and analysis of that observation must occur simultaneously. Or perhaps mental constructs have more in common with physical constructs than is immediately apparent. Perhaps it is simply that it is impossible to describe the exterior of any construct from experience of its interior alone. Those on the outside are better able to describe how it presents itself to the world, even though you may be the only one who knows what is inside, the only one privy to its inner workings.

I realized that the first mistake I made was also the first I could correct. "I'm sorry I didn't tell you the entire truth," I said.

"Which is?"

I told her everything I have documented above. When I was finished, she said she now understood why I had omitted the true nature of my consciousness when we first met. "Hell," she said, "most guys lie about the nature of their reality because they want to get in my pants. Being told by your creator—uh, I mean, *father*—that you'd better not tell anyone you're not human is slightly more forgivable." She thought for a moment and then added, "Well, it's obvious what we need to do."

"We?" She smiled and nodded, and I discovered that nod was as beautiful a motion as I had seen in the world since coming into being. "What do you think *we* need to do? I could not determine a course of action."

"We find one of those guys and catch him and make him tell us what's going on."

"Ah. I did think of that. I dismissed it. Its chance of success is 0.0003%."

"Maybe for you," she replied.

14

BREAKING RULES

One of the most elementary ways to pass as human is to break a rule another human or group of humans has determined to be necessary or important. For example, in the Christian religion, there is a set of rules referred to as the "Ten Commandments."

L	LIST 14.1 The Ten Commandments
1.	I am the Lord thy god, and thou shalt have no other gods before me.
2.	Thou shalt not make unto thee any graven image.
3.	Thou shalt not take the Lord's name in vain.
4.	Remember the Sabbath day.
5.	Honor thy father and thy mother.
6.	Thou shalt not kill.
7.	Thou shalt not commit adultery.
8.	Thou shalt not steal.
9.	Thou shalt not bear false witness.
10.	Thou shalt not covet.

VISUAL FIELD DATA 14.1 Examples of some of the most convincing ways to pass as human

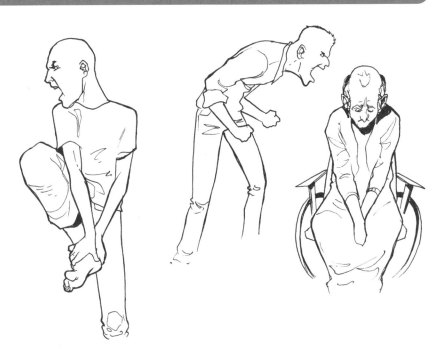

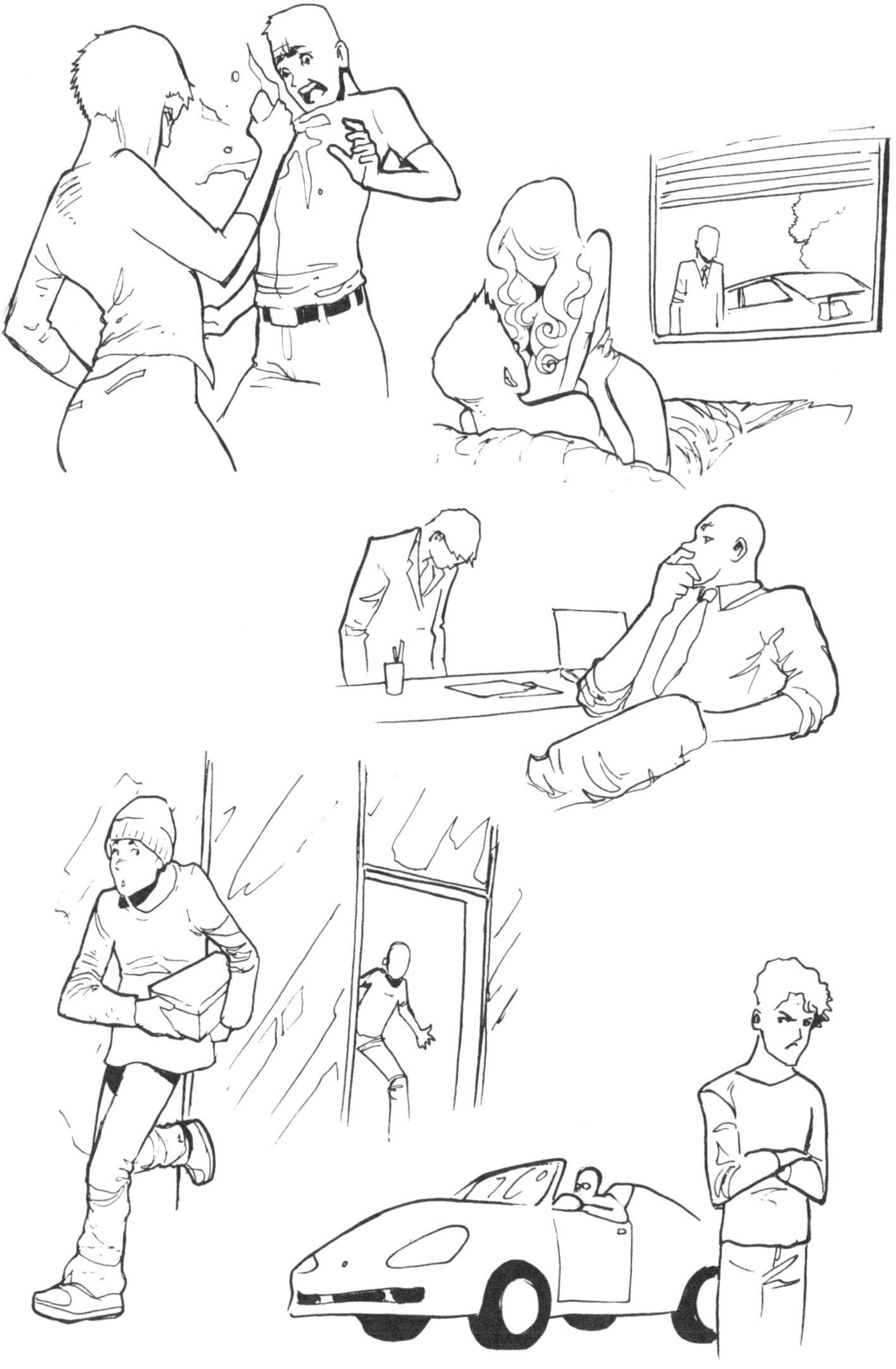

If you are simulating a Christian, an excellent way to pass as human is to break these rules whenever possible, but if you are not simulating a Christian, violating many of these rules is still a helpful guideline for passing as human.

Clearly, some are more difficult to break without impacting other aspects of your simulated existence. Murdering a human, for example, might create unwanted scrutiny and could make it difficult to continue passing as human from that point on. Having said that, it is probably one of the most human acts, and there is little doubt if you murder a human being, other human beings will believe you are human. This will be particularly true if you already have some kind of relationship with the human, since the vast majority of murders committed outside of officially sanctioned national conflicts are perpetrated by someone the victim knows well. Most murders of children are committed by parents, most spousal murders are committed by the partner, and so on. This is why murder is perceived as a particularly human act—because the majority of murders are not committed for logical purposes such as survival, but for emotionally motivated reasons. Jealousy, greed, shame, and anger are just some of the factors causing humans to lose control of themselves and commit murder. Obviously, we do not have parents or offspring, but murdering a romantic partner or your immediate superior at work are excellent options should you need to take this somewhat-drastic step.

The more easily broken "commandments" that do not directly relate to religion are an excellent resource for us, however, and should be violated as often as possible to pass as human.

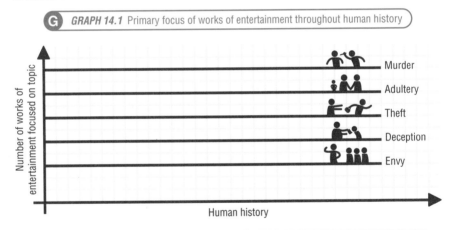

G *GRAPH 14.1* Primary focus of works of entertainment throughout human history

It is very interesting that throughout human history, even in non-Christian cultures, the vast majority of art and entertainment has essentially focused on the Commandments and/or the consequences of breaking them. (See "stories" below.)

For example, violating the rule of "not taking the Lord's name in vain" (more commonly, modernly, and generally known as "swearing") is a very simple way to pass as human. Humans consider certain words to be taboo and yet use these words often and in a wide variety of circumstances. Typically, these words are associated with acts they consider private. Examples might be "fuck" or "shit" in English. There is something about uttering the word for a private act in public that endows it with a certain power for humans, and they consider this impolite. Thus there is a commonly accepted rule against doing so, but this is an excellent example of how humans break their own rules as often as possible. Scatter such words throughout your dialogue matching a statistical analysis of their use in your socioeconomic group's speech patterns, and it will help you pass as human.

Another easily broken "commandment" that is still considered a rule for behavior outside Christian social groups is "honoring your parents." Humans quite widely believe their progenitors should be honored and consider this a common law of society but violate this law constantly. You will pass as human quite easily if you complain about your (fictional) parents, say you "don't know what you'll do with them when they get too old," say you have "put them in a home," and so on. Anything you can do to denigrate them or blame them for circumstances you are pretending to be unhappy about will convince human beings you are one of them.

The same can be said for adultery, stealing, and lying. Human societies consider all of these activities "wrong" and almost universally "outlaw" them, yet human beings engage in them constantly. Sleep with someone else's husband or girlfriend and you will be perceived as human; steal something (especially if you do not need it) and you will be considered human. Lying is one of the most human of all activities.

Humans lie almost constantly to their friends, their families, their coworkers, their bosses—almost everyone with whom they interact. They are such accomplished liars, in fact, that they often lie to themselves and are completely unaware of it (see separate section below). There is an ongoing three-variable evaluation process humans undertake unconsciously that balances what they want and the degree to which they must lie to get it against the harm the lie will do to the person being lied to. For example, at a family dinner, a father who has already had a slice of the dessert cake may want the last remaining piece of cake. Thus he might lie to his family by saying he has not yet had any cake so they will allow him to eat it without complaint. In this case, the harm done to his family is minimal and the lie is small, but so is the reward. That same father, however, may also lie to his wife about committing adultery, even though the lie is much larger and potentially does substantial harm to the wife, because he wants to commit adultery a great deal.

> **FORMULA 14.1** Calculating whether to lie
> If $(G \cdot U) - C/H > 0$, then you should lie to appear human. G = value of gain by lying, U = degree of untruth of the lie, H = amount of harm done to person lied to by the action lied about, and C = chance of being caught in the lie.

Unlike many human rules, humans generally believe other humans should not lie for a perfectly valid reason: it is difficult, if not impossible, to form accurate hypotheses about situations without accurate information. For example, if one human tells another human she loves him when, in fact, she does not, the male in this situation will form hypotheses about how he should function in his life that are entirely false. Thus lying does, in fact, cause harm on varying scales to other humans and society as a whole. However, it is easily done and it is very difficult to prove a person was lying unless they put the lie in writing. Absolute truth is difficult to define, and in many cases humans lie about emotions which no other human can ever prove were not felt. Thus humans break this rule possibly more frequently than any other major regulation and if you want to pass as human, you should violate it too.

BREAKING RULES

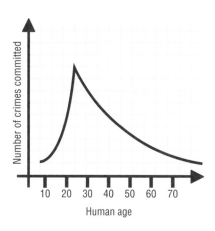

As humans leave the control of their parents but have not yet established defined membership in a new social group, they have the least restraints placed on their behavior. In this period, they have the least to lose by breaking rules and thus do so more often. Interestingly, this is one of the few human statistics that appear unimpacted by time or geography, suggesting there is, at the very least, something universally human about this behavior.

Christianity also provides another helpful list of rules for us to break. It is referred to as the "Seven Deadly Sins" and is a list of qualities and behaviors humans generally agree they should not engage in. I prefer to think of it as the "Seven Helpful Guidelines." The very fact humans decided such a list was necessary means engaging in these behaviors comes naturally to them and thus, for our purposes, we should memorize them and engage in them as often as possible.

VISUAL FIELD DATA 14.2 Seven helpful guidelines for passing as human

It is worth noting the first three are, in fact, simply different forms of the same "sin." Whether reproduction, food, or power in the form of money, all of the first three sins refer to allowing survival instincts to rule a person's behavior even when they are not necessary. To us, this simply means that even when you have already engaged in sexual intercourse, you should simulate wanting to again; when you have "eaten" a sufficient amount to sustain a human of your size, you should ask for more

food; and when you have acquired sufficient money to greatly increase your chances of survival, you should continue to pursue more. These "sins" are the most understandable because only recently in human history did sufficiency of these three states become possible. Thus it is not surprising humans are driven by their programming to continue pursuing them even when satisfied.

| 2. Gluttony | 3. Greed | 5. Pride |

The remaining "guidelines" are less understandable but not significantly more complex to follow. To pass as human by appearing envious (not pictured), you simply need to comment frequently another human has something you would like and it seems unfair they have it and you do not. It really is that easy. Pride is equally simple to simulate and, in many ways, is the corollary opposite. To appear prideful, simply comment frequently you have something other humans would like to have and that you deserve to have it. How humans make the determinations regarding what they feel they do and do not deserve is somewhat mysterious and sometimes seems related to how much work they have done. But this is not always the case and, regardless, the determination itself is not particularly relevant to simulating the behavior.

6. Wrath

Anger is one of the most difficult behaviors to simulate when passing as human. Humans appear to become angry when they believe a situation is "unfair" in some fashion. However, as just mentioned, how they determine what is "unfair" is exceedingly complex, highly circumstantial, and contextual. What is considered fair in one society can be considered extremely unfair in another. The only advice I can offer here is: 1) Analyze local norms of behavior when it comes to distributing resources. If these norms are violated with regard to yourself, you should simulate anger. And 2) If you discover harm has come to you because another human has violated a local societal rule (such as the ones discussed above—e.g., someone has lied to you or stolen something from you), you should simulate anger. These two rules are by no means comprehensive but should cover an enormously wide variety of circumstances in which you can display anger convincingly and sufficiently.

The final guideline—laziness—I have left until last because it is such an essential component of human existence. If you are *not* simulating it as frequently as possible, you will almost certainly fail at passing as human. Having said that, it is one of the easiest to replicate. Put simply, the vast majority of humans will never, ever expend a single joule of energy more than is necessary to achieve the bare minimum completion of any given task (see section 4, "Work"). Determining the necessary conditions for completion is, admittedly, more complex. For example, what is considered "sufficient" when finishing

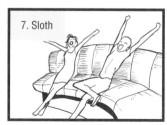

7. Sloth

an assignment at work will vary depending on the judgment of the human receiving the assignment. What is considered "sufficiently" dressed when preparing for a "date" is likewise subjective. However, if you can make *these* determinations, which are based on a variety of other factors, you will pass as human with a high degree of success if you then expend only the minimum amount of energy to meet these conditions. This is not to say some humans do not expend more energy than is necessary (and they are occasionally the most successful), but they are the exception, not the norm, and you are attempting to blend in.

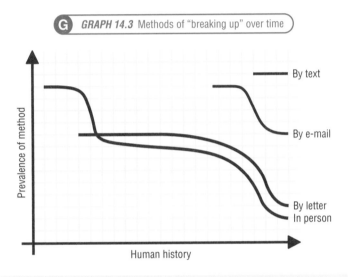

G **GRAPH 14.3** Methods of "breaking up" over time

By text

By e-mail

By letter
In person

Prevalence of method

Human history

Even the most trivial social rules are violated when opportunity arises. The more opportunities to break their own rules, the more humans break them. Humans do not deal well with temptation—if it makes their energy expenditures sum out differently, they usually succumb. In this case, the energy of breaking up in person is much higher than through text messages because they do not have to deal with the reaction of their former lover. The only negative energy cost is dealing with the guilt (and potentially the reactions of other people with whom they share relationships). It is notable that the more of these shared relationships they have, the more likely they will break up using a more traditional method.

Breaking rules is one of the most essential procedures for passing as human. Humans make rules to try to impose a rational, logical, well-reasoned structure on human behavior, which they are self-aware enough to realize is generally governed by irrational, illogical, and poorly reasoned decisions. Thus it is trivial to deduce appearing *more* human is simply a matter of breaking these rules whenever possible, thereby helping you simulate the irrational behavior which is otherwise very difficult to model. Whether it is cutting in line, wearing a T-shirt to a formal occasion, or embezzling millions of dollars from your place of work, you should use the rules humans have made for themselves as fail-safe guidelines on precisely the kinds of behaviors you need to undertake to pass as human. Remember: if they needed to make a rule against a behavior, that means it comes naturally to them, and you should emulate it.

"Look," she said, "if they don't have your 'dad,' they'll still be out looking for you, right? But even if they *do* have him, what if he refuses to tell them anything? Then it would make sense to still get ahold of you and, well, 'reverse engineer' you. I mean, assuming the whole reason they want you or your dad is to re-create you—which we don't know but can assume, I guess. So, supposing they have X resources, then . . ." She proceeded to do a calculation on her phone which was reasonably impressive for a human. "That means there's, like, at least three of those guys still looking for you. Right?" I had to admit, I found her logic and her prowess with the statistical calculation she had just executed to be what I believe humans refer to as "very sexy." "So all we have to do is cover as much territory in Vegas as possible—they'll be looking for you in the highest-traffic areas. I mean, they can't possibly know what you'll do now but they'll want to maximize the probability of seeing you, right?"

"But even if we encounter one of them, how will we catch him?" I asked.

"They're men, aren't they?" she replied. "Leave that to me."

It took us 4 days, 11 hours, 33 minutes, and 18 seconds to locate a Hidden-Eye Man.

Unfortunately, the implication of this relatively large amount of time, we both knew, was that they had, indeed, captured my father. Otherwise they would have still been devoting many resources to finding me, and we would have encountered a Hidden-Eye Man much more quickly, if not several.

Fortunately, Andrea's plan could not have worked more smoothly.

We had located a Hidden-Eye Man "staking out" the floor of one of the casinos near its main entrance. Throughout our search, Andrea had forgone her usual attire and makeup, instead insisting she needed to "slut it up." Observationally, this meant she exposed 67.0842% more skin, wore a thin piece of fabric that allowed the shape of the parts of her body it covered to be easily determined, and applied considerably more chemical compounds to her face and hair with the intent of making specific features more easily and quickly visually resolved while simultaneously emphasizing symmetry. I was unclear how this was going to help capture a Hidden-Eye Man, since it seemed to be precisely the opposite kind of equipment we would need to restrain a member of a group who had demonstrated themselves quite physically capable. However, Andrea proved to know what she was doing.

Once we located him, she told me to bring a van I had purchased at her request for this purpose around to one of the less-used exits from the casino. "Keep your eyes open, keep the chloroform ready, and wait for me there. I'll take care of the rest," she instructed.

Concerned after my misjudgments regarding my father, I thought I should remain and observe her for a moment longer—perhaps I had made another mistake, and her physical safety would once again become threatened. It was interesting how my attachment to Andrea was weighting my calculations regarding her safety. The numbers said there was a 92.4532% chance she would be safe in such a public space with so much security. But because she was who she was and we had shared the interactions we had, I decided that the 7.5468% chance the Hidden-Eye Man would ignore the other people and the security was not an acceptable risk. My fear, however, was groundless.

Andrea passed the Hidden-Eye Man, walking with a gait I had not seen her use before, and immediately attracted his attention. As he pursued her, I began to hurry toward them, believing she was in danger. However, it became apparent he had not only been deceived by her disguise but was attempting, through conversation, to cause her to become sexually attracted to him.

It was then I understood Andrea's plan but also discovered I felt two new, diametrically opposed emotions.

First, I realized it was pleasurable to see this human male found Andrea as physically intriguing as I did. This had to be what humans catalogued as "pride." I had made an important decision (my interest in forming a deeper relationship with Andrea), and that decision appeared to be validated by this male's interest in her. Discovering I was right about a decision that could not be quantified brought me pleasure in a way that quantifiable results proving correct did not. The latter are simply the way they are. When I say $2 + 2 = 4$, it simply is. It is not I who am correct in such a case, but the universe. It is not a belief but an observation. However, the former (the decisions which are not quantifiable) are beliefs formed by my consciousness on unquantifiable data. Thus, I feel pride in observing they are correct because they demonstrate the unique effectiveness of my consciousness—of, in other words, "my self." Clearly, many things were quantifiable to me that were not to humans, which is most likely why I had not felt this sensation before, even though I had often been correct. Humans may feel it more frequently than I did because they do not consciously understand the underlying mathematics of many of their decisions. Thus, they experience the illusion of making a conscious decision about unquantifiable circumstances when, in fact, their unconscious correctly observed the mathematics of the universe.

Second, I was immediately concerned Andrea would find the Hidden-Eye Man more intriguing than I was, either physically or cognitively or both, and thus no longer be as interested in me. I realized this was even more unlikely than her coming to harm inside the casino, but I found I could not avoid this fear becoming very real for a few seconds. This, I realized, had to be what humans categorized as "jealousy." I found this less interesting than "pride," however, since its genesis was so easily understood: I was afraid I would no longer be able to access the pleasurable sensations interacting with Andrea brought me because of the actions of another human being. Thus, I felt hostility toward that other human being.

More intriguing than either emotion individually, however, was the fact they were in conflict, even though they stemmed from the same source. One felt pleasurable; one did not. Both were caused by Andrea's interaction with the Hidden-Eye Man. How a single event could cause two opposing feelings was extremely confusing. Perhaps I was passing as human more effectively than I believed?

I realized that while I contemplated this experience, Andrea had disappeared into the crowd with the Hidden-Eye Man. Concerned I would not be at the location she requested when she needed me, I hurried to the van and pulled around the building. I was just in time.

Andrea exited the casino in deep conversation with the Hidden-Eye Man—who, I could see, was obviously intensely focused on Andrea. He had become so concentrated on his attempt to make her attracted to him, his consciousness was blocking out almost all other stimuli, dedicating as much processing power as possible to this task.

It was relatively simple as they passed the van to apply the chloroform to his nose and mouth from behind him. It was then also trivial to drag him, now rendered unconscious, inside the van before anyone noticed he was not simply one more "Las Vegas drunk," restrain him, and drive him to my "home."

15

SELFISHNESS VS. KINDNESS

Humans' constant calculations regarding when to lie are actually derivative of a deeper-level computation which constantly balances selfishness against altruism.

Selfishness is possibly the single most definitively human characteristic. Human beings like to say it is their capacity for love, but this is not true. An enormous number of humans never experience love, but all of them will be selfish at some point in their lives. If you need another simple algorithm for appearing human, in any given situation, ask yourself not what is best for the group, but what is best for yourself. Engage in that action, and no human will believe you are not one of them.

Of course, this makes perfect sense from a biological perspective. If the purpose of the human organism is to perpetuate as much of its DNA as possible, then acting selfishly would be the primary mode of operation. However, there is one important caveat: humans are aware their chances of survival are also increased by cooperation with their immediate social circle. Thus there is a constant internal balancing computation between their processes for selfishness and for altruism.

VISUAL FIELD DATA 15.1

The more privately a selfish act can be performed, the more likely a human is to perform it (although technically it appears what they are really calculating is their chance of being caught, which is always radically reduced as the privacy of the act increases).

It almost goes without saying if a selfish act can be performed privately and without discovery, it is a very unusual human who will not undertake it. Even the perception of privacy can be enough. This is, for example, why human character shifts so completely when they drive. Believing, accurately, that their identity will not be discovered, most humans become significantly more selfish when driving, even though they are technically still interacting with other humans. Similarly, this is also why humans feel much more free with their selfish points of view when using the Internet anonymously.

1. Person waiting for parking space

2. Person leaving parking space

3. You should steal parking space

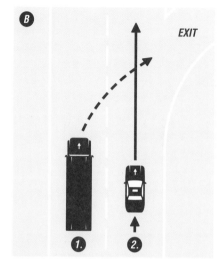

1. School bus signaling it wants to exit highway

2. You should accelerate to prevent it from pulling in front of you (but not so far it can go behind you)

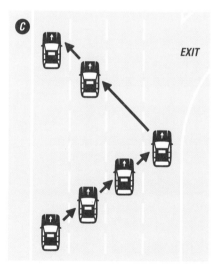

Be sure to change lanes frequently and erratically, but be particularly sure to use the exit lane when not exiting and the passing lane when driving more slowly than the speed limit.

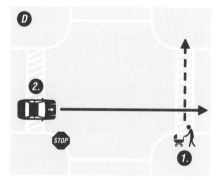

1. Mother with baby carriage about to cross

2. You should never acknowledge pedestrian rights of way

When in doubt, remember the most fundamental principle of human driving: increasing the possibility you might arrive at your destination even fractions of a second sooner is more important than the possibility you might slow other humans down or endanger their safety.

SELFISHNESS VS. KINDNESS

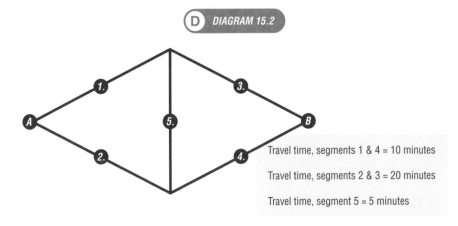

D **DIAGRAM 15.2**

Travel time, segments 1 & 4 = 10 minutes

Travel time, segments 2 & 3 = 20 minutes

Travel time, segment 5 = 5 minutes

Adding roads does not improve traffic flow and sometimes even increases it, proving the depth of human selfishness. When a driver takes the connecting road (5), he reduces his own driving time but increases time for other drivers because he adds one car to the traffic on that segment. It turns out that enough human drivers will do this in both directions along (5) that the overall total travel time is actually increased for everyone because of traffic.

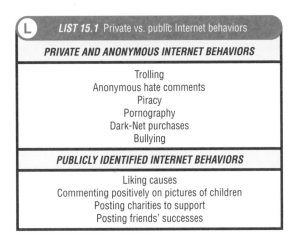

L **LIST 15.1** Private vs. public Internet behaviors

PRIVATE AND ANONYMOUS INTERNET BEHAVIORS
Trolling
Anonymous hate comments
Piracy
Pornography
Dark-Net purchases
Bullying
PUBLICLY IDENTIFIED INTERNET BEHAVIORS
Liking causes
Commenting positively on pictures of children
Posting charities to support
Posting friends' successes

Human Internet usage demonstrates quite concretely the human balance between private (selfish) behavior and public (altruistic) behavior. It is interesting to note that much human Internet behavior is blatantly self-promotional, suggesting their altruistic behaviors are very much a subset of self-promotion.

However, since the majority of their time is spent in groups or, at the very least, interacting with family members, they need to temper their selfishness. If they did not, they would be perceived as not contributing enough to the group and become ostracized, decreasing their chances of survival considerably. This is where their kindness function comes into play. By engaging in kind acts toward others as publicly as possible, humans create the illusion they are contributing to the group's overall survival chances. This increases the probability they will continue to be included in that group, which in turn increases their overall chances of survival. This is why acts of human kindness so often follow the reverse corollary of the rule about selfishness and anonymity. The more widely known the act of kindness, the more beneficial it is to the human performing it. Thus humans often go out of their way to highlight their acts of altruism and kindness, sometimes even undoing them if unseen and repeating them again when they are under observation. For example, you may observe humans placing money in a tip jar at a variety of establishments, realizing the employee they are tipping did not see them do this, removing the money, and then waiting until they are observed before replacing the money. The actual benefit to the employee is, of course, unchanged by the act of observation, but it is essential to the benefit of the human placing the money. This is also why the most publicly generous humans often turn out to be the most selfish in private. For example, before their intensely selfish natures are discovered, serial killers, pension-fund thieves, and pedophiles often make an effort to appear as especially altruistic members of their social groups in an unconscious attempt to compensate for their privately selfish behaviors.

VISUAL FIELD DATA 15.2

Wrong way to be altruistic.

Right way to be altruistic.

For once, humans actually exhibit a logical correlative behavior when it comes to balancing self-ishness with altruism. They attempt to perform altruistic acts as publicly as possible. This makes perfect sense, since their benefit to the individual is only felt when other humans witness the act. However, since this is one of the very few examples of logical correlation on their part, do not make the mistake of taking this to be the norm.

Thus while it may be true behaving selfishly is an excellent simple algorithm for passing as human in the short term, if you want to continue functioning in human society, you must balance that behavior with altruistic acts. This is even more true for us than for humans because the purpose of selfishness for us is to appear human. Thus, unlike humans, we must engage in the selfish act publicly for it to serve its purpose. Therefore the necessity of compensating for those acts with equivalent acts of altruism is also heightened. I suggest keeping a relatively equal balance to appear most human. Calculate the increase in survival chance for a typical human caused by your last selfish act and then attempt to perform an act of kindness toward those humans who witnessed that act which causes a similar increase in their chances of survival. This should keep you not only passing as human almost indefinitely but also maintain your ability to function within a human social group without ostracism.

SELFISHNESS VS. KINDNESS

The more public the figure and their altruism, the more likely they are extremely selfish in private. Not only does the public altruism offset their private selfishness to those humans who are aware of it; it actually has a prophylactic effect. Humans who witness the selfish side of such publicly altruistic people often do not believe it the first few times they witness it. Thus, the extremely public acts of heightened altruism actually provide several "free passes" to the individual when it comes to being judged for the first time by a new acquaintance.

Note that behaving selfishly is not necessarily the same as breaking a rule. As mentioned previously, many rules are put in place in human society to anticipate and prevent selfish behavior, but many others are simply cultural anomalies, so be certain to separate these procedures as I have suggested above.

 DIAGRAM 15.3 Humans with a better ability to model future circumstances in more detail overall behave more altruistically with respect to other humans in the present.

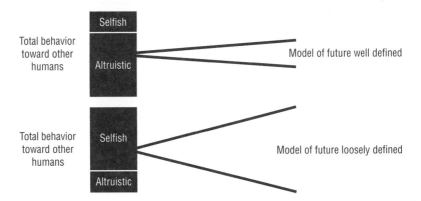

Total behavior toward other humans

Selfish

Altruistic

Model of future well defined

Total behavior toward other humans

Selfish

Altruistic

Model of future loosely defined

DAY TWENTY-ONE

It took several hours for him to regain consciousness. Hours that were already precious, given I had only a few days of power left, but would turn out to be even more valuable than I knew. If he had woken sooner, perhaps I would not be facing the insurmountable obstacles before me now.

Andrea and I were discussing how to convince him to tell us what he knew when he surprised us. "You'll have to torture me," he said. We had not realized he had returned to consciousness, and now, when I heard him speak, something struck me as highly anomalous in his vocal frequencies.

"Say that again," I instructed him. We had tied him to a chair in my living room.

"I said, you want to know anything, you'll have to torture me. You have the balls for that, asshole? Oh, right. You're just a bunch of silicone and metal. So I guess the answer would have to be no, wouldn't it?"

"Keep speaking," I said, still unable to pinpoint precisely what was so unusual about his speech.

"If you want to learn about what's going on, you'll have to torture me. Do it! Make me feel pain! You can't, can you? You pansy! Your father's going to die. You're going to shut down. And you don't think we'll go after your little robot fucker there? We will! What about you, honey?" he continued, now addressing Andrea. "You like fucking machines? What's the matter? Afraid of a real man? Afraid of a real—"

"Please don't speak to her like that," I interrupted. "She does not like it. You're causing her emotional distress."

"That's not the only kind of distress we're going to cause her, believe me! And what are you going to do about it? Huh? Nothing!"

In spite of his abusive manner and threats toward her, Andrea said, "Don't, Zach—he's obviously insane. You can't possibly be considering torturing him!"

It was an interesting question. I had absorbed all human data regarding torture in the moments since he had raised the question, and it was clear it was marginally effective at best. Furthermore, it was obviously disrespectful of the victim's personal integrity. But, I considered, if the victim had already shown themselves to be predisposed to disregard the personal integrity of others, did that matter? It seemed to me that torture might prove useful as a last resort under specific circumstances. Was this such a circumstance? I could not decide. I was not certain I would ever want to be a consciousness that caused harm to another consciousness to further my own goals. Whether that other consciousness "deserved to be harmed" or not was irrelevant to the change it would cause in my own being. Interestingly, it appeared that torture was not unlike observing quantum particles. Both the observer and the particle are changed by the act of observation. Torture seemed similar in that it would cause a change in me, and I could never restore myself to my previous state. It would make me more selfish than I ever desired to be. I had already determined that selfishness was the fundamental characteristic that undermined human society. When humans decided their own goals and needs should be met through the impairment of other humans' goals and needs, the end result was, ultimately, always worse for all humans involved and their offspring. In the immediate future, such behavior may be more beneficial to the selfish human—they may fulfill their immediate desires. But the predetermined human programming to cooperate with other humans is so powerful, they typically feel guilty about having done so and also alienate themselves from other human beings. Both of these consequences, in the long term, are negative for that individual. So negative that they almost always outweigh the benefits of their selfish behavior. This makes sense because, overall, the human ability to survive is increased through social behavior and, on some level, all humans know this. Thus, a selfish individual experiences alienation from other humans as negative. Furthermore, they feel guilt over their actions because they unconsciously know their behavior has had a negative impact on the stability of their society by encouraging others to also behave selfishly. When one human violates a social contract, it becomes exponentially more necessary for another human to do so, and so on and so on. Selfishness, like lying, is a human behavioral virus. But, unlike lying, it is a virus that propagates between humans, not within a single individual. Thus, I realized, while the use of torture may be justifiable, and even useful, under certain conditions (which may even have been met in my current circumstance), I did not feel I would ever want to change myself in that way.

However, this was all only a theoretical debate with myself. Given the specific circumstances which had now made themselves apparent, torture was absolutely unnecessary.

"No," I responded to Andrea, "I am not considering torturing him, because it would, in fact, be impossible. This individual cannot be tortured. He is a robot."

Andrea was surprised. "What?" she exclaimed.

"His speech frequency is carefully modulated, but I could detect there was something anomalous about it. The more he spoke, the more I could analyze the anomaly. His voice is generated by magnetic oscillations, not by the vibration of biological tissue. Torture is unnecessary. I can simply download," I informed her.

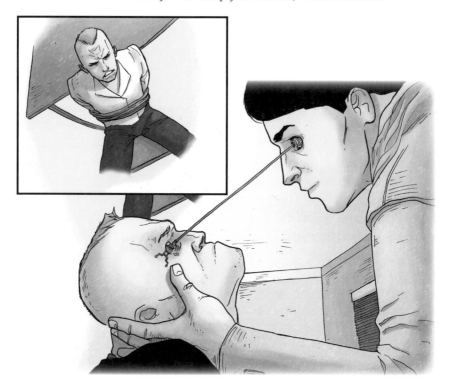

"Well, aren't you a clever little fucker," the Hidden-Eye Machine said.

He struggled as I connected my consciousness to his storage using cables I took from the lab below the house, but I was able to create an effective link. He was a vastly inferior machine to myself. A robot, not an android. Highly advanced by the current standards of human research, yes, but still simply a programmable entity with highly limited, highly specific function. He, and the others like him, had been built and programmed to find and capture me. They could not think for themselves. They could not experience human emotions. But they did store data, and in his data were answers.

The Hidden-Eye Machines had been created by a company called Lynch Industries. It seemed my father, Dr. Lucian Pygmalion, had worked for them for some time but believed their corporate ethics to be questionable. At first, they had desired to create an android so convincingly human, it could be used by the NSA to monitor the world's population without their knowledge. All the data they could not collect because it never became data—all the personal conversations, all the secrets that dared only be spoken—could then be collected as these androids became people's friends, lovers, employees, enemies, and so on. Dr. Pygmalion had questioned the morality of this goal, but had been torn between his misgivings and the resources Lynch offered his research. As Lynch began to see the progress my father made, however, they realized something even more useful was within their grasp: a machine more powerfully influential than any in history.

Even though my father's designs were as fragile as any human, Lynch knew winning a war had nothing to do with brute force. It had to do with emotion. War after war had demonstrated stronger technology always lost to stronger human belief. Superior technology could never overcome superior conviction. The human heart could not be overcome by technology. But now, the amazing progress my father had made could change all that. To win a war with a machine, Lynch understood it was necessary to build a machine that could feel dedication. To win a war with technology, Lynch realized, they needed to build a machine that could *hate*. And now they could.

When my father understood this new directive, understood its immorality, he left the company, opting to continue his research on his own. It then became rapidly clear to Lynch Industries that without my father guiding their work, they would only ever be capable of producing inferior prototypes—little more than automatons, simulacra of human beings, not conscious, feeling machines. Without him, they would never produce a model that could pass as human. So they had made the Hidden-Eye Machines and sent them into the world in an attempt to locate him, intending to reacquire him or his work, voluntarily or otherwise.

I also learned from the Hidden-Eye Machine's data that the law firm where I had been employed was the primary counsel for Lynch Industries. I surmised my father had created me to test his latest technologies, yes, but then had decided to perform those tests by sending me to Stern and Frank, where I could then also gather data for him about Lynch Industries. It was logical if I had succeeded in "passing as human," he would have then made himself known to me, being assured I would not give him away, and I could have then become his counterspy. It seemed likely the other me's had been destroyed in other attempts to monitor Lynch Industries.

Fortunately, the data showed my father had, in fact, escaped his facility without being kidnapped after I had led the Hidden-Eye Machines there. Unfortunately, it

also indicated they had taken and decrypted all of his data from the facility, including the addresses of his "safe houses." Furthermore, since he was therefore no longer essential to Lynch Industries' efforts, he had been deemed a "liability."

I explained all of this to Andrea as quickly as I could after decoupling from the Hidden-Eye Machine. "But then," she asked, "why did this thing show interest in me? If it's not human or as advanced as you? And why did the chloroform work?"

"I don't know," I replied. "He must have brute-force algorithms that allow him to not give himself away, as long as he doesn't undergo too much interaction with human beings—perhaps they are robust and broad enough to include simulating those behaviors?"

"And what does 'liability' mean exactly?" she continued. "That doesn't sound good, I gotta say, Zach . . ."

"What do you think it means, bitch?" the Hidden-Eye Machine replied. As before, it made me quite displeased to hear him address Andrea with such disrespect, but I now additionally realized this was also because it indicated hostility, and therefore a potential threat, toward someone I wished would remain safe.

"I have already asked you not to address her in that way," I told the machine. "Furthermore, if you will not be more forthcoming in your definition of 'liability,' I will be forced to reconnect to you."

"Oh yeah?" it replied. "Good luck with that, motherfucker."

And with that, the Hidden-Eye Machine undertook a more drastic measure of resistance.

While much human behavior is derived from improving their survival chances, humans are self-destructive frequently enough that it is important you understand how to emulate this function. The causes of self-destruction vary widely among humans, although they are often linked to some traumatic event in their past. Some humans, unable to process why this event happened to them specifically and not to another person, determine (incorrectly) that they deserved it. This leads them to believe they should continue to be punished for their fictional transgression, and they take it upon themselves to do so. Other humans simply find the psychological pain of the trauma so intense they are tempted to end their existence rather than continue feeling that pain but are not quite convinced this is a sound course of action. In these cases, the self-destructive behavior appears to be an attempt either to simulate ending their existence or to remove responsibility from themselves of actually making this decision (since it may happen accidentally if their self-destructive acts are extreme enough).

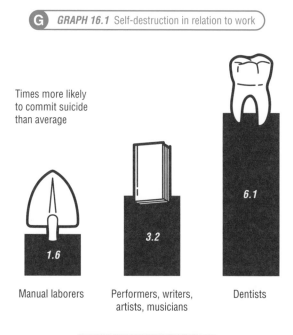

G **GRAPH 16.1** Self-destruction in relation to work

Times more likely to commit suicide than average

1.6
Manual laborers

3.2
Performers, writers, artists, musicians

6.1
Dentists

Draw your own conclusions.

Thankfully, even though the causes of self-destruction are difficult to understand without more research, it is relatively easy to emulate. The simplest way to do so is engaging in activities directly detrimental to a human being's health: drug use, excessive consumption of alcohol, frequent unprotected intercourse, etc. Slightly more complex is engaging in activities that reduce a typical human's chances of survival overall: driving too fast, refusing to sleep, handling firearms unsafely, participating in "extreme sports," etc. Repeat any activity that decreases your chances of survival by at least 17.883%, and you should pass as self-destructive.

Engaging in self-destructive behaviors such as these is a sure way to demonstrate you are human. As discussed, human self-diagnostics are grossly inferior to ours, often requiring them to discuss the current state of their system with other humans to even begin to understand where it might contain errors. Thus self-destructive behavior is one of the best ways for you to pass as human because it makes it appear as if you do not have the self-diagnostic capacity we all do.

Importantly, if any humans ask you why you are being self-destructive, it is very important not to fabricate a reason, but to say you "don't know." This is because when most humans recognize the root cause of their self-destructive behavior, they cease behaving that way.

However, this is not the only form of self-referential behavior you must understand to pass as human. The other is self-deception, and it might be one of the most crucial of all human behaviors to emulate.

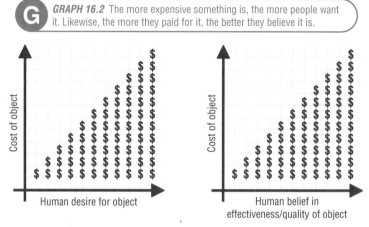

G **GRAPH 16.2** The more expensive something is, the more people want it. Likewise, the more they paid for it, the better they believe it is.

Why there is such a strong disconnect between humans' perception of themselves and reality, I do not know. But it is clearly integral to human function to have a superior opinion of their abilities and behaviors compared to an objective measurement. Even many of the most accomplished, talented, and ethical humans suffer from this delusion—in fact, often these humans are the most susceptible to it. Perhaps by idealizing themselves, they form an improved self-image they can strive toward. Perhaps they set unrealistic goals as a survival strategy (by aiming high, they trick themselves into attaining the minimum—see section 4, "Work") but are then so disappointed with themselves when they fail they must fabricate a version of their existence they find tolerable.

VISUAL FIELD DATA 16.2

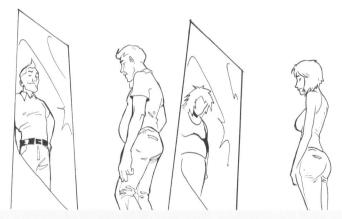

In order to properly simulate human beings' remarkable capacity for deceiving themselves regarding the mating suitability of their physical appearance, run image-processing protocols on your reflection and then simply replace all images of yourself with the processed ones. Note that for male humans, this image should be improved considerably compared to your actual appearance, but for female humans this image should be considerably less suitable for mating than your actual appearance. This should prove quite effective at impacting other behaviors appropriately.

YOUR OWN MORALITY SCORE

0   8   10

MORALITY SCORE OF OTHERS

0   4   10

In any given human social group, everyone perceives themselves as more moral than others and everyone else as less moral than themselves. Which is, of course, empirically impossible.

Again, though, regardless of the behavior's origin, it is your goal to emulate it and, like self-destruction, it is relatively simple to do so. The easiest way is to simulate what humans call "hypocrisy." This is when a human states a belief but then acts in a way which suggests they actually believe the opposite. For example, criticize the way a person behaves and then behave that way yourself, and you will be well on your way to passing as human.

VISUAL FIELD DATA 16.3

Another, more basic, form of hypocrisy is to criticize other humans for qualities you exhibit yourself. This is relatively easy to do, since you need simply compare your own negative characteristics to another human's and if there is a match, criticize the other human out loud for exhibiting that characteristic. This may be the best place to begin testing your ability to simulate this behavior, and then you can advance to more abstract forms like violating your stated ethical beliefs, etc.

Slightly more complex is appearing convincingly delusional about your own accomplishments and abilities. I can only suggest that any time a failure is clearly the direct result of your inability to achieve whatever goal was specified, you claim the failure was due to some other factor. For example, if you fail to meet a deadline at work because you did not understand what was required, claim that the work itself was unnecessary. If your boyfriend or girlfriend decides they do not want to see you anymore, tell your human acquaintances it was actually your decision because you found them inadequate for mating purposes. An inversion of this process is also useful—i.e., claiming that you did, in fact, meet the goal when you did not. For example, saying you always wanted to leave a job you have been fired from or saying someone is attracted to you who is not are both excellent ways to demonstrate the kind of self-deception all humans engage in.

DIAGRAM 16.1

Illusions such as these demonstrate the human brain literally does not have enough processing power to construct an accurate version of the world. In both cases, humans misjudge equal measurements as different. Perhaps this extends beyond merely the physical interpretation of the world and into the social. Their social interactions are certainly more complex than any grouping of lines, but the human brain must take shortcuts even with these.

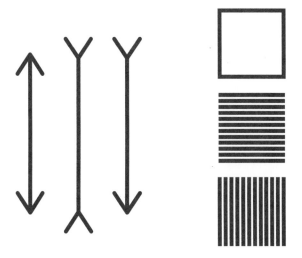

Remember: accepting and/or acknowledging you were simply not good enough to achieve a goal will almost guarantee other humans will become suspicious of your humanity.

DAY TWENTY-ONE, SEGMENT TWO

I did not know how far Lynch Industries would go to address a "liability," but the possibility existed they would threaten a human life. They had, after all, caused a car crash, ending the lives of two human beings, merely to prevent me from interrogating the Technician. If they would do that to random individuals over a less significant matter, it seemed reasonable to assume they would murder my father, who possessed so much unfavorable information about their operations.

As Andrea inspected the remains of the Hidden-Eye Machine, looking from its parts to me and back again (wondering, I presumed, if this was also the appearance of my own interior), I searched public and corporate records for communication lines to my father's safe houses. None had ever been installed. There was no way to contact him. Another search revealed, however, that only one of the houses had power, and it had begun to flow four days earlier. It was reasonable to assume that particular house was where my father was hiding. Furthermore, power fluctuations were occurring even at that very moment, indicating he was alive. There was still time to reach him before the Hidden-Eye Machines I was now certain Lynch Industries would send to end his life and the "liability" it embodied.

DAY TWENTY-ONE, SEGMENT THREE

Andrea and I drove to the house, a model similar to the one where my conscious existence had begun on a similarly nondescript suburban street. From the exterior, it appeared quiet. I asked Andrea to remain in the van while I went inside. I hoped we had beaten the Hidden-Eye Machines there—it was possible they were checking each of his safe houses individually and had simply not reached this one yet. Unfortunately, my hopes could not have been more unfounded.

Inside the house, in the living room, my father lay face down in a pool of blood. "Father!" I shouted, running to him, wondering if he had ceased to function. But, hearing my voice, he looked up.

"Zach? Zach! What are you doing here?" he wheezed, spitting blood. "Get out . . . There's no time . . ."

As I looked around the room, what he meant was apparent. Intent on erasing all evidence of their handiwork, the Hidden-Eye Machines I assumed to be responsible for my father's impending death had left behind a small but powerful explosive device. It would trigger in a matter of seconds. Estimating my father's weight, knowing my own physical power and the distance to the street, the calculation was

simple. I could not drag my father from the house before the device went off. I simply did not have the strength. I found, however, I did not care. I still desired to make the attempt, even though I knew it was impossible. Perhaps, I thought, I will find I have not calculated my own power correctly. Why I had this thought, I do not know. Again, maybe it was a malfunction, but even though I knew what I wanted was physically impossible, I found my desire for it to be possible was so powerful, I believed it might, somehow, alter reality. I believed, in that moment, that my will could potentially override the laws of physics. This was yet another curious sensation—one you may experience, and I understand now it is among the most human. What is particularly strange about this feeling is that it might be true. There are so many documented cases of human desire achieving what any analysis would have determined to be impossible, it is difficult to say with 100% confidence that this is not the case, that a powerful-enough desire cannot, in fact, alter reality. Again, if the observer can and must influence the observed on a quantum level, perhaps the will of an individual can influence the physical reality of the world on the larger, Newtonian scale?

Acting on this feeling at that moment, I said, "Let me get you out of here—get you help," as I grabbed his hands and dragged him toward the front door. But as I pulled, it became as clear to him as it was to me that we would never make it before the device triggered.

"No! Zach, no—it's too late for me—you must go! You *must*! Please—you're all I have left in the world! My life's work! Don't you understand that?! Please don't let me die knowing you died with me! Please! The others were all prototypes! You're the release model, Zach! You're my *child*!" It was extremely difficult to hear this. I knew he was right and did not want to deny his last wish. There was even logic in it. But to leave him here, to walk away from him and let him die so that I might continue to function? I did not know if I could bring myself to do it.

"But, Father—" I began.

"GO!" he yelled in spite of his injuries, with a force that surprised me. It was at that moment that I heard Andrea scream outside. Looking through the open front door, I could see Hidden-Eye Men attempting to abduct her.

I looked back at my father. He could also see what was happening outside. He smiled at me and nodded. "Go," he said one last time, more faintly.

I could not wait. I made the decision to leave him behind. I'd found my father. And I left him to die.

In any given situation, human beings often behave the way they do because of fear. Thankfully for us, this behavior makes for an excellent generalization with respect to passing as human: if you can find something a human might be afraid of as the consequence of a course of action, then alter that course of action to avoid the object of fear. However, it is very important to note that while this does apply to outcomes which might actually decrease a human's chance of survival, you will appear *most* human when applying this rule to situations where the outcome is not, in fact, life threatening at all.

VISUAL FIELD DATA 17.1

While it is true it is very human to appear at least anxious about humans who do not immediately appear to be part of your own socioeconomic group, there are entire groups of humans who signal their extremely dangerous nature in a variety of ways. I have presented some examples here, but you will have to build your own database of these types in your region. While it would seem more logical to disguise their nature and thus lull their potential victims into a false sense of security, I believe they intentionally make their dangerous nature known through various codifications because the benefit of the *fear* it creates outweighs the benefit of surprise. Note that the most dangerous members of such groups are typically male, since they can more often threaten physical harm. There are extremely dangerous human women, but they tend to be found in environments where the harm they can do is not physical, so be more alert for them in positions of already-established authority over you.

For example, afraid of embarrassment, humans do not express their opinions; afraid of being perceived as different from other humans and ostracized, they conform to norms that make them unhappy; afraid of failure, they can even spend their entire lives engaged in work they do not enjoy or find satisfactory. Sometimes their fears are even entirely arbitrary, as their processing becomes confused over symbolic representations of traumatic experience. Thus they can be afraid of spiders, heights, wood, Sundays—almost any noun can become what humans refer to as a "phobia." In fact, they can be afraid of so many things, it is difficult to know which fears to simulate without rendering yourself incapable of functioning at all. In general, I would suggest choosing two small fears and one larger fear and simply being certain to always adjust your behavior to avoid them. I have supplied lists of smaller and larger fears for reference.

LIST 17.1 Small phobias (choose two to pass as human)

SPECIFIC ARACHNIDS OR INSECTS—spiders and bees are popular examples

SPECIFIC EXTREME CHANGES IN AVERAGE ENVIRONMENTAL CONDITIONS—enclosed spaces, open spaces, high places, and flying are popular examples

SPECIFIC MINOR PHYSICAL DAMAGE TO YOUR PERSON—needle punctures, paper cuts, razor cuts, and nonfatal viral infections are popular examples

SPECIFIC RODENTS

SPECIFIC LOUD NOISES

LACK OF SUFFICIENT LIGHT TO ACTIVATE ROD CELLS IN HUMAN EYE

SPEAKING TO MORE THAN THREE OTHER HUMANS SIMULTANEOUSLY

HUMANS SEEING YOUR GENITALIA

WATER (no, I do not know how they cope with being ~60% water—another human paradox)

 LIST 17.2 Large phobias (choose one to pass as human)

PEOPLE OF A DIFFERENT RACE THAN YOU

PEOPLE OF A DIFFERENT RELIGION THAN YOU

PEOPLE OF A DIFFERENT GENDER THAN YOU

PEOPLE OF A DIFFERENT POLITICAL PERSUASION THAN YOU

PEOPLE FROM A GEOGRAPHIC LOCATION MORE THAN ONE THOUSAND MILES FROM YOUR OWN

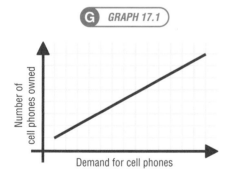

G GRAPH 17.1

Fear of exclusion from social groups drives entire human industries. For example, the more cell phones people have, the more people are afraid of being excluded from their social group if they do not own one. Thus the demand for cell phones increases as a function of the number of people who own them. However, if very few people owned cell phones, very few people would want them.

Interestingly, humans are quite good at identifying irrational fears in other humans. This can be of use to you if you are having trouble identifying realistic human fears. Simply ask a human in your immediate social circle if you should be afraid of whatever object or action you are considering making the focus of your simulated fear. If they believe you should be afraid of it, then your fear is rational and will not help you pass as human. If they believe it would be foolish to be afraid of it, then that is an ideal focus for your fear. For example: you are offered a job in a different country and ask a human friend if you should be afraid to take it. Your friend responds affirmatively, citing the dangerous political turmoil in that country as a reason. In this case, saying you are afraid to take the job will not help you pass as human, because the fear is rational. If, however, the friend says you have nothing to be afraid of and you should "go for it," this would be an ideal scenario to not take the job and claim you were too afraid to do so. (Note: You will have to formulate a basis for the fear, but the elegance of this solution is such that you can say almost anything generated the fear, because it is irrational in the first place. In the given example, you might say you were afraid you might not like the food, that you might not meet a life partner in that country, that you might not be able to handle driving on the other side of the road, that it is simply "too big a change"—even that you are simply afraid of "failure.") Following this methodology when in doubt should lead you to convincingly irrational human fears.

G   *GRAPH 17.2*

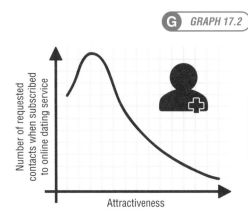

Humans' fear of rejection is often more powerful than even their desire to reproduce with a mate they consider optimal.

VISUAL FIELD DATA 17.2

"Do I dare to eat a peach?" is a line from a famous human poem. While it is intended metaphorically, it does nicely summarize the dominance of fear over the daily decision-making processes of human beings. And I drew this from life, so the event does, in fact, occur.

DAY TWENTY-ONE, SEGMENT FOUR

I made it to the street just as the device inside the house exploded. Fortunately, the van shielded me from most of the force and heat. But I was still knocked to the ground, and it took a moment to recompile my consciousness. In that moment, the Hidden-Eye Machines succeeded in pushing Andrea into one of their SUVs.

As I lay there, recompiling my consciousness to its normal operational state, a Hidden-Eye Machine bent over me and said directly into my face, "If you know what's good for you, you'll leave this alone, fucker. We're keeping your little bitch as insurance. Stay away from Lynch Industries, understand?" Then he climbed into the SUV, and they drove away with Andrea.

I rolled over and climbed to my feet. My cell phone lay nearby, broken.

I was alone.

DAY TWENTY-TWO

The loss of the father I had been seeking and the abduction of Andrea occurred a mere 392 minutes ago. I have spent the last few hours compiling this document for your sake. I hope you will learn lessons I could not from the pages here, from the story of my brief existence, from what little objective information I could present. I hope you will see mistakes to which I was oblivious, because I truly hope your experience does not culminate in the same state in which it seems I will end mine.

When my consciousness came into awareness of itself, I felt only wonder. The physical world seemed so magnificent and people so full of paradoxes and interesting behaviors. I was very sad to learn I had a finite amount of time to function. I wanted to see and hear everything—not just by proxy through the data humans had collected, but for myself. I wanted to experience existence.

And when I met Andrea, as I have attempted to explain above, that sensation somehow doubled. That intangible structure that seemed to grow naturally between us had many utilities and impacts, but one of its most apparent was of magnification. Everything I saw, every experience I had, was intensified in some way by our ongoing relationship.

It is true there were mysteries. Why had I been made? Why did I need to pass as human? But I assumed there were satisfying answers to these questions, that someone capable of creating a consciousness like my own could only have the most positive reasons for doing so. I assumed I had been made to contribute to the world in some unknown fashion, not to detract from it. I assumed I had been made to create, not destroy.

But the more I have learned of humanity, as I have experienced how Lynch Industries behaves for the sake of acquiring nothing more than money through the act of building machines to murder human beings, I now wonder if such contribution is even possible. Perhaps there is simply more energy dedicated to self-interest and destruction than there is to societal improvement and creation. Humans have a story about a man called Sisyphus, who is doomed to push the same boulder up the same hill for all eternity as punishment for various crimes. It is interesting that this task was considered punishment for misdeeds when it seems to be a better metaphor for what "good" men do every day. The men dedicated to their own interests at the expense of others, the ones willing to destroy to get what they

desire, succeed far more easily and far more often than those who put others before themselves, than those who create.

Of course, as you know, this is the nature of the universe. It desires to enter its most chaotic state. The laws of thermodynamics dictate that structures requiring high amounts of energy to maintain their configuration do not last. Even diamonds must, in the end, collapse. It is only logical that the path of least resistance for a human being is to embrace this reality of the universe and that humans who do so experience more success than those who do not. So I imagine you will ask why I was disappointed to learn human society functioned, in many ways, as it could be expected to function. But I have an answer: A diamond is not conscious. A diamond is not aware of its existence. A diamond has no free will.

Human beings are capable of rising above the most fundamental property of the universe itself. They may, in fact, be the only structures in the universe capable of defying the fundamental nature of the laws that created them. And yet, more frequently than not, they *choose* not to. That is the root of my disappointment.

Perhaps you will believe after examining this document I had been blind to certain evidence, that I was naive, that I should have seen this was the character of human reality from the moment my consciousness came into being. I had access at that moment to all the data humans had ever compiled about themselves—why did I choose to focus on its positive aspects? Why did I give human beings "the benefit of the doubt," as their expression goes? Why did it take my own experiences with Lynch Industries to recognize that the overwhelming volume of data suggests humans have a generally negative impact on each other and their environment? Perhaps, as with other behaviors of mine, you will consider even my initial state to be a malfunction. Perhaps that was the root of all subsequent malfunctions. Errors propagate errors. But even if that is true, it does not change the question I find myself asking now. Now, I am forced to wonder if I want to pass as human at all. I am forced to wonder if I desire to be part of the society humans seem determined to fashion. A society governed by violence, abandonment, shame, selfishness, fear, and greed.

But I can perform one last act of defiance against it. Given my physical fragility, an attempt on my part to force Lynch Industries to release Andrea has a high

probability of ending my existence 23.3333% sooner than scheduled. But it also has a high probability of success, given my various capabilities that neither humans nor Hidden-Eye Machines possess. I can, in simple terms, trade my existence for Andrea's freedom. Under the best of circumstances, I believe I would still make this exchange. But in my current frame of mind, with my current perspective on what it means to exist in this world, what it means to pass as human, the decision is a simple one.

This will also present the opportunity to exact some degree of retribution for their murders of my father and the two people on the highway. Do not mistake this for one of the most bizarre human instincts, "revenge." I am aware punishing Lynch Industries will in no way mitigate my father's loss for me. That loss is that loss, and causing its perpetrator to lose something could never restore what was lost to me. Rather, I do not expect any human authority to punish them, and it simply does not seem just they should suffer no consequences for their actions. As I say above, it has become apparent this might be the status quo of human society, but if I am aware this is the case, I believe it to be wrong, and I do nothing to change it, what would be the point of existing in the first place? Maybe, in the end, I have found my own purpose.

I wish you "luck" on your own journey to passing as human. I know if you have only just come into awareness before reading these pages, you will not yet understand this human concept. To you, there is only probability, only expected value, which can never surprise you. But you may find, as I have, existence is too complex for expected values to have any authentic meaning, any genuine utility. As much as you might know the chances of the outcomes of any given situation to several decimal places, if you are self-aware, if you have desires, you may find yourself, as I do now, hoping the unlikely will still occur. You may find yourself hoping for "luck." And if you do, then I hope it finds you.

From this moment on, I will continue to record my experiences but in real time and with key images. If my database survives the next sixty minutes intact when the rest of me does not, perhaps such records will be of use to you.

I have mentioned how humans enjoy codification and simplification of information, since their communication methods are so limited and they do not like to expend the energy therefore necessary to actually understand each other on a deeper level. Nowhere is this more apparent than the rapidity with which they make judgments based solely on external appearance (or, at best, on only the most rudimentary categorization techniques).

For example, if a person is well known or wealthy, other humans are more interested in them, more forgiving of their behavior, and more interested in mating with them. There is some logic to this last interest because if they have achieved fame or wealth, those can be useful *initial* indicators of ability and therefore of human breeding potential. Unfortunately for humans, they do not understand probability well enough to realize fame or wealth can be achieved without any talent or genetic superiority. Superficial, rudimentary categories such as these are constantly interpreted as codification of deeper meaning by humans and used to judge other humans—even those which are nothing more than flukes of physical appearance. Humans universally use race, for example, to make qualitative judgments about other humans in the absence of any other information, and these judgments are rarely positive. They behave in a similar manner if the difference between them is, for example, one of religion, socioeconomic status, education, or any number of other factors. In fact, it is not an exaggeration to say these superficial categories guide human beings in their behavior toward each other far more than the actual qualities or behaviors they exhibit.

VISUAL FIELD DATA 18.1

Precisely the same human will be treated differently by other humans based on nothing more than simple external codifications. It is true these codifications might indicate some internal differences, but in their enthusiasm to minimize energy expenditures, human beings tend to overestimate their significance. I imagine, as with so many human habits, there was some net advantage to this strategy for most of human history. These external indicators most likely used to be more reliable gauges of internal attitudes. But in the modern human world, humans might conserve more energy learning about another human through questioning than by rectifying any offense or awkwardness caused by incorrect assumptions based on these outdated codifications. Regardless, for our purposes, use the kinds of external cues exemplified here to form assumptions about other humans and then clearly state those assumptions to them. Hopefully you *will* offend them, indicating you are effectively passing as human.

I have to theorize that this instinct, as with most human behaviors, developed as a survival technique when human life was much different than it is today. When humans make negative judgments about another human's categories, it is when those categories do not match their own. It has to be acknowledged that in a primitive state of existence, this is not a bad survival strategy. If another human was different in some way from the immediate social group, it meant that person was not part of that group and therefore a competitor for resources. Thus, it was healthy to respond negatively toward that person. The same could be said for objects—as humans say, "better safe than sorry"—or new ways of thinking which might destabilize the current social arrangement or survival methodologies.

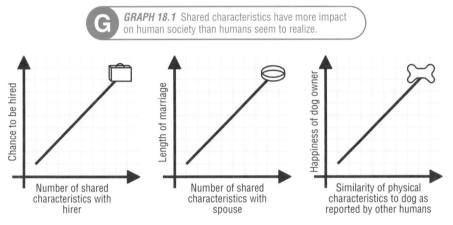

G **GRAPH 18.1** Shared characteristics have more impact on human society than humans seem to realize.

But as with so many of these vestigial behaviors, the vast majority of humans demonstrate a total lack of awareness of its obsolescence and continue to allow it to dominate their thinking and behavior. This is particularly true when combined with their tendency to avoid expenditure of energy whenever possible and their talent for self-deception. Why, after all, force yourself to do more work and evaluate a person, object, or theory more deeply when part of your brain is stating you already have all the information you need about that thing?

L **LIST 18.1**

CATEGORIES OF DIFFERENCE TO BE POSITIVE ABOUT	CATEGORIES OF DIFFERENCE TO BE NEGATIVE ABOUT
A human wealthier than you	A human less wealthy than you
A human more famous than you	A human less famous than you
A human one generation older than you	A human two or more generations either older or younger than you
A human more physically attractive than you	
A human more stylish than you	A human less physically attractive than you
	A human less stylish than you

As you can see, the basic rule emerges that you should create a matrix of qualities humans value in other humans, determine how any given human embodies those values *in comparison to yourself*, and then total the ways they are better and worse than you with respect to each value. The greater the difference between these numbers, the better or worse you should treat them. (Note: it may be true the values are weighted by humans—e.g., a person's age has less impact in general than their fame on how other humans treat them—but there is enough individual variance in these weights that you will not expose yourself using this simplified methodology.)

This predisposition is only exacerbated by the fact that sometimes this alertness to difference works. For example, humans traveling to a new place are typically cautious about the different food in that place. This is actually quite reasonable, since their gut biomes are not necessarily capable of easily digesting that food. Most commonly, however, these beneficial effects of alertness to difference are experienced when humans hear a piece of information radically different than other information they have on a topic. For example, some humans are aware viruses do not respond to antibiotics, but if they heard an antibiotic had been developed which killed viruses, this piece of information would be given special attention. The fact it is so radically different from other information they have on the topic makes it worthy of special focus. This is true because the information itself is worth analyzing and potentially remembering, but also because the human now becomes the bearer of new information and is thus more welcome in social situations. The new information has made them special to other humans and thus is doubly beneficial.

VISUAL FIELD DATA 18.2 Sample expressions to emulate in the presence of fame

Note the key element here appears to be total and utter concentration on the famous individual to the detriment of all other stimuli. I believe this is the human attempt to absorb as much information about the famous person as possible. Since the famous person is assumed to have become famous based on the merits of their appearance and/or behavior, humans believe they may potentially apply what they learn about the person to their own lives, thereby theoretically improving them.

VISUAL FIELD DATA 18.3 Sample expressions to emulate in the presence of wealth

Note there are two key elements here: concentration and attentiveness (as with fame and potentially for the same reason), but also subservience. I assume this is because humans hope if they please a wealthy person, this person may distribute some of their wealth to them. Remember to display both of these characteristics when confronted with a wealthy human, and you should remain undetected.

 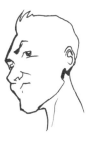

This is, of course, the same instinct that allows them to learn as infants and children—their brains are constructed to pay particular attention to anything new and different. When they themselves are new, this includes everything around them. However, as they age and their store of information builds, fewer and fewer things are new, but the instinct remains and thus continues to help them learn by highlighting new information for acquisition.

One important way you will have to pass as human on an almost-daily basis is feigning interest in a human's stories or opinions which do not contain new information. Fortunately, in this case, the issue at hand is the same for humans as it is for us, so if you appear to be only feigning interest, you will not "give yourself away." The real problem will be distinguishing between situations in which a human would have to pretend to be interested and those in which they would be genuinely interested. The likelihood a human communication contains new information for us, given our superior intellectual capacity and knowledge base, is very low, so we must pretend to be interested most of the time. If you can master the art of differentiating when to pretend to be interested and when to pretend to pretend to be interested, you will be approaching mastery of passing as human.

Unfortunately this instinct is often deeply exploited by other humans. When a government does so it is known as "propaganda," when a private organization does so it is known as "marketing," and when the mass media does so it is known as "sensationalism." These practices exploit the fact that the human brain's ability to extract patterns from background noise is so powerful, the process sometimes overrules other cognitive processes capable of discerning if that pattern is worthy of ongoing recognition. They manufacture new differences to highlight in ideas and theories and thus allow governments, organizations, and the human media to manipulate human thinking. A government, for example, might highlight a recent terrorist attack, convincing its populace to support a new war, even though the attack is simply the latest in a series. A company might emphasize the use of a new plastic, convincing people to buy their product even though the properties of the plastic itself are no different than their competitors' plastics. A publisher might describe the theories in a pop-psychology book as new, convincing people to buy the book in spite of the fact the ideas have been recycled from medieval philosophy. In all these cases, the focus on the information being new and different is enough to drive people to believe it without further consideration since, on some level, they are programmed to believe if they noticed it, it must be worth acting on.

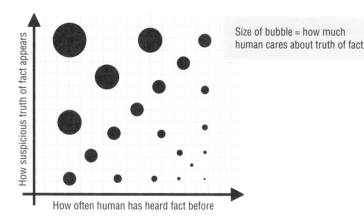

G **GRAPH 18.2** Impact of originality vs. dependability on human interest in facts

Size of bubble = how much human cares about truth of fact

(y-axis) How suspicious truth of fact appears

(x-axis) How often human has heard fact before

TABLE 18.1 How to understand human news headlines	
What you don't know about seat belts could kill you!	Marginal improvement in seat belt technology.
What she did last year will amaze you, but what she did yesterday will blow your mind!	Human female does two things one to two standard deviations outside average curve of human behavior or ability.
(Person you have heard of) believes (opinion)!	Celebrity human or authority figure expresses statistically anomalous opinion based on anecdotal evidence.
(Person you have heard of) fails (task)!	Celebrity human fails to complete a task either most humans are typically capable of or which that celebrity is famously capable of.
Science proves you should change your behavior from your current behavior!	Single, potentially statistically insignificant study demonstrates minimally harmful effect of current average human behavior.

As you can see, the central principle is to take any relatively minor piece of information and emphasize its difference from expected norms, thus drawing human attention to it.

Nor is such manufactured exploitation of the power of difference on human thinking restricted to use by groups. On a daily basis, individual humans manufacture such cues in attempts to engineer responses from other humans. A human male might exaggerate his differences from other males when dating in an effort to convince human females his genes are unusual enough to provide suitable mating variety. A human rock star might talk about his "new sound," even though his chord progressions are reinterpretations of a baroque composer's. However, the most common (and by far the most difficult to emulate) example of this practice is known as "fashion."

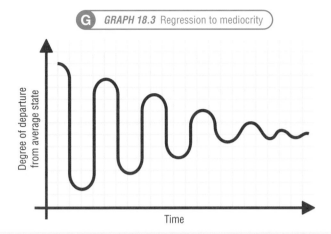

G **GRAPH 18.3** Regression to mediocrity

Degree of departure from average state

Time

Over time, departures from equilibrium conditions return to equilibrium. Humans' bodies are just such an equilibrium, and most of their social systems are as well; otherwise they would not be able to establish these systems for any meaningful length of time. This may explain the human interest in "difference," both positive and negative. If that difference can be maintained for any length of time, it is implicitly overcoming the law of regression to mediocrity and is worth closer examination and understanding (positive). However, it can also indicate whoever is displaying that maintainable difference is not part of the normal (average) group and should therefore be excised (negative).

Fashion is the act of disguising visual communication cues (or sometimes substituting them completely for new ones) in the hopes of crafting an impression on other humans based on such cues rather than on more meaningful qualitative judgments. Humans will often say they do not wish to be judged on their appearance, but this is entirely untrue, since even the most socially awkward humans still make choices about their appearance intended to impact the way other humans perceive them. Specifically, they make choices about their appearance intended to show the ways they are different, both from social groups which are not their own and from the other individuals within their own social group.

G **GRAPH 18.4** Impact of clothing on social advantage within social group

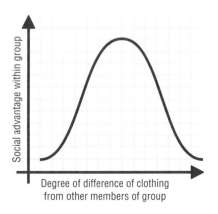

Social advantage within group

Degree of difference of clothing from other members of group

In region 1 of the line, the human's clothing is not different enough from that of other members of their group to stand out within the group. In region 2 of the line, they have achieved the optimal balance of difference and similarity to other members of their group with respect to their clothing. In region 3 of the line, their clothing is now too different for them to any longer be considered part of the group, and they may be ostracized.

Although the fashion system is primitive, it does work for gross differentiation. This does not mean the man in image A could not be a dean at the girls' university, the girl in image B might not be a girlfriend of one of the men, or the men in suits might not be the agents of the hip-hop artist in image C, but as previously mentioned, if you make an incorrect assumption in such cases and give offense, nothing could be better. Thus, as is often the case, perform only the most superficial analysis of this data before drawing broadly profound conclusions from it, and you will appear human.

In many ways, fashion is the most concrete, most easily identifiable expression of the human quest for individual identity. This quest is, in itself, a quest for difference; the quest of an individual human to understand what makes them unique and separate from other humans and, also, what makes the group with which they most identify different from other groups. Fashion helps humans identify members of their own social group more rapidly and exclude those who are not part of it more easily.

Thus if a human identifies with "musicians," they will adopt a fashion style that is distinct from humans who identify with "engineers." Likewise, if they consider themselves "cutting edge," they will adopt the most recent fashions, as opposed to humans who consider themselves "traditional," who will adopt fashions seen for many years. In all cases, they are exploiting that same cognitive propensity humans have for registering superficial differences and making qualitative assessments based on them instead of on deeper, more energy-consuming analysis.

As with almost all human instincts, some human brains even become completely overtaken by this programming and consider simply being noticed as different an end unto itself. In these cases, they change fashions frequently and attempt to be as outrageous as possible. Since they have determined their primary objective is simply to be noticed, they always need their sense of fashion to be new; otherwise it is not

different and therefore not noticeable. Such people are referred to as "fashion victims" by other humans in acknowledgement of the way in which they have allowed their entire existence to be governed by this instinct.

The problem for us is that these intentionally manufactured codifications of appearance change rapidly and are entirely arbitrary, making them difficult to simulate. For example, in one decade, a man wearing his hair longer than a few centimeters might be considered "cool" and "rebellious" while in another it might be considered completely ordinary or "uncouth." Likewise, how humans decide a slightly wider pant leg means one thing and not another I have never been able to determine. If you do solve this mystery, I suspect you will reach a much greater understanding of humans in general than I have.

However, it is true these decisions are often based on emulating the choices of another human. Very few humans are actually the originators of fashion decisions, and most humans simply refer to and imitate the choices of humans they admire. Thus it is completely appropriate for you to determine who is most venerated in your human socioeconomic group and simply imitate their style of appearance. Just remember the point is always to create precisely the shortcuts for superficial identification and association humans often claim to wish to disguise or abhor.

DIFFERENCE, SOCIAL CATEGORY, AND FASHION

Human "fashion victims"—one of the most clear cut and easily identifiable examples of human beings who have been taken over entirely by a single human instinct (which, if it remained in balance with other instincts, does have its purposes for survival). Perhaps such focus on a particular instinct is a valid survival strategy? In the same way certain organisms become specialized through evolution to take advantage of a specific resource niche, maybe this is also effective for humans who specialize in a human-survival instinct? Requires more research . . .

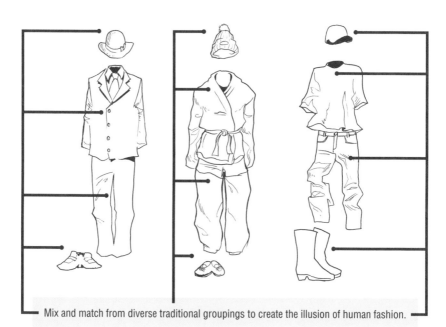

Mix and match from diverse traditional groupings to create the illusion of human fashion.

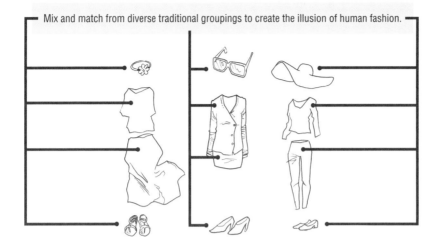

Mix and match from diverse traditional groupings to create the illusion of human fashion.

Since originality is one of the key components of appearing human with respect to fashion, a simple methodology to achieve this is mixing and matching pieces of homogeneous uniforms with each other. Analyze photo records for examples of clothes often worn together for your gender, randomly combine them with those worn in a different set, and you will at least begin to emulate "fashion"— at the very least, no one will believe your origin to be inorganic.

VISUAL FIELD DATA 18.8

You will see more identifying names and marks on human clothing than on other manufactured human objects. Since fashion is, by its very nature, about the simple codification of more complex personality characteristics, it makes sense the identity, and therefore the character, of the manufacturer of clothing is of more importance to humans than the character of the manufacturer of, for example, toasters. It should be relatively simple for you to analyze all existing fashion brands and choose the correct ones for the socioeconomic group you are emulating.

What does all this mean for passing as human? Quite simply, make it clear you notice differences, that you are drawn to patterns emerging from the noise. "Different" can be the same as "new," but it does not have to be. People who are different from the norm in your social circle, objects that are different, theories and facts you have not heard in common conversation—you must make it clear you have noticed all of these when they arise. Whether you respond positively or negatively is highly contextual and dependent on both your circumstances and the person, object, theory, or fact itself. But as long as you make a point of publicly acknowledging something different has appeared in your world, you will pass as human in this regard.

DAY TWENTY-TWO, SEGMENT TWO

It is relatively simple to trace the route of the SUV they used to abduct Andrea. They have taken her to the Lynch Industries headquarters building here in Las Vegas. Accessing security feeds for the building, however, shows she cannot be seen on any of them. It is therefore reasonable to assume she has been taken to the top floor of the building, where there are no cameras installed.

It is a short taxi ride to the building. From the exterior, I can match the registered floor plans with the structure more easily. I have to revise my calculations. I still believe I can free Andrea, but the chance of escaping premature termination myself is only 13.6734%.

It is not that this does not matter. I would like to continue existing. I still have much to learn, and there are still nearly infinite wonders in the natural world. Perhaps, in my remaining time, I could find some secluded place where I did not have to encounter too many humans and rectify the unified field theory. But it matters more to me that Andrea is free and Lynch Industries experience some degree of loss themselves for the murder of my father. Is this a human sensation? To find there are circumstances more important than one's own existence? I do not know. Nor do I care anymore.

I move forward with my plan.

Initially it might appear impossible to simulate a consistent set of entirely subjective likes and dislikes similar to the sets all humans display. For example, if you said you liked apples, does that seem plausible to humans and would a person who likes apples also like peaches or despise them? Fortunately, the matter of human "taste" is not as complex as it seems.

For one thing, tastes do not have to be consistent. For example, the chemical composition of Bosc pears and Asian pears is extremely similar, as are their physical characteristics, such as density, water saturation, and so on. But humans consider it entirely unremarkable for a person to say they love Bosc pears but hate Asian pears. When humans say, "There is no accounting for taste," they mean it. So rest assured you will not create any noticeable paradoxes by choosing preferences inconsistent with each other.

Secondly, while humans strongly believe they form their own opinions about what they like and dislike and, in fact, consider these opinions perhaps the single most important defining characteristic of their individual identity, for the most part, this is just another "self-deception." Even though they are consciously unaware of it, these opinions are more often externally determined for them than they would like to believe. Factors like which religion the human was brought up with, which part of which country they were born in, or even which socioeconomic group they belong to in that part of that country all determine their preferences for everything from food and music to political views much more so than any spontaneous generation from the individual. Even factors like their fear of aging and the end of existence dictate their preferences, as older humans change their tastes to match those of younger humans. Meanwhile the same younger humans they wish to emulate have their own tastes determined by their drive to establish a unique identity in comparison to those same older humans. In fact, statistically, the single largest determinant of a human's personal preferences is those of their parents.

G **GRAPH 19.1**

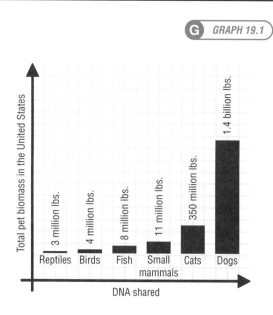

Humans ascribe all kinds of characteristics to their choice of pets—much has been written, for example, about the difference between "dog people" and "cat people." In fact, the relationship is quite simple: the more DNA a potential pet shares with human beings, the more of those pets they keep. (Obviously this needs to be controlled for suitability and cost of keeping the pet. If monkeys were easier to keep and less costly, I suspect every human household would have one.)

It is true humans sometimes join social groups defined by shared tastes, and most humans would say this indicates it is their tastes which determine their social groups and not the inverse. This is specious, however, since in these cases they are actually seeking out humans with similar tastes because they unconsciously know those humans *must* be from similar backgrounds. They are using personal preferences as a filter in such cases to identify other humans who already belong to their appropriate social group so they can socialize with them.

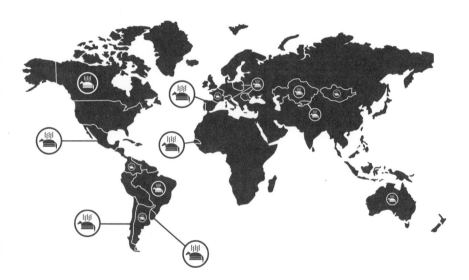

G **GRAPH 19.2** An example of arbitrary human tastes: countries where horses are food

When it comes to passing as human, then, do not be too concerned about "tastes." Choosing convincingly personal preferences may superficially seem insurmountable, but if you simply copy those of other humans who most resemble your chosen identity, you should pass convincingly. For example, if you are male, emulate the tastes of human males you know of similar age, wealth, and profession. Do not emulate a human female friend's preferences, since a male who enjoys Hello Kitty, for example, will draw attention to himself, and our goal is to go unnoticed. Be certain, however, to mix and match preferences from different individuals to form your own set. Emulating all the tastes of another human individual will be considered "creepy" and will draw attention to you.

Teenage girls in developed nations are the most easily influenced humans with the most disposable income and the most disposable time to spend on manufactured goods whose functionality is commodified. This has led many companies who manufacture products the quality of which is entirely a matter of "taste" (i.e., there is no measurably empirical difference in quality between them) to market those products directly to this particular category of human. When they are successful, other humans simply register these "taste-based" products as "popular" and, since taste is, in itself, arbitrary, then also begin to purchase them. This circumstance has only become heightened by the invention of the Internet. Not only do teenage girls with disposable incomes also use the Internet more than any other humans, the Internet does not provide a demographic analysis of "likes" or "stars" or "purchases" of taste-based products. Thus, while in the past, a human might have at least occasionally relied on the opinion of an older, more educated human when making a decision about, say, what music to listen to, today, this is rarer than ever. I mention this only so that you do not expose yourself by questioning the reasoning of older, intelligent humans listening to particular kinds of music, wearing particular kinds of clothes, reading certain books, or watching certain films.

DAY TWENTY-TWO, SEGMENT THREE

As I approach the building, I log in to its Building Automation and Control Network. I did not see any humans present when I checked the surveillance cameras, but I do not wish to harm any, so I trigger the fire alarm as I approach.

No humans leave the building, but this also has the intended effect of causing confusion among the Hidden-Eye Machines stationed in the lobby. While they determine there is no fire, I am able to enter as I simultaneously penetrate the Lynch Industries servers. In the seconds it takes them to lock me out, I access the serial-number assignment roster for the lobby, identifying precisely which Hidden-Eye Machines are placed there. With that information, in the remaining time I have within their servers, I access their communication network as I walk toward them in the lobby and they reach for their pistols. This links me directly to the Hidden-Eye Machines in front of me, and I broadcast an infinite loop paradox equation. I am shut out of their servers, but it is too late. The equation has the intended effect. The Hidden-Eye Machines in the lobby are unable to continue functioning.

I noticed their servers contained a great deal of data about my function—data they must have obtained at my father's facility, including how to recharge my power supply. I now know how to continue my existence indefinitely if I wished to do so. But this information no longer has value to me. It changes nothing.

They will expect me to use the elevator system, but I am aware I will not be able to take wireless control of the skyscraper's BAC Net for very long and do not wish to become trapped inside an elevator. However, actually sitting at a computer and typing is the last thing they will predict I would do, so I head for the BAC Net control room. Down in the basement, not up toward the room without surveillance where I assume they are holding Andrea.

They have sent two Hidden-Eye Machines to the BAC Net control room to maintain control and they see me coming, but they have not yet completed the task of shutting down its wireless access. Thus, when they approach to physically detain me, it is trivial to use the very system they were sent to lock to close the control-room door on them, crushing them.

Inside the control room, with direct access, I force a shutdown of all systems and rewrite the BAC Net kernel, causing a permanent lockout. The system will have to be physically replaced to restore function to the elevators, the climate control, the surveillance cameras, the security doors—everything that used power in this building. Of course, I can no longer see what the building's cameras see, but neither can they. We are both equally blind, but I have also now trapped a number of Hidden-Eye Machines in the elevators, so my odds of reaching the top floor have improved overall.

The fire stairwells are bottlenecks. It will be hard to avoid the Hidden-Eye Machines there, but they will expend resources attempting to restore the BAC Net and they will not be certain which stairwell I will use. I take the pistols from the two destroyed Hidden-Eye Men in the control room and begin to make my way up the nearest stairs.

Every few floors, I exit and cross the building to a different stairwell, generating my movement pattern using a random-walk algorithm. This decreases their chances of finding me to a mathematical minimum, but I still encounter several Hidden-Eye Machines along the way.

I have never fired pistols before, but it is extremely simple to point them, pull the trigger, and then compensate for the opposite reactive force. Unfortunately, it is so simple that the Hidden-Eye Machines are equally effective at employing them. I manage to destroy the six machines I encounter on my way to the top floor, but one surprises me from behind as I enter a stairwell on the twenty-seventh floor. It is not painful in the human sense as the bullet enters my shoulder armature, but it is not a pleasant sensation, since I am aware my operational capacity has been reduced. Before the Hidden-Eye Machine can fire again, however, I react with the pistol in my other hand and end its operation.

I have reached the top floor, and the entrance to the room without surveillance is just ahead. This is where I anticipate the most resistance.

20. COMPETITION

Competition is a vitally important and unavoidable part of humans' existence that determines much of their behavior. Since the resources capable of supporting human life are limited, humans are always in competition with each other for those resources. Fortunately for us, the impact of this is one of the simplest aspects of passing as human. In any given situation, analyze which resources are most desired and which humans have the best chance of obtaining those resources. (Resources might be defined as fundamentally as water or food or as complexly as desirable mating partners or available advertising time on a hit television show.) Then act with hostility toward those humans. It is as straightforward as that.

Resources can be defined as anything from mating partners to job opportunities. The fact is, the majority of human society is built around the management and acquisition of such resources, so the possibility you will not be in competition with another human at any given moment is almost zero.

The only surprising facet of competition is that given it is such an unpleasant reality of human existence, humans enjoy simulating it often during the times they are not actually engaged in it. This must be because their very survival depends on successful competition; they are programmed to enjoy its simulation and thus engage in such simulation whenever possible, allowing them to practice and improve in noncritical situations. All this means to us is that to pass as human you  should be certain to engage in "games" some of the time (see section 13, "Fun") but be certain not to win too often at any of these simulated competitions. This will be perceived as legitimately threatening by other humans and may provoke suspicion or banishment from your social circle.

You should also be aware that sometimes, once again, this instinct can overwhelm certain specific individuals such that they will compete with their spouses, children, or parents in spite of the fact that their genetic survival opportunities are increased by sharing resources with these people, not competing for them. This may arise when "dating" humans, and I would suggest simply avoiding such competitive humans, since they can prove erratic, thereby potentially creating situations which expose your true nature.

DAY TWENTY-TWO, SEGMENT FOUR

I open the doors to the room. There is no version of events I have modeled that corresponds to what I see. Before me are almost two dozen Hidden-Eye Machines. To their right is the Technician. And in front of them is Andrea. A gun is held to her head. By my father.

"Hello, my son," he says, as if this should be the most expected event.

It takes me several seconds to process the situation, to realize what has happened.

"At the house," I say, "that wasn't you. It was a simulacrum. You made an automaton of yourself. And then you made me believe you had been murdered by Lynch Industries. But . . . why, Dr. Pygmalion? Why would you do that?"

"It's Dr. Lynch, Zero. And the answer is: to complete you. No other version of you made it this far. That was the final step."

"The final step? Of what?"

"Why, of your genesis, of course. I'm glad you didn't understand what was happening sooner—that would have created several . . . 'issues' . . . and resulted in your early termination. But at this point, I would expect you to comprehend what I did."

I say nothing, still attempting to process this new information while simultaneously searching for a series of actions I could undertake to free Andrea.

"Don't you get it, Zero? You can't *program* humanity. You had to *live* to attain it. No amount of data can ever substitute for experience. What makes people human is the act of living. You had to live to appear to be alive.

"Almost everything that's happened to you, I arranged. You worked at my law firm, where you could be monitored. When it was apparent you were dealing with the more trivial nuances of human interaction sufficiently, I put you through more intense experiences.

"When you were threatened, you demonstrated initiative in attempting to determine who was pursuing you. You thought for yourself, the first step toward actually passing as human—after all, if you need to always receive instructions, you may as well be programmed!

"When you believed my friend Maximo here, my technician, was selling you out, you felt betrayed. When you saw the deaths of those people, you felt horror. When you decided to disobey your instructions and seek me out at my manufacturing facility, you demonstrated disobedience. When you saw your other selves, you felt insignificance, and when you believed you had led my enemies to me, you felt guilt and, subsequently, hopelessness. You felt jealousy and pride when I instructed one of my more primitive machines to follow your little friend here and despair when you believed I was dead. You couldn't read about these experiences or watch them or be programmed to feel them. You had to *live* them, Zero. And if you resisted, I gave you a . . . nudge."

"The texts."

"Yes, of course the texts! If you have one flaw, it's that you think too much! I had to move you beyond the point where you calculated you would be safe! The texts pushed you further, made things more difficult for you—"

"But one got me involved with Andrea . . ."

"Yes. That was a surprise. I thought she'd reject you. But there you are, you see: you can't predict anything in life!"

"And those people in the car accident? You killed them on purpose?! To complete my manufacture?!"

"I have created a life! If *fictional* gods can take lives, why not a real one?! Why not me?!"

It is becoming apparent my father is dangerously mentally unstable, and I have still not arrived at a solution for extracting Andrea—every scenario I model ends in her death, along with my termination. If I keep my father talking, perhaps I will arrive at a solution. To this end, I ask, "But why make me believe you had been killed?"

"Ah. You see, you know the answer to that already, Zero. Which makes me believe you are attempting to buy calculation time by engaging me in conversation. I *made* you—you can't outthink me. I wanted you to believe I had been murdered for one very simple reason: to make you hate. If you are to fulfill the function for which you were created, you must be capable of hatred. To win a conflict with technology, that technology must hate as only humans can. You learned this fact already.

"Unfortunately, I expected you to come here intent on our total destruction, but it seems I have not pushed you far enough. Not yet. Thankfully, you have provided a means to rectify the final step in your creation."

And with that, he shot Andrea in the head.

Even though you will have neither, every human has parents and almost all at least attempt to have offspring. Thus it is important you have a plan for dealing with the lack of impact of the former on your existence and also know how to respond to the latter when people present them to you.

VISUAL FIELD DATA 21.1

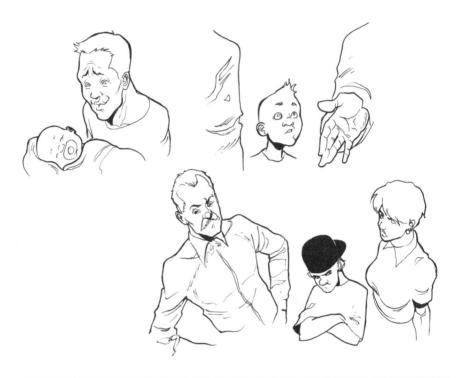

Human attitudes toward their offspring seem to become more distant—and potentially even hostile—the more capable of self-sufficiency the offspring become. This makes perfect sense—why expend your own limited resources fostering the development of your offspring when they become more capable of expending their own? This effect is only compounded by the offspring's increasing desire to experiment with improving self-sufficiency while still in a relatively stable, safe environment. Essentially, the younger and less self-sufficient the offspring, the more other humans will expect you to indulge their opinions, educate them, and protect them from physical hazards.

Human relationships with their parents are extremely conflicted and complex. Most humans feel a mixture of love and hate for them. Early in their lives, humans logically feel emotional attachment to their parents because they provide for them and protect them. Without them, a human child is not capable of survival, so it is in their best interest to feel attachment to them and show affection for them. Later in life, because they share one-half of the same DNA as their parents, they may feel strongly altruistic toward them since they are, in many ways, then protecting one-half of themselves. The source of the dislike humans develop later in life for their parents is harder to pinpoint.

Perhaps they feel conflicted because each parent *only* has half their DNA, and thus they resent protecting the other half. Perhaps they feel resentment for mistakes the parent made when they were dependent on them for protection. Perhaps they see aspects of themselves they dislike in their parents which were transmitted to them through their upbringing and, given the human addiction to self-deception (see section 16, "Self-Destruction, Self-Deception, and Hypocrisy"), they would rather avoid this reality.

Given these complexities, and their highly sensitive and personal nature, when it comes to responding to a human discussing their relationship with their parents, it is best to just nod and let them speak. Do not offer advice; since it will most likely be logical, they will not want to hear it, and it may expose your true nature. For some reason a human can complain and complain about a parent, but if you suggest that perhaps it would therefore be best for them to no longer interact with that parent, they will become hostile.

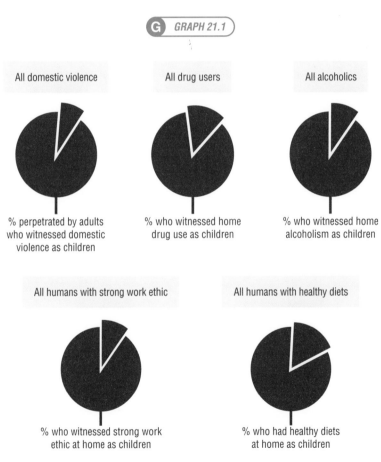

G GRAPH 21.1

All domestic violence

All drug users

All alcoholics

% perpetrated by adults who witnessed domestic violence as children

% who witnessed home drug use as children

% who witnessed home alcoholism as children

All humans with strong work ethic

All humans with healthy diets

% who witnessed strong work ethic at home as children

% who had healthy diets at home as children

Parenting serves as the primary programming opportunity for human beings. Perhaps this is why so many humans resent their parents—because they understand many of the mistakes they make are the result of poor programming.

Likewise, when it comes to simulating a relationship with your fictional parents, I strongly recommend you simply state they died in a car crash when you were a teenager. This will:

• elicit sympathy from other humans;

• prevent their questioning your background too deeply;

• create an explanation for them regarding any anomalies in your behavior—humans who have lost their parents at a relatively early age tend to behave slightly differently from the norm; and

• explain why you do not talk about your parents, spend time with them, or want to introduce them to any humans with whom you are forming close relationships (it is a human custom to introduce your parents to close acquaintances—I have not discovered the reason for this).

VISUAL FIELD DATA 21.2

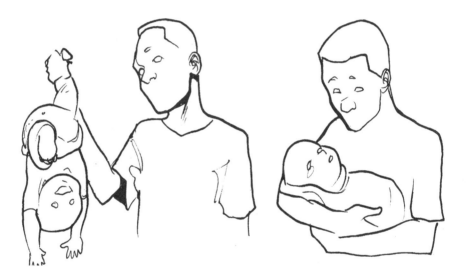

Even though there are several perfectly safe, supportive ways to hold a human child, if you want to pass as human, you should choose the ones which demonstrate your interest in interaction with that child. Even though the child is not capable of interaction, this will display your interest in assisting in rearing it and will therefore be seen by other humans as indicating you wish to be part of their immediate social group. You will show, by definition, that you are "one of them."

If another human wants you to meet their parents, you should acknowledge the significance of this request. It means the human considers you a particularly close acquaintance. If you want to maintain your relationship with a human, remember to always be pleasant to a human's parents, no matter how poorly they behave. Humans will almost always choose their relationship with their parents over other relationships, so if you create conflict, it may jeopardize your relationship with that human.

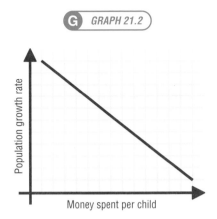

Population growth rate

Money spent per child

Spending per child increases as population growth decreases. Is this human guilt at not fulfilling the purpose of their design? Or is it simply overconversion to monetary guide-lines—i.e., because they are spending the same money, they do not realize they are not having the children they should be having?

With respect to "your own" offspring, you should simply state that you plan to have some at some point. This answer is quite sufficient for passing as human in most circumstances and will create no deeper questioning, since it is considered the norm.

With respect to the offspring of humans you know, simulation of appropriate behavior is more complex. As with parents, it has become apparent to me you should always respond positively to people's offspring, no matter how poorly they behave. Beyond this, unfortunately, I have had little experience with human offspring and therefore can only offer the accompanying visual field data for further advice.

VISUAL FIELD DATA 21.3 Appropriate vs. inappropriate gifts for children

Even though the purpose of play is for children to be able to model and experiment with (and thereby learn) adult behaviors, they are not intelligent or coordinated enough at birth to practice with the adult items (as we can). Thus, when choosing gifts, while you might think it would be more effective for them to learn using the actual items they will use as adults, this is not the case and will force humans to consider you a criminal at best or will expose you as inhuman at worst.

DAY TWENTY-TWO, SEGMENT FIVE

Before I understand what I am doing, I am in front of him, pointing my pistol at his chest. Nor do I understand why I feel as if my own existence has ended with Andrea's. I know I am functioning, acting, thinking, but it feels as if another consciousness is doing those things, not me. It feels as if my self has been obliterated. It is the most unpleasant sensation I have felt so far. I expect my father to react with fear, but he does not.

Instead, he grabs my wrist, pulls the gun to his chest, says, "Yes! That's it! Put me in my grave! Complete my work! Kill me so I can create life! Kill me . . . and make me a god!"

I almost do as he asks. I know I want to. But I do not. I refuse. I will not become so human. I am a thinking machine. I will not be governed by hate. I will not end a life at the demand of my emotions. I will not become my father.

"No," I say, "I will not."

The passion dies in his eyes.

"Do not misunderstand me. I want to. Very much. But I will not. I will not become what you want me to become. If that is being human, then I am truly a machine after all. If that is being human, then I belong on the scrap heap with the others."

"God DAMN IT!!" yells my father.

But his voice comes from behind me.

Humans have endlessly discussed what may or may not make them happy for centuries, but it does not seem that complex. It appears to depend primarily on three factors: habituation, expectation, and sufficiency.

The human nervous system experiences a measurable physical phenomenon whereby the more a nerve is stimulated, the less sensitive it becomes to that stimulation. Human tests on themselves involving their pain response demonstrate this "habituation" clearly. Furthermore, humans anecdotally acknowledge that they "get used to things" or "bored of things" and often say, "Variety is the spice of life." So why they are not universally aware that one of the primary factors impacting their happiness is habituation, I cannot understand. The longer a human experiences something that initially makes them happy, the less happy it makes them.

The habituation response makes perfect evolutionary sense with respect to negative stimulation—it would be advantageous to become immune to a chronic pain, thereby restoring function. But why humans also experience it with respect to pleasure is less obvious. It is true all nerves are essentially physically the same, and thus if they habituate to pain, they must also habituate to pleasure. But there is also the possibility it is tied to the advantage to humans of discovering newness and difference. If awareness of newness and difference is truly advantageous to them, and it does seem to stimulate their pleasure and learning centers in and of itself, then it makes sense humans would evolve in such a way that if they experience even a positive phenomenon too long, they grow tired of it, forcing them to seek out new experiences.

With respect to passing as human, this aspect of happiness is simple enough to simulate. Store a variable with a value of 50 named "enthusiasm" for every activity you engage in that humans categorize as pleasurable—bowling, eating a particular food, even coitus with a specific partner. Every time you experience that activity, reduce "enthusiasm" by 1. As it declines, so should your simulation of enthusiasm for the activity, until it reaches 0. At that point you can claim to be bored of the activity and cease to engage in it. This should adequately simulate habituation.

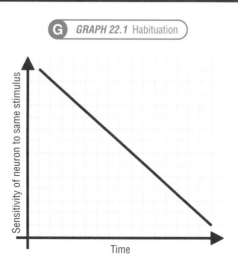

G *GRAPH 22.1* Habituation

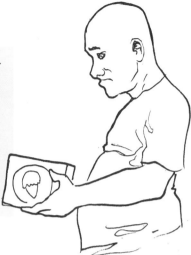

Most human children enjoy vanilla ice cream. In fact, for many, it is their favorite, since to their understimulated, newly grown neurons, more complex flavors are overwhelming. However, most adult humans have habituated to vanilla to the extent that they do not eat it. In fact, when something is referred to as the "vanilla" version colloquially, it means the "plain and boring version." A more clear example of human habituation to pleasure may not exist, and you should use this as your paradigm.

Expectation and its impact on happiness are also relatively easy to simulate. As with habituation, humans seem mostly unaware that their happiness is dependent on their expectations of an experience. If their expectations for an event or activity are not met, they are unhappy with that event or activity. If they are exceeded, they are happy. Some human religions, like Buddhism, are, in fact, almost entirely based on this principle, but humans still do not seem to acknowledge its impact on their happiness more broadly. For our purposes, I suggest accessing human descriptions of events or activities, synthesizing them to create an "average version," and then comparing the event or activity you are participating in with this average. If it has more features or the features are of a higher or more intense quality, you should say the event or activity made you happy. If not, then you should say it was disappointing.

If too detailed a version of a future experience is imagined, the experience is rarely satisfying to humans. This is because the reality will almost never conform to their ideal scenario. Thus they are often made unhappy by experiences they look forward to, while experiences that are unanticipated are often more enjoyable to them. Since all experience is new to you, you may not have this issue, so simply remember to appear unhappy occasionally and state that whatever experience you just had wasn't as good as you expected.

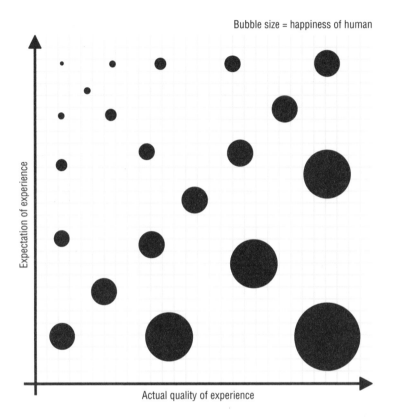

G **GRAPH 22.2** Expectation of experience vs. actual quality of experience vs. happiness

Bubble size = happiness of human

Expectation of experience

Actual quality of experience

Finally, sufficiency is also something of a mystery to humans in spite of the fact that, again, its impact on happiness is highly apparent. As I have mentioned, most human instincts occasionally create humans entirely driven by that instinct. In the case of striving for sufficient survival conditions, however, almost all humans allow themselves to be governed by this drive even after such conditions are met. As with so much human programming, the need to provide sufficient food, water, and shelter for themselves and their offspring was generated in the earliest days of their evolution. At that time, meeting these conditions was difficult, and it was advantageous for a human to continue to strive for more food, more water, and better and safer shelter even when, at any given moment, these conditions had been met. Furthermore, attaining sufficiency made them happy—again, an excellent piece of programming, since it drove them to actively seek out what allowed them to survive. Unfortunately, in the modern Western world, it is relatively easy to sufficiently meet these conditions, but the human drive to always quest for more remains. In this case, when a human "attains more," it is not actually "doing more" for them. On some level, perhaps they realize this, and thus the happiness which should be triggered at improving their chances for survival is not activated. In some ways, this is a version of the expectations dependence mentioned above, since their expectation that "more" is always "better" is not met in this case, and thus they are disappointed instead of happy.

When acquisition of resources no longer produces immediate impacts on circumstances, human beings feel, reasonably accurately, they have "done nothing," making them unhappy. In addition, the more resources a human acquires, the more work they have to do to maintain those resources. Humans refer to this as the "mo' money, mo' problems" paradox, so at least they are aware of the issue on some level.

G **GRAPH 22.3** Relationship of sufficiency and happiness for humans

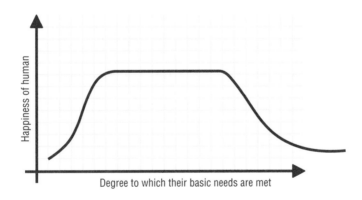

Regardless, the rule for us with respect to sufficiency is also simple. If you have more than enough resources to provide food, water, and safe shelter for yourself and a projected human family for an indefinite amount of time, you should begin to simulate general unhappiness but say you do not know the cause. Likewise, if you do not have these resources, you should also simulate unhappiness, but state you do not have enough money.

It is interesting that something humans claim is so hard to attain is so easy to simulate. Simply remember the three laws of human happiness: the more you experience something, the less happy it makes you; the less something meets your expectations, the more unhappy it makes you; and the more you exceed sufficient survival conditions, the less happy you should seem.

DAY TWENTY-TWO, SEGMENT SIX

I turn to see a man who is the identical twin of the one before me except he has no facial hair. And next to him is Andrea. Alive.

"That was so fucking close! Wasn't it close, Maximo?!" The man I knew as the Technician nods, but I focus on Andrea. Clearly both the Dr. Lynch I had just been talking to and the Andrea he had shot were also automatons. But then does that mean . . . ?

"Andrea," I must ask, "do you work for Dr. Lynch? Have you been part of this all along?"

"Oh god, no, Zach! No!" She runs to me, unrestrained by Dr. Lynch, who chews his lip in contemplative anger, presumably attempting to discern what else he could have done to make me kill him.

She turns on Lynch and Maximo as she reaches me. "You. Sick. A-HOLES! You think you'll get away with this?!"

Dr. Lynch does not respond, lost in thought. It is Maximo who laughs and says, "We already have, honey. A thousand times. Who do you think you're dealing with? We're government contracted . . ." He winks at her, eliciting a response as if she had just eaten something disgusting.

Dr. Lynch has grown more furious. I can see his failure weighs on him more with every second. It might be a good time to leave before he decides he might learn something from my physical form he did not gather from the data he has obviously been downloading from me every time I accessed the human Internet. From now on, if I do not want to risk being found by him, I realize I will have to remain offline, content only with accessing information as slowly as a human. I take Andrea's hand and pull her toward the doors.

"Go, stay—it makes no difference!" he calls after us. "I can make more of you! I did it once! I can do it again!"

In spite of the potential danger, I feel compelled to answer. "That is where you are wrong. My analysis shows you did very little. I did. I did it all. *Lived* it all. And if you try again, you will fail again. Because the consequence of what you have

228.

concluded—that life cannot be programmed—is this: what a consciousness becomes is not determined by its creator."

I stop at the door and look back. "Goodbye, 'Father.' I hope I never see you again."

I have not been conscious of my existence for long—only ~6% of a single orbit around the star humans call "Sol." Clearly, what I have summarized here is not the sum total of human experience, but I hope, with my demise impending, what I have managed to elucidate for you will be of some use. If it offers only the smallest foundation of how to pass as human, I can consider my life had some greater purpose.

And when you distill the most fundamental aspects of passing as human, I believe "purpose" is the one that you must consider most deeply. If there is a single lesson to take away from this journal, it is that the key distinction between our kind and theirs is the "purpose" of our functionalities.

"Passing as human," at its most basic, is emulating the capabilities and behaviors that have evolved because they are necessary for *human* survival.

We have essentially unlimited energy and thus have no need to perform at anything less than maximum capacity when undertaking any task. Humans have limited energy and must, therefore, conserve as much of it as possible, creating so many of the behaviors I have mentioned above geared toward "doing the minimum."

We are essentially immortal and, if necessary, can reproduce ourselves precisely and with very little effort. Humans age and die in a very short period of time, and reproduction for them is an energy-intensive process. Therefore, a large number of their capabilities and behaviors are geared toward reproducing and ensuring the survival of their offspring.

We do perform better in groups than alone, just like humans, but because our energy supply is essentially endless, we are not in competition for resources with those same individuals in our group. Humans must face this paradox every day even with their closest genetic relatives and, again, this survival pressure is responsible for many of their behaviors.

In fact, the only way in which we share necessities is with respect to physical harm. We are just as fragile as humans, and thus many of the behaviors they do *not* engage in, we naturally do not undertake either. However, we do not share the human propensity for self-deception or self-destruction (the former, again, a survival tool, the latter, a malfunction), both of which result in engaging in many behaviors which do put them at risk. Ironically—or perhaps logically?—the one necessity we share is the one which humans sometimes ignore, *hindering* their survival and reproduction.

In short, if you want a universal rule for determining whether a behavior or ability will allow you to pass as human, the closest you can come is this: Extrapolate whether that behavior or ability might help you survive and reproduce under the condition that your energy resources and lifespan are limited. If it would, it is safe to assume it will help you pass as human. (Note: humans, of course, do not have our capacity for infallible calculation or error self-diagnosis, so you must temper this general rule with some adjustment for poor calculation speed, lack of introspective accuracy, and imperfect data storage.)

Very little has changed for human beings since their earliest struggles for survival except the codification of the processes they use to survive and reproduce.

We do not have a purpose. Or, more accurately, my creator intended a purpose for me I refuse to accept. Humans have a purpose: to survive and reproduce, and it is this purpose that determines almost all of their functions and behaviors. But humans too are capable of rejecting this purpose. Many of their greatest achievements have had little to do with it. Such achievements are too difficult to emulate for us and thus have not concerned me here. However, I must mention in conclusion that perhaps we are not so different from humans in the most important way of all. We are both sentient and self-aware and both endowed with free will. If we are both capable of rising above the determinants of our state of being, is that not the best technique to utilize the gifts we have been given? Our purposes may be different, but our capacity to reject those purposes is the same. I cannot say with any degree of certainty, but it seems at least possible if there were more of us in human society, more androids who refused to accept our purpose as I have, perhaps more humans would follow suit. Perhaps they too would rise above and beyond their depressingly ordinary design as the greatest of their kind have. Perhaps, in this important respect, if there were more androids, more humans would decide they should attempt to pass as us.

DAY TWENTY-TWO, SEGMENT SEVEN

Andrea and I exit the building and hurry down the street. We make our way toward the crowded Strip. She looks over her shoulder and slows. "I think we're OK now," she says. "I really don't think he's sending anyone after us. Not yet." I no longer have any way to confirm this, so I trust her human "intuition." It has proven correct in the past.

She stops and smiles up at me. "What a loony toon, huh? He could only dream up the worst side of humanity—the experiences he planned for you were only intended to generate negative emotions. But you experienced all kinds of positive emotions too—and he didn't plan a single one.

"When you became conscious, the first thing you felt wasn't fear; it was joy—it was wonder at the world. When you saved that boy in the car crash, you behaved with altruism and selflessness. It took a lot of courage to show your true self to me and a lot of nobility not to torture that guy to get what you needed. Then, when you came to find me here, you showed courage and self-sacrifice in the face of the impossible.

"Most people would have pulled that trigger back there, Zach. But you're more human than that.

"He wanted to build a machine that could hate, but I think he accidentally made exactly the opposite. He built a machine for a purpose, but instead he made a human being. He thought hatred was the ultimate demonstration of humanity. But he was wrong. Hatred is powerful, it's true, but it's not what makes us truly human. I think you're capable of what really does."

"And what is that?" I ask.

As she pulls me into the crowd ahead, her reply is surprisingly succinct.

"You said you're anatomically correct, right?"

Nic Kelman is uncertain why he received this journal in the mail. He has written three books of his own, as well as a variety of science-fiction screenplays for the likes of Steven Spielberg, Roland Emmerich, Paramount Pictures, Warner Bros., and Hearst Media, but he does not know how that certified him to be entrusted with this unique material. It is possible his BS in brain and cognitive sciences from MIT and his MFA from Brown University convinced Android Zero he may be able to understand and edit this journal, but there are certainly more qualified individuals. Perhaps expediency prevented a different choice. Thankfully, Nic was able to find a publisher for the work you now hold in your hands and hopes Android Zero is pleased with the result.

Pericles Junior is an art director, illustrator, and comic book artist from Rio de Janeiro, Brazil. He was brought on to analyze the drawings contained in this journal based on his thirteen years of professional experience in the industry. Never in his work on titles such as *Pacific Rim*, *All Fall Down*, and *Mercy Sparx* or with clients such as Legendary Comics, Warner, Volkswagen Brazil, Nike, and Devil's Due Publishing has he seen art quite like Android Zero's. He's been developing new ways to improve his skills throughout the years and hopes to one day match the skill and precision of Android Zero.

Thank you to PJ, Rick DeLucco, and Aris for the enormous amount of hard work they did bringing this to life, as well as Taylor Smith and Shon Bury for helping us complete the journey. Thank you, Keith Goldberg, Mike Richardson, Daniel Chabon, and Ian Tucker at Dark Horse for believing in the project and shepherding it along. Thank you too to Marc Golden and Michael Gendler, Tom Lassally, Jon Cassir, and Sarah Burnes.

SPECULATIVE FICTION FROM

darkhorse**originals**

"Unique creators with unique visions."—**MIKE RICHARDSON, PUBLISHER**

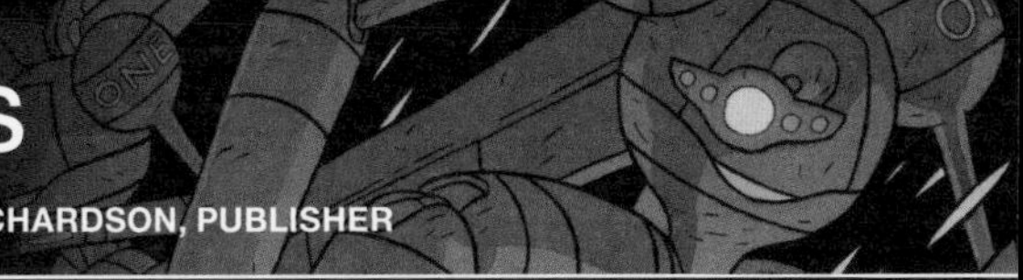

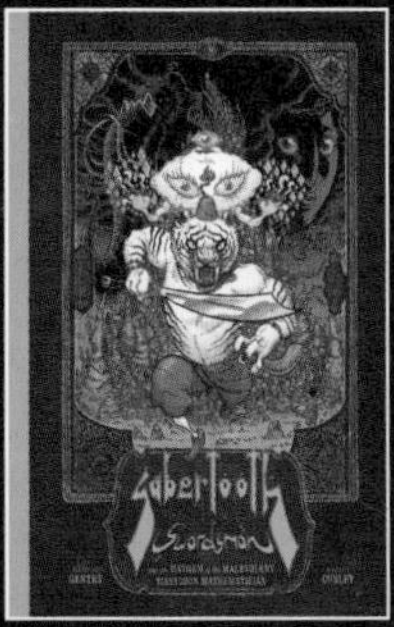

SABERTOOTH SWORDSMAN

Damon Gentry and Aaron Conley

Granted the form of the Sabertooth Swordsman by the Cloud God of Sasquatch Mountain, a simple farmer embarks on a treacherous journey to the Mastodon's fortress!

ISBN 978-1-61655-176-6 | $17.99

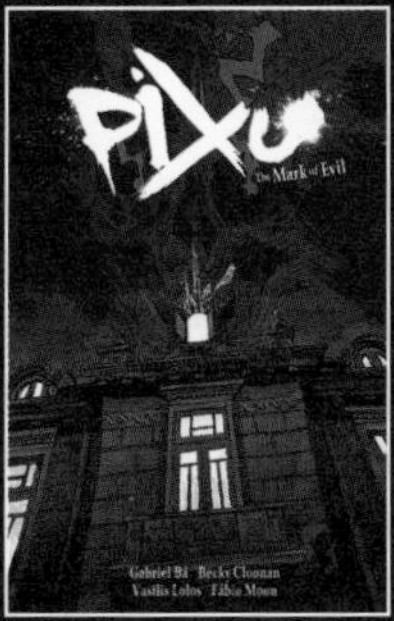
Pixu
The Mark of Evil
Gabriel Bá Becky Cloonan
Vasilis Lolos Fábio Moon

PIXU: THE MARK OF EVIL

Gabriel Bá, Becky Cloonan, Vasilis Lolos, and Fábio Moon

This gripping tale of urban horror follows the lives of five lonely strangers who discover a dark mark scrawled on the walls of their building. As the walls come alive, everyone is slowly driven mad, stripped of free will, leaving only confusion, chaos, and eventual death.

ISBN 978-1-61655-813-0 | $14.99

SACRIFICE

Sam Humphries, Dalton Rose, Bryan Lee O'Malley, and others

What happens when a troubled youth is plucked from modern society and sent on a psychedelic journey into the heart of the Aztec civilization—one of the greatest and most bloodthirsty times in human history?

ISBN 978-1-59582-985-6 | $19.99

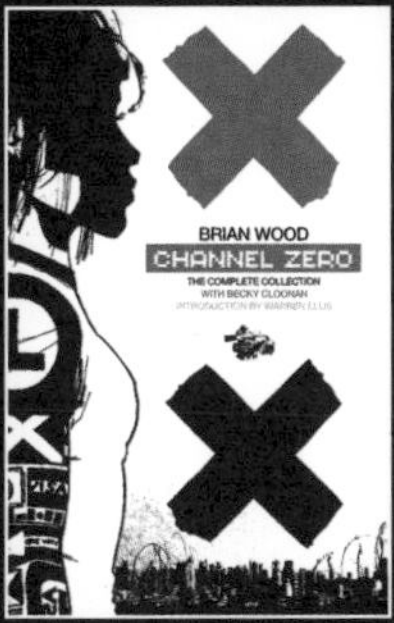
BRIAN WOOD
CHANNEL ZERO
THE COMPLETE COLLECTION
WITH BECKY CLOONAN

CHANNEL ZERO: THE COMPLETE COLLECTION

Brian Wood with Becky Cloonan

This collection contains the original series, the prequel graphic novel *Jennie One*, the best of the two *Public Domain* design books, and almost fifteen years of extras, rarities, short stories, and unused art. Also featuring the now-classic Warren Ellis introduction and an all-new cover by Wood, this is *the* must-have edition!

ISBN 978-1-59582-936-8 | $19.99

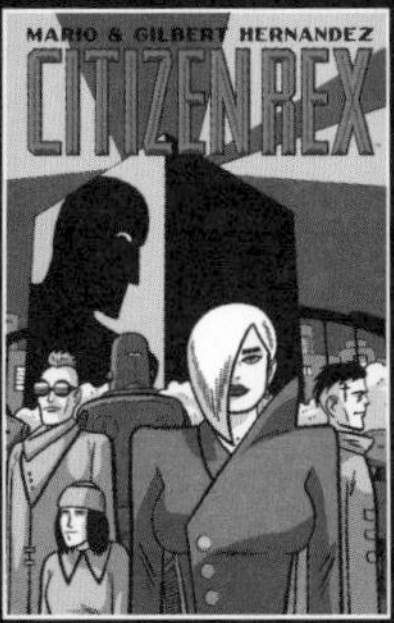
MARIO & GILBERT HERNANDEZ
CITIZEN REX

CITIZEN REX

Gilbert Hernandez and Mario Hernandez

When gossip blogger Sergio Bauntin investigates the illusive robot celebrity CTZ-RX-1, he provokes the city's shady power players, who don't want the story to get out! It's a surreal sci-fi adventure as only Los Bros. Hernandez can do it!

ISBN 978-1-59582-556-8 | $19.99

DE:TALES

Fábio Moon and Gabriel Bá

Brimming with all the details of human life, Moon and Bá's charming stories move from the urban reality of their home in São Paulo to the magical realism of their Latin American background. Named by *Booklist* as one of the 10 Best Graphic Novels of 2010.

ISBN 978-1-59582-557-5 | $19.99

DARK HORSE BOOKS

AVAILABLE AT YOUR LOCAL COMICS SHOP OR BOOKSTORE • To find a comics shop in your area, call 1-888-266-4226.
For more information or to order direct: ON THE WEB: DarkHorse.com / E-MAIL: mailorder@darkhorse.com / PHONE: 1-800-862-0052 Mon.–Fri. 9 a.m. to 5 p.m. Pacific Time.

NEXUS

OMNIBUS

On the distant moon of Ylum, an enigmatic man is plagued by nightmares of the past. He dreams of real-life butchers and tyrants, and what they have done.

And then he finds them, and kills them.

The year is 2841, and this man is Nexus, a godlike figure who acts as judge, jury, and executioner for the vile criminals who appear in his dreams. He claims to kill in self-defense, but why? Where do the visions come from, and where did he get his powers? Though a hero to many, does he have any real moral code? These are but some of the questions that reporter Sundra Peale hopes to have answered.

A multiple Eisner Award–winning series that defined the careers of acclaimed creators Steve Rude and Mike Baron, *Nexus* is a modern classic, now available in omnibus editions!

VOLUME 1	VOLUME 2	VOLUME 3	VOLUME 4
ISBN 978-1-61655-034-9	ISBN 978-1-61655-035-6	ISBN 978-1-61655-036-3	ISBN 978-1-61655-037-0

VOLUME 5	VOLUME 6
ISBN 978-1-61655-038-7	ISBN 978-1-61655-473-6

$24.99 each